Postponing Armageddon

Book I: The Amaranthines

Adele Abbot

BARKING RAIN PRESS

Postponing Armageddon—Book I: The Amaranthines

Edited by Ti Locke (www.urban-gals-go-feral.blogspot.com)

Cover artwork by Michael Leadingham (www.michaelleadingham.com)

Barking Rain Press
PO Box 822674
Vancouver, WA 98682 USA
www.barkingrainpress.org

ISBN print: 1-935460-80-3
ISBN eBook: 1-935460-81-1

Library of Congress Control Number: 2013942041

First Edition: July 2013

Printed in the United States of America

9 7 8 1 9 3 5 4 6 0 8 0 0

Acknowledgements

I'd like to thank my family for their help and advice on the storyline. Thanks are also due to John Jarrold, who made both rude and encouraging remarks about the manuscript. Finally, a very heartfelt "thank you" to my editor at Barking Rain Press, Ti Locke, who patiently translated my UK English to American English while making substantial suggestions to improve the story.

Dedication

This book is dedicated to my son, William, and to my honorary nieces, Katy and Alicia, who all come up with the most astounding ideas.

I

AD 33

e left the barracks and began walking down to the gate. The auxiliaries were already there when we arrived, as well as the regulars making up our maniple. Max and I, and his men, had enlisted in the Roman Legions some years before. Max considered joining forces a far better strategy than fighting and resisting this implacable military empire.

There was much for all of us to learn.

We waited for them to bring the prisoner out—and waited, and waited. It's what all soldiers have done since the beginning of time; we've become quite good at it.

"I'm not looking forward to this, Max," I said to him quietly. "Too many of the population think he's a God."

Max made a rude noise and bent to adjust a boot lace. "Too many gods around, too many."

"You know them personally?"

"Some," he said, and stopped in the middle of tying a knot, thinking his great slow thoughts.

Max for short, Maximus was his chosen name—Latin for *Big*. Max was built like a Roman bath house and had been around since before I was born. As far as I knew, no one had any idea where he came from or perhaps nobody was telling. He looked primitive, as though he had been built by a God who was working on his skills.

Max had overheard my thoughts, a habit that I occasionally found disturbing.

"Where you think we from?" he asked suddenly.

"You? Or all of us?"

"My kind."

I shrugged and buckled my belt. "Some god molded you from clay, perhaps. Then he breathed life into what he'd fashioned. Must have taken a very big puff." I grinned.

Max snorted and shook his head, draining the last of his cup of water. "We come from beyond Egypt. Beyond Nubia. Like your kind, only before. Many,

many gen'rations before you." He stopped and frowned, great brow ridges folding up like a plowed field. "Don't think a god made us; I never saw any at beginning. Seen enough since… big ones, small ones."

"Gods or people?"

"Both."

"So all of us came from Africa?"

He nodded slowly. "We come, not many, very few—twenty hun'red maybe. Like you," he tapped me hard on the chest and left his finger there, in contact with my flesh; suddenly he sounded clearer, better words. "Like you, Gerard, we do not die except through accident."

"You just walked out of Africa? A whole tribe?"

Max nodded. "Remember journey. Ver' long."

"Why? Why leave Africa?"

Max looked round at me. "Too hot. For us, big, growing too hot. We all came, whole nation, no seen brothers for many cent'ry. Maybe all dead now."

"Except you?"

Max lifted his shoulders and let them fall, his big mail shoulder plates rising and falling with a ringing sound, then nodded. "Listen me." He put fingers on the back of my hand and he spoke to me, mind to mind, again. *Your kind came later, first a few then many thousand. You multiplied, you covered the world. And we… mix us together.*

Clearly, Max was not satisfied with his choice of words.

We put ourselves into you. We made the Families We chose the finest of you and gave you our best gift.

"Ah!" I said, a long, drawn-out breath.

He moved his hand. "For us, too few children. So we give *your* kind a gift, long lives like us… us Amaranthines. Why you call me Uncle?" he asked suddenly.

I shook my head. "Everybody does."

"No. Your Family only, Ger'd, just yours. Reason is, I your uncle, for real. We make many families. I make yours." He frowned." Held out a hand. "Ten hands."

"Fifty? You made fifty men?"

Max nodded. "Men and women. Live all over. Some die, others grow big, make more." He put his hand back on mine so I could understand his thoughts. *We make you, understand? We make new children, to start the Families. Different from the rest.*

There was movement at the front of the Praetorium and the fellow was brought out.

"Here we go, Max. Put half your *numeri* ahead, the rest of us will follow. Any trouble…"

Max smacked his scabbard with a hard hand.

We marched towards the western gate; the sun was just rising above the Temple walls. Its red beams threw our shadows, dark and long, before us, and curls of steam lifted from the damp pavements. It was going to be a long, hot day. There was a suggestion of stink from the drain down the center of the street, too.

Bedding and covers were hanging over the balconies of higher buildings and people leaned on them to watch us passing below. Others regarded us from the windows of lower stories, from doorways and alley ways.

A group of legionaries led by one of my *decuriones* was stationed just in front of the condemned man; I was a couple of dozen paces behind the squad and strung out behind me were another fifty or so men. Both groups covered each side of the street, eyes peeled for any sign of trouble.

Everywhere sounded voices; some strident, some low; muttering—complaining, arguing: a many-throated beast which might lie supine or suddenly snarl and harass without warning. I was ready for anything, from pushing and rough behavior to a hail of stones to a coordinated attack. The anarchist had a following across Jerusalem and well beyond the city. However, there was nothing more than a bunch of citizens keeping pace with us. A few women, weeping and wailing—one of them even gave him her veil to wipe his forehead. It was a depressing sight but there was no rioting, not even a mass swooning or a rush to embrace him. Somewhere along the way, someone—probably one of my legionaries—had made a circlet of thorn twigs and pushed it on his head: a crown of thorns. He bled now from his scalp as well as from the scourging he'd received.

We were a quarter mile from the gate when he stumbled and the burden he carried went crashing down onto the feet of the on-lookers who were pressed too closely about him. I ran up the street and grabbed one of those who was keeping pace with him.

"Back, back, all of you. And you—" I shook the arm of the young man I had seized, "—take up the cross and carry it for him." The fellow obeyed without question, looking at me first then trying to lift the heavy thing from the other's back. He wasn't going to manage it.

I tapped another couple on their shoulders with my vine-staff. "You two, give him a hand." And again, it was as though my order had been foreordained or perhaps—for once—I looked the part of a centurion. I was often accused of being too young to exercise that sort of authority but I had grown my beard and even thinned out my hair to give me a semblance of maturity. It could be hard work being one of the Amaranthines.

We went on with no more pause than that—as long as it takes to draw a handful of breaths.

My Uncle Max had a century of his own men at the gate itself—Max and his men were officially part of the Roman Army and therefore under my control here. They came from tribes that lived up in the Alpine mountains—Max's *Little Legion* was well known and respected. He made a sign to me, a drinking motion and pointed to the sweating Nazarene. I nodded to Max and he dipped a cup in the fountain and offered it to the prisoner.

There was a moment's surprise before the cup was taken, a pause as the water was drunk and then, "Thank you, friend." The voice was low and courteous, a little slow and tired, perhaps.

We reached the place of execution without incident. They called it Golgotha because, so it was said, it had the look of a skull. That needed more imagination than I had; to me, it just looked like an unpleasant stretch of bare hillside, well suited to its purpose: a place of execution.

The bearers laid down the cross. One of the legionaries wrote a sign and nailed it to the top of the crucifix while the criminal was stripped of jewelry and clothing and as tools were made ready.

I looked at it: *Jesus of Nazareth— King of the Jews.* "Very droll, Aulus. Didn't know you could write."

The legionary looked up and checked my expression. He saw I was not going to bawl him out and grinned. "Just practicing, Sir."

The man was stretched out on the crucifix, and in short order his wrists and ankles were nailed down. Unlikely though it seems, he did not cry out, not a sound beyond an in-drawn gasp for breath. The willpower he showed was remarkable; I was astounded. The same, too, when they lofted the cross upright and his full weight came onto his wrists, not a sound and silent still while they jockeyed it around and dropped it into one of the holes bored into the limestone rock.

The rest of the day went as these things do, though extraordinarily quickly. The legionaries had a bit of cruel fun with the dying men and they auctioned off their clothes and possessions. In fact, the one they mischievously named "the King" had a particularly fine cloak—they placed wagers for the garment, not wanting to tear it into smaller parts for sale.

By mid-afternoon—around the ninth hour, the would-be Messiah was dead. I was not convinced and got one of my men to poke him in the ribs with a spear before I sent word to the Governor. Life had definitely fled. The same legionary went to let Pilate know.

Our orders were to stay on until the twelfth hour. One of the Sanhedrin, a Joseph of Harimathea, has permission to take possession of the body. We were to stay until he was done.

Heavy cloud hid the sky most of that afternoon and as the hour grew later, it became darker still and cooler. I had a brazier lit to dispel the gloom and sent most of my legionaries back to barracks. Max was still with us, but I had dismissed his men some time before.

The other two condemned were still alive and groaning; the noise did not put me in a charitable mood. And when, eventually, a small group of people arrived with a ladder and a pry bar and were making more noise than was strictly necessary. I was rather curt with them. Joseph identified himself to me: he was a wealthy Jew and a follower of the dead man. I told him to get on with his business.

Manhandling a corpse from a ladder in the darkness is not the easiest of tasks to perform, especially when nails have to be pulled out and too many eager hands are trying to assist. An accident was almost inevitable and Joseph slipped off the ladder and sprained his ankle. Maybe he had broken it, I wasn't sure and I didn't care much either.

Max, on the other hand, who wasn't normally sympathetic toward others, helped him stand. He pulled a branch from a nearby bush and with his thick, calloused fingers, stripped it of twigs and thorns and thrust it into the older man's hand. Joseph smiled and thanked him, patted Maximus's arm and hobbled carefully off to his friends.

"*Succ'ro le'ma...* he'p them," said Max in mangled Latin.

"What?"

He tried again in Germanic. "I help them lift. Has tomb for dead one."

"Fine, Max, fine."

Speech was one of Max's stumbling blocks. His mouth had not been made for language. Nevertheless, he persisted and could usually make himself understood in one language or another.

Max and I got back to the garrison about midnight. We warmed a measure of vinegary wine to help the dry bread go down and sat close to the fire still guttering in the hearth.

"What have you there, Max?"

He showed me. "Spec'lum. One of dead man's frien's gave me. Frien' like you."

I wasn't certain what he meant by that. He liked me? He was like me? A fellow centurion?

Max passed it to me. It was a mirror, two pieces hinged together. Both sides were cloudy when I looked at them, as though I'd breathed over the two halves. "From the Families," he added.

That surprised me and I wondered who he meant until I looked at the mirror and forgot his last remark. As I looked at it, the left hand side cleared; it showed Max as I was thinking of him; shaggy, bulging brows, and teeth like temple altars. Then the right hand side came into focus. It was Max again; but a very different Max. He could have passed as a senator: noble brow, tightly curled hair, well-barbered beard; scheming and duplicity written in every crease and furrow.

"Keep," he said. "No good to Max."

"But…"

"Know already." Max winked slowly and went to his bunk, while his urbane image faded slowly from the polished bronze.

He had been playing with my head.

II

AD 41

ermanicus had saved the Roman Empire's face by a decisive victory in Germania Superior and had then been recalled by Tiberius, leaving the Germans to reclaim many of their old lands the following year. We were transferred to one of the Macedonian legions, and years after Germanicus's Triumph in Rome, we were posted to the line of fortifications along the borders of Germania Inferior. Rome's influence finished here and that of the German tribes began.

It was ironic. There was Max and his Little Legion of primitives and me: all of us more German than Roman and defending the Empire against incursion from our kin. Even Mandor, my family's home, was only a few days march away.

There were all sorts of military works along the border, great sprawling fortresses big enough to cater for a full legion all the way down to marching forts and the occasional minor emplacement like ours, manned by a century or two of legionaries.

The true Romans didn't like our cold, wet forests festooned with moss and slimy pools of water hidden beneath bracken and fallen branches—we felt at home, of course, our forebears had lived here for generations. Perhaps it was the unvoiced kinship we felt with the nearby tribes which caused us to be a little less stern with our neighbors. Max's Little Legion was recruited from homelands along the higher regions of the Alps—this duty was like a summer camp to them. Max himself was a different matter; I had never seen another like him—primitive, certainly, but only in form. He had once confided to me that he was one of the first people, the first to appear in the World. Did I believe him? Not then, but later, oh yes.

We labored to keep the undesirables out of the Empire though the job was trivial enough. We were rarely subject to more than stone-throwing or target practice from their bowmen.

On that day, we had been attacked by a force of young men—youths, really. They were probably just out to cause a bit of mayhem and it was their bad luck to choose a day when Legatus Quintus Darius Capro had toothache. Half the camp's complement was sent after the youths and chased them all the way back to their settlement. Not content with this, Capro picked a handful of the young men whom he judged to be among the elite and another handful of young women including the chief's wife. They were marched back to the camp. It turned out to be an astute move, it had an immediate effect—the sporadic raids we had been experiencing since we'd got there stopped immediately.

No one knew what the Legate intended to do with the hostages and accordingly, they were treated with a sort of amused condescension. Isagunde, the chief's wife, was a delight to see: dark hair to her waist, eyes bright enough to light a candle, a face that might be the ruin of many a young man. Her lips formed a pursed look of contempt for all things Roman yet asked to be kissed. You might say I was very taken with the lady.

I laid siege to Isagunde's affections. She was not easily swayed and would gaze at me, as I praised her charms, with a mixture of mystification and slight amusement. I persuaded the cook to make me honey cakes which I brought to her. I traded items with a slightly sardonic centurion from Raetia for a dusty jar of rich red wine. Isagunde and I opened it and tested its quality.

Slowly she melted; slowly, as the ice does at the beginning of spring. Her mystification had long since vanished and her amusement grew as my intentions became clear. Perhaps she was lonely and missed the attentions of her husband or more likely, she found herself in a place of men with no control of her destiny and wanted a protector. She consented to come to my chamber—fortunately a centurion at this camp warranted his own room—and we enjoyed the pleasures of the couch.

Came the morning after, I was on the walkway with Max gazing north into Germania and I mentioned my good fortune. When he understood what I meant, Max's laughter boomed out across the dark woodland, startling a crowd of rooks out of the tree tops. "We send her to husband with child. Good gift from Rome."

I put my elbows on the top wooden rail and looked at him. "Pregnant?" I asked. "Come on."

It is unusual for one of us to make a child; with near-immortality, our fertility is low, otherwise we would overrun the world. But one from the Families with one of the short-lived, pregnancy is possible, though not likely.

"Ah, her fertility rises now and for fathering, you are at your prime."

I sniggered. "And who tells you all this?"

Max propped his chin on his knuckles and closed his eyes. "Max smells, Max knows."

We fell silent and contemplated the mist, wondering what it hid. The air was cool; there was the smell of growing things, the smell of decaying things, of natural forces at work. Perhaps Max *did* know.

"This woodwork is rotting away," I said. "We ought to get it replaced."

Isagunde slept with me three nights. On the fourth, unknown to me, she brought a gift with her and her lovemaking was spirited, almost frenzied. I was asleep when she unwrapped her gift—a knife with which she ripped open my belly from crotch to sternum. Guards came in the instant I screamed, but far too late; *instantly* would have been far too late. She tossed away the knife and crouched in a corner, her face buried in her hands while I tried to hold in the mess of slashed guts.

"Jupiter's cock," said a decurion looking at me with shock in his eyes. "Was it her?"

Without waiting for an answer, he crossed to the woman and yanked her to her feet. "What have you done, whore? I'll strangle you, I'll personally strangle you." And he swung her around as though she was no more than a bundle of reeds. Minutes later, there were enough Romans and primitives in the room to subdue an army of brigands. I was past noticing, whimpering as blood and shit dribbled from my belly onto the bed.

"Wha' goes on?" Max looked from me to the officer to the German woman. He could see what had gone on. "Shit and corruption, Gerard. Shit!" And Max rarely swore or cursed.

He went to the woman and held her hand up to his face; he smelled her palm then forced her mouth open and smelled her breath. "Have you fornicated with anyone else?"

"Yes, I fornicate with my husband all the time." She spat at him but Max ignored the gesture, oblivious of the gobbet of spittle running down his face.

"Hold her on the couch. She is not to be injured, not to be allowed to hurt herself, you understand?"

How was Max able to speak so clearly? I asked myself as though nothing was amiss with my guts. Ah! He was using *voice*, we heard the intent behind the words and obeyed without question; even I, in my extremis, paid attention.

"Out," he said to the junior officer. "Take all but four of my men and leave us. The Centurion will not live through the night and I need as much time as I can have."

The others filed out. Working to Max's command, two of his men held the woman who was trembling like a spider's web in a breeze. The other two held me by shoulders and ankles and stretched me flat on my back, holding me still.

Max put a hand on the woman's stomach, just above the pubis. She flinched, her eyes pools of terrified darkness, her body rigid with expectation. Max shut his eyes, remained still. "Ah!" he said in a low voice and stayed silent and motionless for an hour. Nothing moved, then: "Union happen, "he said, "woman is with child."

On hearing this, there was a snort of derision from Isagunde.

Again, Max ignored her and turned to me. "You dead man, Ger'd. Too much damage to mend, 'specially with foulness of the bowel."

I knew this, of course, and strangely calm, I nodded.

"Now lay still. Do not question me, do not move or speak. I have much to do." The *voice* again.

Max had the couch dragged next to my bed and put his left hand back on the woman, his right hand on my brow. He squatted between us.

Calm as if I lay in the grass on a summer day, I drowsed.

The pain went away and I dreamed of things long forgotten, so long in the past I had never remembered them before. I recalled suckling at my mother's breast, my teeth breaking through, the day I didn't shit myself and everyone was so proud of me. I remembered my first uttered words: *Da's sword.*

I lived the whole of my life in a blinding rush of images and sounds and feelings. The first time I killed a man, the fiftieth time, that charge we'd made, that clash of shields, the rush to put down a rising. Spring mornings, summer days, nights in the fall and winter feast times. I lived it all as clearly as if I watched in the brightest sunlight, right up to the ripping open of my stomach.

Max spent the rest of the night with us, scarcely moving until dawn came. At last he rose. "She will remain here for five days," he told the Legate forcefully.

The commandant looked down at the woman, who seemed to be sleeping, then across at me.

"Is he dead?"

"Not long now." I heard Max say, though the words meant nothing to me. Turning to Isagunde, Max touched her forehead and her eyes opened. "You will sleep with your chief when you return and later you will tell him that he has a son."

The pain had gone away, and the early morning brightness, too. Eventually there was only the slow lift of my chest, the gentle beat of my heart, then these too, went away.

III

AD 57-67

t was an odd childhood; my growing up was different. I would play in the forest and while my friends would take on the role of a boar or a wolf—looking for a totem to adopt—I was always a man. When we were given wooden swords to play with, I knew how the attack went and then the riposte, how to hold the little round shield. Even with child-sized bows and arrows, I knew how to draw the string back to my cheek, how to allow for crosswind, how much to lift the aim for distance.

All the skills the other children learned, I remembered from before. Practice was all that I required. Hunting, tracking, living rough, travelling; all there in my mind, memories waiting to be unleashed.

No one thought this unusual. I was a chief's son and a very able one. My parents were proud of me, my mother even a bit frightened of me. She tried to hide this, but I could smell the fear on her.

While tribal chieftains were elected, not inherited; it did no harm in future elections if one was the son of a chief. It made no matter that I did not want to be chief, certain assumptions were made and I was taken on visits to other tribes, I was present when other clans paid visits to ours. I was old before my time and knew, as well, that I should hide these memories from another life. Not all was clear to me, memories would wait, invisible, and startle me as they came to life when roused by something new.

That was my inner view of life, growing apace, and understanding far beyond my years. However, I did not grow older as quickly as the other boys of my age. Oh, I had stature and strength but my beard was slow in coming, my balls dropped late and my body filled out more slowly. I had little interest in girls beyond a natural curiosity at our differences, little ambition to decide my future path and was impatient when told to stop what I was doing and sleep. I could not be shaken from the feeling that all the time in the world was mine.

This dichotomy between the interior and exterior lives I lived worked to the advantage of my father's politicking. As a youngster I heard and understood conversations not meant for my ears and reported back not only the discussions but insights which, like so many other things, were stored in my memory waiting to be used. It was a gift which was more than useful to my father.

"This is a great clan." My father told me as we climbed the entrance ramp between stone towers. "Powerful, with great influence and better still, they do not seek to gobble every small tribe and expand their territory. They call themselves the *Schonau*."

The world lurched about me and my heart beat to a faster rhythm. *What?* Whatever had just happened, it was not yet finished, hazy recollections of people, confused echoes of... something. The memories were not yet ready to burst open.

"Trade?" I asked, "Is that what they do best?"

"They do," he agreed, nodding, gesturing. "They do not waste their men in warfare nor send them out to control their neighbors. It's an interesting point of view."

We entered the holding—more a sprawling stronghold than a castle—and were escorted into the interior, a gloomy place of stone walls with dusty hangings and dark oversize furniture. It would not have suited my tastes except that... I shook my head, wondering.

Talks about grain and vegetables, furs and metal ores would be held the following day. Tonight was for feasting and drinking—another quirk of mine, I had no taste for mead or beer or even the odd jug of wine filched from Roman supply trains.

When the time came, the food was brought in both by women and by men, as though both were equal; certain of those who had brought dishes in from the kitchen and served the meal then sat down with us and ate. Customs here were stranger than I was used to. The food, though, was good and I enjoyed myself, sitting at a small table reserved for esquires, some of whom were young women— who were just beginning to intrigue me.

"I've not seen you before," a girl with hair the color of chestnuts and eyes like mint tea said to me. "What are you called?"

"Gerdeg," I told her, "and you?"

She inhaled gently as though there was a scent in the air. "You're from here?" She asked, eyebrows curving. "Schonau?"

"No. No, I came with the delegation. And you are?"

"Aha, the chief's son. You don't smell the same though." She sniffed the air again. "You *do* smell like the Family though."

"Whose esquire are you?" I asked her. "You are with one of the Schonau?"

"In a manner of speaking. I work with Maximus or... perhaps Maximus works with me."

An image in my mind's eye: a huge man, not tall but broad, a head like a vast war helmet, hands like hams, knuckles like walnut shells. I saw him, recollected him. "I remember Maximus, one of the first men."

"You know him? You've met him?" Russet eyebrows rose. "Where was that?"

"I don't know. It was a long time ago. Must have been when I was small, I think."

The following morning, we were due to breakfast early before getting down to business. I was up still earlier, before the dawn, to run a circuit of the holding and when I was finished, I was still the first into the dining room where a woman was bringing in food.

"Greetings." I nodded. I turned away to find a chair and behind me there was a resounding crash, a magnificent clatter of broken crockery.

Looking back, I saw the woman who had been laying the table standing almost knee deep in the remains of a great enameled bowl. Fragments of the dish lay muddled with apples and plums and woodland fruit and berries. Dark juices were bleeding into a bear pelt on the floor.

"Gerard?"

My spirit leaped, memories flickered behind my eyes faster than ripples in a mountain stream.

"Mother?" I asked.

She rallied, squeezed her eyes shut for a moment and looked at me. She shook her head. "No, silly of me. My son was a grown man before you were born. He must have died many years ago for I've not seen him since… for a long time."

"Yet, I know you. I remember you—from somewhere." I said.

"No, young man. We are both mistaken." And she called for assistance and began to clean up the mess she had made. I brought an empty bowl from the table and gathered apples and still-whole fruit from the confusion.

"What's that?" she asked, pointing.

"What?" I was puzzled.

"On your arm." She reached across and pulled my sleeve back. "A birthmark?"

"Yes. I've had it since I was… born." I laughed at the inanity of my answer.

"Like a snake." She added.

"My father would have said it was like a worm."

She smiled and shook her head. "*Your* father?"

"The father who speaks in my mind, in my memories."

"Who are you, Gerdeg? Why do I know you so well?"

I shook my head. "When we're gone, Lady, ask Maximus."

The girl with brown hair and green eyes was waiting for me as we packed our gear onto each other's backs and made ready to leave. "Farewell, Gerdeg. Perhaps we'll see each other again."

I grinned. "What's your name?"

"Morion. Will you forget it?"

"I don't think so," I told her. "I'm sure I shan't." She smiled at me; I don't think I had seen teeth as white as that before, nor as sharp.

It was a three-day journey to our tribal holding. Not long enough to sort out all the new things filling my head but the main story was coming alive. When the woman called me *Gerard* all sorts of things had fallen into place. My tour of duty in the Twelfth Roman Legion when Max signed up his men; the border post on the banks of the River Rhine; and then… *Gods and daemons*!

I stumbled and tripped, rolled over. Someone helped me up and straightened my pack. I mumbled my thanks and walked unsteadily onward.

I could not go home. Half a day's march away and I could no longer go home! I had taken pleasure with my mother—perhaps not physically but this presence in my head had done that, I remembered so clearly it might just as well have been me. Me, a virgin boy of sixteen.

Others spoke to me throughout the day, I answered, but did not remember what I said. I was trying to find a way out of my impasse. There really seemed to be only one course to follow.

When we stopped for water and a rest, I wrote a note for my father trying to explain that a compulsion had been put upon me, that I was forced by the gods to travel to an unknown land. I folded the scrap of parchment and gave it to a youth of my own age—one who could not read—and asked him to give it to my father.

I slipped away between the trees and was gone within minutes.

Strangely, no one came after me, no one called my name; I had entered a world where I was the only sentient thing. Here, I walked or rather, stumbled, all through the rest of the day and the night, drinking from black pools in the darkness, choosing mushrooms by smell. Dangerous, dangerous—wolves and bears, hogs, deadfalls, abandoned pit traps—but I was still alive at sunup and stayed that way, my life was charmed.

I journeyed through the lands of the Northmmen—joined a Roman Legion in Britain and retired as an officially recorded corpse. I found a fallen Briton, exchanged uniform and identity with him, and crept from the field of battle. I never went back to the small settlement in Germania Superior.

Battles and injuries, even bar fights, had taught me what sort of being I was and I had grown exasperated with the petty ambitions of Ephemerals. I went instead to Mandor, the holding of the Schonau Family. My father in that place was dead of some fatal poison; administered or accidental, neither his brother— my uncle—nor my cousins would discuss it. My mother astonished her family by welcoming me as a distant nephew and I took over my father's chambers which had been closed since his death.

I hung my belt and my Roman sword, my only souvenirs, on the wall and went to find more suitable furnishings and less threadbare clothing. If I was going to be adopted into the now familiar surroundings of Mandor I was going to do it properly, as a member of the Family.

IV

ABOUT JUNE AD 1016

 was quiet for a while, trying desperately to make sense of my memories. My head felt tight, too small. "Am I dying?"

"Dying, Gerard? Of course not."

"I already died, Morion. I *died*."

"No, maybe you were dreaming." I could hear the smile in her voice.

"There was a raid, a massacre in some place in the east." I rubbed my eyes, pressed my palms against the temples, trying to squeeze my overflowing brain back into its skull. "Masada? In Palestine?"

"Judea." She bathed my burning forehead with cool water. "The Romans killed off everyone there."

"But they didn't. They didn't. Not in here." I tapped my head. "I remember just like yesterday; the Jews tried again… sixty, seventy years later. There was a general uprising… Fields of gold, Mori. Fields of red gold."

"Morion. There are two sets of memories in my head. I was in the Roman army and then, later, I travelled. I wandered, I suppose. At the same time, I was with the Romans in Palestine and Judea and there, Mori, I was killed." I shuddered. "It's something I'm never going to forget."

In my memory, I squinted against the brightness, the sun burning the rocks and the sand. It seemed as though the whole of that desert was draped in cloth-of-gold and the sun shone and reflected off it like knives. Even the water, the Salt Sea, looked like a great tray of beaten brass.

I was a centurion then—as was often the case. I was in charge of a hundred or so—what *had* been a hundred or so—men.

It had gone desperately quiet after that last rush; the Jews had retreated back into the red and ochre rocks. Yesterday, buzzards had squabbled over the piles of dead left by the earlier engagements but today, now, even they were silent. I didn't want to be here, the place felt grim, dangerous, even though our line of defense was solid. I could not decide what made me feel so apprehensive. I went to check with each of the groups of legionaries who like me, waited for the next charge. The shield wall covered me. "Any movement?" I asked the officer. He shook his head and looked out again, his eyes slitted against the fierce glare striking molten highlights from his helmet.

It was the same for each one—some ten emplacements protected by strategic rock outcrops and a semicircle of interlocked shields.

I had almost reached the last defensive position, close up to the fractured hill which closed off escape to the north. There was a small noise just louder than the sound of my sandals crushing the sand and the decurion in charge leaped and pushed me to one side.

The boulder smashed down where I had been standing. It crushed the officer, killing him slowly. It was one of several suddenly dislodged from a ledge above us by three or four of the enemy. Two more crashed down inside the enclosing rocks; two legionaries were killed outright and another lay with his legs mangled and useless. There was another rumble and stones and dust rained down on us so we were briefly blinded—long enough for another fall of broken stone.

One landed on my shoulder, knocking me over just in time for a second one to fall across my legs. For a few heartbeats I felt nothing. I attempted drag myself out from under and then the pain struck, so fiercely I blacked out with the agony. I came to with the ring of steel clamoring in my ears and my numbed legs trapped by the huge slab of rock.

Those of my comrades remaining were fighting a desperate engagement—three of us against big men with heavy black beards, hair braided tightly and each one—I saw it quite clearly—had a finger missing, cut off at the joint closest to the hand.

My remaining legionaries stood no chance, only one had escaped injury; they were cut down like corn before the hook. I reached and slashed at one of the Jews, cutting the tendon in his ankle and he fell cursing and chopped at my hand; I lost three fingers. My last man went down then and the Jew turned to me and grinned.

He raised his sword and brought it down. There was a thud and my view of the world whirled around and suddenly became still. A little way away I could see torn flesh, blood spurting from severed arteries—the blood was mine, soaking into the thirsty sand. I turned my eyes away and saw grains of sand like nuggets of gold, stones of brass all the way to that terrible sea.

Golden light grew dim, turned red, purple, black and I died. I died on the golden shores of the Salt Sea in Judea.

"I died, Morion." I shuddered. "Died…"

"And yet you didn't." She stroked my hair. "You're here, with me."

"I remember it, on those fields of death—every last detail."

"But none of that happened. Syria had its boot firmly on the Judean neck until Sylvester led the First Crusade."

"No, it cannot be. The first crusade…" I frowned, "…never reached the Holy Land." I knew she was wrong, but I also knew that she was right. Again my mind was recalling two histories.

Morion patted my hand. "Forget all that. Tell me, can you remember the last few days? The last few months? That's what matters. Do you remember Mandor, the holding?"

"Give me an inkling? When did we meet, for example?"

"You were blindfolded," she chuckled. "You had your head in a bag."

Ah yes. Mandor. Before we left, they put a bag over my head and tied it at the neck. I could still tell a lot about where we were going, there were clues; the sound of my horse's hooves on forest tracks, bird calls, the scream of a hare caught in a snare once, wind, scents. Nor was I alone of course, there were muttered conversations, the occasional query or command from Morion; enough words to gather that we were going westward.

The blindfold was taken off after the first day, once it was dark, and my wrist chains were unlocked and discarded. There was still the last blush of sunset in the night sky and the direction from which we had come into the forest clearing was plain. We had travelled west as I had guessed, though rather more south than I had expected.

So went my first day in exile.

There were sixteen in my guard. Sixteen and Morion—my Uncle's *right arm*. All sixteen were from Uncle Max's private army: brutish, hirsute. To look at them, you'd think they had only brain enough to be loyal to the last drop of blood but several were more than that; they had intelligence—not your kind of intelligence or mine, more an animal cunning—but for Max it worked just fine. With training they became good at whatever they were taught. Morion trained them, commanded them, and gave them Max's orders.

Uncle Max came to see me after supper. "Morion take them on to Brittany, now. Go on, go Terr'conens' maybe, over mountains. And stay away."

He had tried to say *Terraconensis*. I nodded. "There's no point in going back for a while."

"Long while, better never," he rumbled and turned away.

My exile was delivered by the head of the family though it was clear that my cousin had had a hand in it—a favor called in or a favor promised. Considering the reason for exile had been an accident, the punishment was harsh.

I had received an invitation to my cousin's wedding; a marriage arranged with another Amaranthine Family. It seemed only polite to go. Fertility within Families was poor; the condition seemed to go hand in hand with our longevity, and hybrid children born from Family and ephemeral parents only rarely shared our extended lives. Consequently, marriage agreements between Families were not uncommon.

I left my farm estate on the south side of the Alps, within sight of the warm Adriatic Sea and reached Mandor in upper Germania. After various greetings and meetings I went to the old suite of rooms that I'd inherited from my father for a bath and a rest. I'd arrived too late for dinner, but I had spent time here when I was younger so, later in the evening, I took the familiar back stairs down to the kitchens to raid the pantries and the wine cellar.

There I met someone else on a similar mission.

The other was an attractive woman. Tall, athletic, a sense of dress; you know that sort of mental *click* which tells you both that such a meeting is decreed. Beyond big grins and an exchange of names, we didn't speak much. By common consent, we took our ill-gotten gains back to my rooms and stayed there as daylight deserted the sky.

The following morning, we were interrupted.

"Well, Gerard, time you were... oh, your pardon, cousin."

This was Hugh, the man about to be married. "I'll come back," he said, then he paused and looked at the woman in my bed. "Bugger me gently."

Oh dear. Now I guessed with whom I had spent the night.

"You little slut, Phyle! Whore!"

His affianced, of course. It was one of those things—a mistake.

Cousin Hugh was not amused, however, nor were his Father and Grandfather when he barged in on the conference they were having with Uncle Max. Darian, my great-uncle as well as Hugh's grandfather, was the uneasy head of the Family. Since my offense was against his line of the Family, he naturally took Hugh's side.

I don't know what happened to Hugh's wedding arrangements, but I was banished from Mandor forthwith. Max had intervened on my behalf for a lesser punishment, however. As the door had closed, I heard Max's raised voice; it was angry. "No ex'cution. Ger'd is *my* boy…"

The term of banishment was not mentioned. Would it be until rule passed to another line? Until my cousin forgave me? Until I had learned better manners? *Forever*, surely not?

Hugh was on hand to see me off, of course, to wish me well. "Don't ever show yourself here again in *my* lifetime, Gerard! I'll have the skin flayed off your back before I have you killed."

I smiled to show I took no offense.

Uncle Max's heavies escorted me on my way. They marched, double time, while Morion and I rode. The air was mountain fresh, the birds cautiously welcoming the spring as green crept back into the world while winter's frigid draperies had melted away. It was a pleasant few days.

Morion: russet colored hair, cropped; eyes the color of woodland leaves and long and narrow. She was shorter than I remembered, small, one might even say slight in fact but for me, the inner stature was quite breathtaking. She moved like an animal, a hunting dog.

I had known Morion when we were little more than children. I met her when I had gone to Mandor on a trading visit many, many years before. Even then she'd been allied with Max; even then, she had been a little unsettling. And now, she was just the same… but far more intriguing.

How she managed the guards, I couldn't say. One evening, the guards had dispersed to forage and two came back grabbing at a single partridge, arguing in great shouts about whose bird it was. Morion's whip snaked out and wrapped itself around the small carcass and snatched it away from the bellicose pair. They looked at their empty hands, then at one another. Then they looked at Morion.

She spoke with a combination of gesture and sounds. I had no understanding of either but the meaning was plain enough. *Behave like men*. The two of them straightened up. *Make friends*. Each put a hand on the other's shoulder for a moment before dropping it to their sides. Morion threw the dead bird away into the brush. *If you cannot share, you cannot eat*. They accepted the judgment, going to get a drink of water then getting ready for the night.

Astonishing.

"How?" I asked Uncle Max later on.

He tapped his thick skull. "Voice," he said, "in here." I remembered then that the *voice* came from within the head.

The following morning, before we were properly awake, Uncle Max left. He rode a huge dray horse, fully twenty hands at the shoulder: nothing less could carry him for long and the sound of its departing hooves woke me. He took all but four of the guards away on whatever business he had discussed with Darian.

The guards were there to make sure I left the Mandor estate, no more. As darkness fell, they slept while Morion and I talked to each other. We had come to know a little about each other—had become interested in each other, even liked each other. We would soon be going our separate ways and as far as I was concerned, it would be months if not years before our paths crossed again, so we left it at interest and liking.

On the fifteenth morning, Morion came to me. Usually, we were getting our kit together, our horses saddled. However, today, Morion joined me on the log where I was sitting, tugging my boots on. The whip—her badge of office? her weapon? I didn't know—was uncoiled and she jerked the little tuft of frayed leather at the end up and down, up and down.

"How do you do that?"

A flash of white teeth. "Three things."

"And?"

"Practice, practice and more practice. Oh, and a little bit of wisdom from your Uncle Maximus."

"That's four."

"I lied."

The leather wiggled some more and eventually wound its end around my ankles. "Today you are free."

I gestured toward my ankles. "It doesn't look like it."

Morion grinned, white teeth shining, then she gentled it to a smile. She recoiled the long leather thong. "Well, we must leave now; I have to meet up with Max today. Can you manage on your own?"

"Not so agreeably without you. Who might Uncle Max's business be with?"

The flashing grin again. I was not supposed to be given any information of a confidential nature, but she told me anyway. "The Bishop of Hypolita Keep."

It meant nothing to me... actually, there was a fleeting memory; it seemed to me that it was or had been a derogatory title. "It doesn't mean a thing to me."

"Of course not. Still, I will be back. Perhaps I'll see you at Mandor?"

"You know why they sent me packing?"

"Yes, you told me. You made a mistake. Perhaps an enjoyable one at the time?" She smiled again.

I smiled back, and while Morion's boys tidied up I wondered about Max. He seemed to have an inexhaustible supply of armed men which he recruited from the high mountain regions where humankind's ancestors still lived.

There were few who knew this and though I knew, I would never tell, it was a secret known only to the families. I wondered what he was doing with them— selling guard contingents to local lords and barons? Hiring ready-made bands of mercenaries? Or just positioning forces for his own military advantage?

Uncle Max was capable of anything.

Like his guards, Max was short, wide and built like a prehistoric, but he had a mind for the politics and intrigue—a factor in his arguing against my execution and volunteering to escort me from the estate. It was a small favor to Darian and to Hugh but a huge one to me, putting me heavily into Max's debt. Having someone in debt to you was always good management... although, on second thought, I think Max cared for me too much to use it in that way.

"Do I get my sword?" I asked, now that I was free.

Morion gestured. The guard was already carrying my sword belt—I had not noticed. With a jagged toothed grin, he swung his arm down, back; then forward and up, my weapons sailed up, up, up and snagged among the higher branches of a tall fir tree.

"It's yours." We both chuckled, mine echoing hers and a little hollow. A few minutes later they were away, taking the horse I had been riding and disappearing along an all but invisible track to the south.

Just before they vanished, Morion turned and looked back at me, a big grin still on her face.

"Hmm! Is this how friendship disappears?" I wondered.

I climbed the tree for my sword and its accompanying dagger. By the time I was back on the ground, I had decided there was no point in following them. In any case, I suddenly realized, I had as much time as I wanted. There was no need to follow anyone—the world was mine.

Fate beckoned.

I pulled the turf away from the fire site and found some still-hot embers. I blew them back into flame and then sat by the newly re-kindled fire, waiting for a little more light to seep into the sky. That morning I waited in vain; heavy, leaden clouds rolled in and the rain began to fall. I decided to stay within the woodland where the tall conifers offered some shelter. I had a vision then—ugly, brutal, barbaric:

> *A half-moon cast a wan light on the forest covered hillside and the squat monastic building below. A cold wind came from the east, clearing away the clouds, shaking the trees and blowing into concealed places.*

The wind acted as some sort of signal; there was movement; at first minimal, then chaotic. Out of the trees came the shapes; some on two legs, others on four. They were lupine, huge, and ugly, and they picked up speed as they moved toward the monastery below.

Inside no one stirred. It was a full hour to matins and most monks were abed, some in cells, others in a communal hall. The ones whose deaths were immediate were lucky; the unlucky ones were those left for questioning.

The one who led the raid was angry now. The attack had been a waste of precious time, he had not found that which he sought, and his master would go crazy. The last soul in the monastery had gone screaming to his God rather than reveal the whereabouts.

Disgusted, he allowed the less human among his followers to feed on their prey before they left. His head was turned northward to the next target, the next possible place that might conceal what he was searching for.

I felt as though the future had turned back and was polluting my dreams, for I had been among the merciless hoard. I didn't remember taking part in the raid, but I was there, watching it unfold. And when I woke up, I saw that I had been sick, for vomit stained my clothes.

V

ime passed in the pursuit of life. This morning my stomach was empty; I needed breakfast though I needed to wash even more urgently. I walked down to a sizeable stream that purled contentedly between stones and muddy banks. I stripped and washed myself, then washed my clothes and tossed them on to the bank. Upstream, fat fish swam lazily below the widening circles of raindrops. Soon, thereafter, two of the fish were filleted and baking on the hearthstones around my fire while I too warmed and dried my clothing. Beautiful—every meal should taste as good as this. After breakfast, I leaned back against a tree bole and looked around me.

It was all very restful; I had been riding for fourteen days from before dawn until after dark. Why should I not enjoy a day of rest? There were no urgent matters, no one was chasing me. I drew my sword from its scabbard, laid it by my side with the hilt in my hand and lay down to sleep.

At least that was my intention.

I couldn't sleep. What was Max doing? Max, and Morion, and the primitives? I got up, killed the fire, packed up and started off—westward once more—Terraconensis was a long way off.

I came down out of the mountains and tried to think of somewhere else to go. North? North was colder. South—that was where Max had advised me to go… and I didn't like advice. Westward? To the Great Ocean? What then? I sat down beside a stream of cold mountain water and mulled it over. *South, I suppose it has to be south after all; it is warm and sunny to the south, orange blossoms and a clear blue sea…*

I must have dozed because a shower of ice-cold water woke me up. I was lying on a bank of new green bracken just thrusting its curled shoots through the soil; my bag was perched on a small rocky outcrop. Off to my left was a young brown bear scooping fish out of the water and spraying me with droplets.

I froze and pretended to be invisible.

Brown Bear ignored me. He finished his fishing and ate his catch; when he'd finished, he grumbled to show he was aware of me and waddled off. He didn't seem to care about me, but I had to be careful.

I followed the leaping water downhill, looking for a place where I might cross safely… in vain. The stream and I reached the lowland where it grew placid and slow and meandered between rush filled banks.

A tree trunk bridged the stream, it had sunk into the ground on both sides, the grass was short and flattened—a place much used. I followed the bank and an hour or so had passed when a heron exploded out of the water with a furious flapping of wings. I don't know which of us was the more startled; I nearly fell into the water and he lost a few feathers. Unfortunately, the commotion caught the attention of another animal—this one was a mean, stinking, warty, hairy boar.

I jumped to the right as this solid mountain of flesh rammed into my left side, sending me spinning to the ground. The hog ran on, taking several paces to kill its momentum, and then it turned again. This time, shaken and bruised but with everything still working, I faced it with my sword, ready for action.

The animal assumed itself to be invincible, and certainly recognized no danger in me; little eyes ablaze with the fury of frustration, it hurled itself at me. The jaws gaped, the muzzle tipped to the side to bring its right tusk to bear. I slashed and stepped aside as the creature came again. My stroke opened a deep gash below its right eye, enraging it still further. It dug its forefeet into the ground and this time, stopped instantly. It rounded on me, snapping and snorting; I made another wound on the opposite side of its skull, an ear hung loose and bleeding. Crazed by pain, the boar came at me recklessly—I thrust my sword into its gaping mouth and it bit down on it, injuring itself still further on the razor sharp edges. I twisted the blade and thrust it onward, trying to find the animal's brain. I pulled the sword back and swung it two handed, around and down, onto the almost non-existent neck, deep into the spinal column. The heavy boar fell on its side and kicked in the instant of dying.

I sat down on the trunk of a fallen tree and shivered in a cold sweat. I felt sick. I looked at the heavy corpse and knew how lucky I had been. Twice that day, the spring sunshine, the smells of earth and growing things had lured me away from caution. A bear and a boar; it could as easily have been a venomous snake, or a man. Any of these might kill me or injure me so badly that life would become a burden—a burden which any one of the Families would find difficulty in laying down. I had been too long away from the wild; easy living had dulled my natural vigilance.

I plunged into despair. What purpose did I have? No plans, no goal. Nothing. I could not bring myself to resume my journey to nowhere. Making a slow and unusually inept job of it, I built a shelter and fire; I went back to the boar to cut some meat for my meal. Somehow, that small act of defiance turned my mood, and by evening I was feeling better.

I considered my recent existence. I had led a hedonistic life. Slaves tended the growing and harvesting at my farm while I sailed my boat down the Adriatic and back again. An expert crew did the hard work; a delightful lady friend made the hours fly by.

I had squandered the skills I once had owned, contributing nothing to the Family, nothing to my own evolution. No wonder I had been discarded! What a waste!

In a mood of despair I fell asleep in my rude shelter. Just at the moment between sleeping and waking came a most curious sensation. A pair of unseen lips touched mine and kissed me so long and so sensually I forgot to breathe. I tasted the tip of a tongue which flicked between my lips, felt a kiss on each eyelid and a ghostly breath against my ear. *"Where are you now?"*

For an instant I saw myself as my imaginary visitor might see me—light brown hair tightly curled, a long, thin face with eyes the color of autumn leaves and a nose narrow as a knife blade. I confess, my inner eye painted me in flattering colors, for my chin needed shaving, my mouth did not smile so engagingly nor were my teeth as white or as even as they seemed in that moment. Still, one is not brought to account for misrepresenting the truth in one's own dreams.

"Sleep safely and well."

I did sleep both safely and well, and in the morning I recalled the strange dream and wondered what had brought it about. Was I getting lonely, or was it the memory of the last smile from Morion?

I didn't move from my shelter for another day. The next morning, before my eyes opened, I heard the whispered voice again.

"Follow the river, go to Marcon, where it crosses a road. I will look for your there by nightfall."

Again I was kissed with ghostly kisses and indeed, I responded. My despondency lifted. The dream left me with a surprising and unexplained anticipation.

For breakfast, I ate some thinly sliced meat roasted on last night's coals and drank water from the nearby stream. I walked away with the sun at my back.

In the middle of the afternoon I smelled wood smoke. It grew stronger as I continued west and occasionally it was joined by the faint smell of cooking and the odors of penned cattle and pigs. I crested a small hill and there, below me, was a village made indistinct by the canopy of smoke floating above the huddled houses and market stalls. There was a timber bridge nearby, crossing the busy rushing river that my bucolic stream had grown into.

I salivated. Down there was food far superior to the boar's greasy meat. I hurried on, eager to sample a little of civilization. There would be a tavern, how could there not be? There were herdsmen all about and a blacksmith and a farrier and all the people who come together at a river crossing, There *must* be a tavern, maybe more than one.

There was a tavern of course; warm and smelling of brewing, filled with low voices and an occasional shout of laughter. I drank back a cupful of ale and took the jug outside to savor as I sat by the river, legs dangling over the stones holding the water to its channel. Later, I went around to the back and found a horse-trough fed by a small freshet of spring water; I cleaned myself up somewhat and as the day died, inquired about food.

"We'll take partridge if there is any and if it's been hung long enough."

The voice came from behind my left shoulder, the voice from my dreams: slow, quiet, deliberate. I turned and gazed at her while she smiled and then grinned as she reached up to hug me. *Morion.*

We found a corner and sat down. "You sent dreams to me," I said.

She nodded, leaned back and smiled a little, uncertain. "Did you mind?"

"Mind?" I raised my eyebrows. "Why should I mind? I admire you; I never thought you might feel like this."

"Too tough?"

"Too self-sufficient."

Morion shook her head, still uncertain. I took her hands, held them tightly. "I thought it was just my own desire that was making me dream. You... I never..."

We gazed into each other's eyes, realizing our feelings were mutual.

"How do you do it?" I asked.

Morion frowned. "What?"

"Make me dream like that."

"Oh. Max taught me to prompt the guards with my thoughts. When you were with us, I found I could feel your thoughts a little, too. Why, don't you like it?" She smiled.

My face felt warm and I probably blushed, but the place was only dimly lit.

"I liked what *I* felt," she added.

The innkeeper brought two trenchers of hard, black bread soaked in gravy; on each one was a small roasted fowl.

We ate. If the food was good, I don't remember it. If the tavern was noisy or silent, crowded or empty, I don't remember. I'm not sure where we went afterwards. There was Morion's horse tethered to a bush, there were tall trees and stars and a sliver of moon, there was a soft bank of pine needles and there was the warmth of our two bodies; her downy skin was like silk beneath my fingertips. There was softness and touching and belonging...

"I had to see you," said Morion the next morning. "We weren't far away; I couldn't waste the chance of seeing you again."

"Where have you been?"

"I told you, remember? But he wasn't there—the man we wanted."

"The Bishop?"

"It's just a foolish man. He had gone; we will go on. Somewhere west of here, I think." She shrugged.

"What do you want with him?"

"It's Max's business, and he tells no one. All I know is that it won't take long and then I'll come and find you again. Do what Max told you—go to Cordova, and I'll find you there."

We made love, again, in our woodland glade and then she dressed; I saddled her horse and she was gone.

Morion. *My* Morion.

How had I not seen what she was like at Mandor? I would not have dallied with anyone—let alone Hugh's betrothed. Why did we have to leave that knowing until now?

Madness!

VI

he weather turned. The world was a cold, rainy, misty place again. Unpleasant. Rain had soaked into the earth and covered the path with a layer of mud deep enough to hide potholes, cracks, and my feet.

Max had told me to go south to Cordova, but Morion had said she was going north and west; therefore I, too, was going north and most definitely west.

I shouted a curse as, once more, I almost measured my length when I saw the old man as I looked up. I saw movement from the corner of my eye but so fleeting that it was gone before it registered. Someone running away?

The man was sitting in the mud at the side of the road, his hand on a bundle wrapped up in tan-colored cloth. As I came closer, I saw the pile of cloth was a cloak and occupied, though the occupant was probably dead judging by the stillness and the amount of blood pooling in the mud.

The one who still lived sat in the wet grass shivering; shaking so hard I could hear his teeth chattering. His hands were blue with cold and one of them rested on the head of his dead comrade. A drop of water trembled on the end of his hooked nose, another on an earlobe. I squatted down and felt for a pulse in the throat, to make certain I was right, that the dead one *was* dead. There was no doubt.

"He is dead, my friend," I said in an attempt to comfort him. I patted his hand. "Are *you* all right?" I asked, trying for the attention of the living and wondered if he had suddenly died as well, for the pale gaze never moved; he seemed not even to breathe.

At last the fellow *did* look up, slowly and foggily. There was something about him… I recalled having seen him somewhere long ago, though I could not recall more than a fleeting image. There were crowds, I thought, a long hot street, an execution to be performed. His eyes focused on me momentarily and he nodded.

"Cold," he said. "Cold and yes, I know he's dead." Then he drew a great breath of air into his lungs.

There was a bruise on his temple, a smear of blood on his hand, and his cloak was torn a little and spattered with mud. I took his limp hands in mine and tried to chafe some warmth back into them.

"A thief?" I asked. "Foot pads, hmm? Someone's attacked you, old man. Are you hurt badly?"

"Foot pads?" He said, picking my words at random. "Yes. Probably. Though a monk has little enough to be robbed of."

A *monk?* "Let's get you warm again, you could die if you don't get warmed up." I had passed an old hut a while back; if there was enough of a roof left we could probably find somewhere dry to sit. In fact, the idea quickly grew more attractive—a chance to get dry after the rain which had lasted most of the day. I should have done that when I had first seen the ruin but then, this monk, too, might well have died from exposure.

I put a hand under each arm and pulled him upright. "Can you walk? Nothing broken?"

He looked down at his feet, one was bare, mud squashing up between his toes. "There's Ricard and I've lost a sandal somewhere. Must do something for Ricard."

"Bury him, you mean?"

The other nodded.

I looked about. Everywhere ran with water, even if I could find something to dig with, the pit would fill with rainwater. There were plenty of stones though, along the stream which edged the road, but I didn't want to leave a dead body to befoul running water. Well, what did another quarter hour matter? I was wet through anyway. I shed my cloak, lifted the body and carried it across the way beneath the trees. Then I carried rock after rock from the stream's margin to make a cairn over the body.

"All right?" I asked at last and suddenly spied his sandal. "Here, is this what you lost?" I picked up the badly worn sandal, as sodden as everything else around here. He stood and leaned on my shoulder while I bent and fitted the sandal, doing it up as if he were a child. "All right?"

"I had a bag." He frowned. "There was a bag. I think I threw it down there while they argued about us."

Down there was the small, swift stream which burbled between stones and yellow iris flags at the edge of the road. "If you threw it in there, it's surely gone by now."

But it wasn't.

The bag turned out to be quite large and too heavy to drift away. It was lodged at the edge of the stream and hidden by a tuft of grass. I retrieved it, hung the heavy thing over my shoulder, and took his arm. We stumbled slowly back the way I had come.

Clouds scurried overhead with tendrils of rain drifting down like the tentacles on a jellyfish. It was occasionally windy and the rain stabbed at us viciously, each falling drop leaving little craters in the mud for the next one to obliterate.

As we went, the fellow's steps grew steadily firmer and although he limped, his stride lengthened. He began to look less aged and less infirm. In fact, I needed to revise my initial thought. He probably looked no older than I did. I laughed inwardly at the thought, because even I was unsure how old that was.

"You seem to be recovering pretty quickly." I let go of his arm.

"Shock, I think. Wearing off now. I've not been set on before—not for many years, and killing Ricard like that—I haven't seen someone killed since… well, for a long time."

"So they took nothing?"

He shook his head. "I threw my bag away while they…"

"Argued, you said. About you."

"About attacking a pair of monks, I'd guess. A foolish thing to do—whoever heard of thieving from a cleric?"

"How many were there? Two?"

"Yes. Two of them. Something wrong with them…" His voice trailed off as he tried to remember.

"Wrong?"

"I don't know what it was," he said. "Just something in how they looked; stooped, but big."

We reached the hut; the decaying remains of a serf's home. When it had been whole it would have housed a man and his woman, children, and maybe grandma and grandpa, too. Now the roof sagged to the ground at one end where the wall had fallen and a crop of weeds had taken root in the rotting remains of the thatch. A dark doorway gaped near to the wall that was still standing, and it was obvious that wild pigs had made it their home at one time.

I investigated and found it tenantless for the moment and we moved in. At some time in the past a former lodger—probably not the family of pigs who had preceded us—had thoughtfully laid out a circle of hearthstones.

"You were limping. Is something the matter with your leg?" I asked as I lowered him to sit down against the wall.

"It's nothing. Perhaps I was kicked." He shook his head and he eased himself to the ground. "It'll mend."

"There's quite a bit of dry stuff in here," I said, half to myself, "an old chair or something, no, a table. I can break it up for fire wood. Be good to get warm and dry again."

I found a stout twig the length of my forearm and pulled a couple of threads from my cloak which had, I must admit, already seen better days.

"What's that?" he asked. "A bow?"

I nodded, looking up at him. "To make a fire drill."

He struggled with the bag I had left beside him. It was a big, leather scroll case and quite a weight. "There's flint and iron in here. It'll save a deal of effort."

"That it will." I chuckled gratefully. "What's your name?"

"Why?" he asked, immediately suspicious of something and put the bag down as though he would deny me the use of his flint.

"Friendship?" I said, puzzled by his attitude. "If we're going to be here a while, drying out, it's nice to know who I'm sharing the warmth with."

He relaxed a little. "Yes. Yes, of course." He paused for a heartbeat. "Simeon," he said after the pause. "Brother Simeon."

"Gerard." I told him, though I doubted he had told me his real name.

Presently we had a small fire going. I had cracked the table into manageable pieces for immediate use but when the rain eased a little, I went out to drag in some damp but usable dead branches. Back inside, I sat and leaned against a wall and closed my eyes in the welcome warmth.

My clothes steamed and my boot soles stiffened and later, I suddenly came awake to find Brother Simeon regarding me steadily. I raised my eyebrows and threw a couple of pieces of wood on the fire.

"Where were you coming from when you found me?" he asked.

Coming *from*? Usually, the question was *going to*. "Marcon. That's south and a little east of here; a couple of days' walking."

"I know Marcon. I know all the villages and towns around here. Who's the mayor there?"

"No idea. I was passing through." I described a few of the things I remembered about the place. "I was meeting someone there."

Simeon scowled at me. "Who was that?"

"A woman… a friend." Put like that, it sounded a little unlikely, so I embroidered. "Unfortunately, her husband returned in the small hours, as he had played too many losing hands."

"Ah. The woman's name was…?"

"Well, I don't suppose it matters now. Bernadette."

"Bernadette who?" he pressed. Then, when I shrugged, "Describe her."

"Brown eyes, hair down to here—a lovely glossy black. Small, lively." I described a woman I had seen in the market.

He squeezed his eyes into slits and gazed at me. "Yes, I know her."

"Well, there's a thing."

Simeon relaxed. Somehow I had established my bona fides. He was far younger looking now than when I'd first seen him. Forties perhaps, though it was difficult to tell. His hair was black and the tonsure had not been shaved in a while. He had very light brown eyes—much lighter than mine—bracketing a nose of noble proportions; again, unlike mine which was thin and straight. The eyes were unsettling; they were almost sand colored, not at all what might be expected with his olive complexion.

He kept his beard well-barbered, a narrow line of whiskers running down the crease in front of each cheek-bone, he grew it to a slight point at the bottom of his chin. More time passed and the fire burned down a little before he spoke again.

"I see you carry a sword?"

I patted the scabbard. "Short and broad."

"Can you use it?"

I grinned. "Oh yes. I had my first sword from a ruffian whose master thought I'd look good on the slave block. They were both wrong in what they supposed. That was a few years ago, though. I've learned many more skills since then—as well as a certain doggedness."

"Yes. I can see how the situation could have come about." He looked at me some more. Speculatively. "Well proportioned, healthy, a little rakish but you would find favor with the woman of the house. You look excellent slave material to me."

"I only *look* to be slave material."

"Yes, yes, I believe you." He leaned over and squeezed my forearm. "Strong sword arm, you look capable of killing if necessary."

I laughed. "Want to count my teeth as well?"

My companion remained quite serious. "Do you hire yourself out?"

"What, to kill?" I was prepared to be offended.

"No, no," he said testily. "As a protector. My protector."

I shrugged. "I don't think you need to worry. As you said, whoever heard of a monk being attacked? It won't happen again."

"It might," he said thoughtfully, uncertain. "It might happen again. How much?"

"For how long?"

"Go with me at least as far as Mont Saint-Michel."

"The Mont? That must be twelve days from here, at the least."

"Say fifteen or even sixteen. I'm not as young as you; at least I don't think I am, and I've obviously led a more sheltered life."

"Sixteen days? Two dernier a day." That was a good rate.

"Done."

"And food."

"Just so."

And where did an itinerant monk get enough money to hire a bodyguard, I wondered? Still, I could swing westerly later, and it would be much nicer seeing Morion with a gift and coin jingling in my purse...

I went outside into the gathering gloom to bring in more firewood, ample to last us through the night. When I returned, Brother Simeon was sorting through his bag. He had tipped out the contents together with a certain amount of rain-water and was checking that each of the items—scrolls mostly, rolled up in oiled silk—was dry. I noticed the cuts on the middle finger on his left hand, they were smearing the rolls with blood. I remembered the blood I had seen on his hand when I first came across him. His finger had started to bleed again.

"Your hand's bleeding," I told him. "Is the cut a deep one?"

He looked at both hands then noticed his left middle finger. "Damnation!" he said vehemently—not the most suitable expletive for a cleric to use. "They took my ring! It was always a bit tight; it must have cut me when they took it off."

"Valuable?"

"Only in a manner of speaking." He rummaged among the mound of parcels from his bag and came up with a small one. He unwrapped it and showed me a ring of what looked to be silver; the firelight tinged it with gold. There was a stone set in it, ordinary, nothing valuable... except, on closer inspection, there was a light within the stone, not bright, but the color of new milk. "They took a copy of this."

"Important?" I asked as he wrapped up the real thing again.

"Oh yes, important. Quite important. Very important, actually."

"I don't follow you."

Simeon dug into his pouch and brought out a palm full of silver coins with a few copper ones among them. "An ordinary thief would have taken these. They didn't. They took what they thought was my ring of... office. I hadn't realized it was gone, I must have been unconscious at the time." He turned his hand this way and that, looking at his finger. "They had quite a job taking it off, look."

The monk's finger had been bruised and cut as the ring had been screwed from side to side, to get it off. The cuts were bleeding; smearing blood on every-thing he handled.

"Fortunate it wasn't tighter," I suggested. "They might have taken your finger with it."

"Hmm. They knew what they thought they were taking."

I found that quite worrying; it suggested knowledge of something, a purpose other than thievery. He began to put the things back in his bag.

"Are you hungry?"

My stomach rumbled. "I certainly am. Is there a tavern nearby?"

"No but…" he felt around in one of the voluminous pockets of his robe, "there's cheese here, some black bread and also, a rather marvelous sausage." He took what I thought was a scroll from his case, it turned out to be the sausage which fitted in among the other cylinders very nicely. He unwrapped the food as he talked.

"Is there a bottle of wine in there? It would round things off rather well."

"That I cannot provide."

By now it was quite dark outside and it was beginning to rain again. The rain found several ways through the sagging roof and began to puddle on the floor. We moved as far as possible from the leaks to enjoy the food. Simeon sliced the sausage and served it up on the bread.

"What *is* that, Simeon?" He was using a sort of knife, its blade split up the center.

"Hmm? This? Oh yes, useful. For serving meat, saves your fingers from burning. One of those oddities you find when you travel."

"You travel quite a lot?"

"Yes, quite extensively, in the past. Byzantium in this case—they call it a fork. Clever."

Well, the sausage was as wonderful as Simeon had said, spicy and filling. We talked of this and of that. My companion had metamorphosed from a shaken old man into quite a sharp minded conversationalist with eyes that gazed at you and dared you to tell lies.

I did lie though, when he asked about my past. I had a well-worn history that I would trot out on such occasions, it was all true—to an extent—I almost believed it myself sometimes. I also told him an edited version of my reason for leaving the family home. I explained that thoughtlessly, I had caused ill-feeling and that my absence would allow things to cool off. As the hour progressed, conversation lapsed. Sleep was close for us both. Simeon was heating up a last drink on the fire.

"Where are you from?" I asked, hoping I might catch him off guard.

"Mont Saint-Michel," he said, which was some distance to the north. Given that he knew villages in quite the opposite direction, I wondered still which was truth and which fabrication. Perhaps he was prevaricating; dancing around the truth like a sword fighter awaiting an opening. I took a cup of hot broth from him and drank the mixture, which tasted of herbs. I felt warm and comfortable as the mixture went down; here was a good friend and a trustworthy companion.

There were rustlings in the drooping thatch: mice, rats—a bird perhaps; a spider floated down on its silken cord and reaching the floor, stalked off into the darkness. The livestock didn't trouble me; I went to sleep and dreamed of a mad monk with disturbing eyes. Outside my dreams there was chanting and Simeon insisting we were friends and should remain so.

The dream became something much more real and frightening. I was looking through someone's eyes at a map; it showed hills and water courses which were familiar to me. But whose eyes was I looking through? They looked up, signaled to something away to the left, and I saw that which should not be seen. It is written that what I witnessed then was tantamount to watching my own death. I closed my eyes as I realized the familiar smell came from the form I appeared to inhabit: hairy, stooped, my knuckles close to the floor. At least one of my companions inhabited the nether world.

I woke to the smell of the sausage Simeon had carved last evening. Slices of it were warming nicely on a hot hearth stone.

"Ah," said Simeon. "I wondered if the smell of breakfast would bring you round. Look outside, it's a beautiful morning."

I looked towards the door where a shaft of sunlight lit up the haze of smoke. I went out and scooped water from a stream a few strides away. With my mouth feeling a little fresher and some cold water on my face, it did indeed look to be a beautiful morning—if one ignored the saturated ground under foot and the quagmire the road had become. I returned and Simeon offered me a dock leaf bearing half a dozen slices of hot sausage meat.

"And I'd like to thank you for your help yesterday."

I made a dismissive gesture.

"No. You helped me greatly, it was too late for Ricard but you may have saved *my* life. I was quite overwhelmed by my assailants and I think that only your coming preventing them taking my life along with the ring."

I munched on the sausage and shrugged. "Killing a monk seems a little extreme."

"Like you, I have not told the whole truth. There may be reasons for the killing. Reasons of a sort."

I nodded. "What makes you think that... that *I* lied?"

"A simple wanderer? A country boy running away from home? You are far too mature for that. Your speech is educated—you ape a country accent but the words you use are not those of a country boy."

"Hmm." *Careless*, I thought to myself. "Still, let us strike a bargain, you tell me your truths and I'll tell you mine."

Simeon found a twig and began to clean his teeth in between words. "I'm a cleric, or was, an abbot in fact. The Abbot of Hypolita Abbey, although the office is no longer relevant. I am collecting a number of... documents from various monasteries which have to be taken to a certain center of learning."

I snorted and chewed a couple of mouthfuls of hot meat. *Hypolita. I had heard that name before, not too long before.* "You may be telling me the truth, but you're not telling me much of it. Documents, center of learning?"

"The matter is sensitive."

"Do you still want my protection?"

"Well, yes of course. That is why I wish to be frank with you."

"*Be* frank then. There is more to be told."

The cleric frowned, I could see furious thoughts passing through his mind. He opened his mouth to speak; to protest, I thought. He closed his mouth, thought better about what he would say and started again.

"All is as I told you. The documents I mentioned are old, a thousand years old. There are twelve of them all told, each one written by one of Our Lord's disciples. I have ten of them."

I heard the capital letters; usually it was Christians who referred to their God in that way.

"Which Lord is this one?" I asked, checking, for I preferred to steer clear of faiths requiring strenuous devotions or frequent sacrifices.

"The Risen Christ."

"Christ?" The Christians had overrun half the known world. They were an intolerant lot and because of that I kept in touch with their beliefs—there were occasions when it was useful to pretend to be one of them. Here though, I did not consider bluff to be necessary. "You're a Christian?"

From my tone of voice, he realized his choice of God was not mine. He stretched out his hand in a calming gesture. "It doesn't matter now, anyhow. God is gone away."

Gone away? Do Gods do that? For a priest of the God in question, it was quite a bold statement. I tried to remember; there were two more Gods to his faith, then it became clear—their Trinity was not three deities but three *aspects* of the same one. Why did they have such complicated arrangements?

"Gone away? You don't seem particularly upset about it. How can you be so certain?"

"I don't think I could tell you, not so you would understand."

"I'm not unintelligent."

"No, I know that. Well... I'll try.

"There are many... variations in the way Christians worship the One God, variations in belief."

I nodded. *A new one every year.*

"My own particular branch traces its origins directly from Matthias the last apostle. He established our order."

"How does this make your, er... your order more knowledgeable about this God's movements than others?"

"Because Matthias still lives and leads us."

I realized then that when he had said *understanding,* he meant credulity—or at least faith. Simeon had no idea that I would find such a thing easier to believe than most, of course. To one immortal, another one comes as no surprise. I grinned, raised an eyebrow and allowed a healthy hint of skepticism to shine forth. "Well then. I have to believe you. This Matthias talks with your God, I suppose?"

"Actually, yes. Though not exactly *talk.* Communication, communion," he said. "With Our Lord Jesu. Until He left us to work by ourselves."

This was a little bizarre! I had expected him to be quite vehement—either in denial or affirmation—but not reassuringly agreeable.

"Well then, what purpose does this pilgrimage serve?"

"It isn't a pilgrimage. I'm bringing together these old records in one place. I—we, at the monastery, have always possessed one of these and I've collected the other nine over the years. The eleventh is held at the abbey of Mont Saint-Michel. My task is to collect this one and the final one and to deliver them."

"You told me you *came* from Mont Saint-Michel."

"Did I? I don't remember saying that."

"Last night, before we slept."

He thought back to the previous evening. "I thought you asked me where I was going."

Which could have been true, I suppose. Perhaps that was what I *had* asked him and the mistake was mine. "No matter," I shrugged, as I was often too suspicious. But he *hadn't* told me all of it; I was certain of that. "So we go to Mont Saint-Michel?"

"Yes. Then I go on to Britain."

"To Britain? And where then? Where do you have to take them?"

"Since you are going only as far as the Mont, you needn't know that."

No, he was right, I didn't need to. "Can I see one of the documents?"

"It's better that you don't. There's a power in them that will enthrall you; you'll feel dizzy for some time, perhaps even rather ill."

I shrugged to express my disinterest.

We packed up and left, passing the place I had first met him and we stopped, briefly, to pay our respects to his dead comrade. Then onward, over a slight hill and down to a valley where a river—one of many rivers—crossed our way. Reeds lined its banks and there was thyme and forget-me-nots among the iris spears.

Closer to the water, I saw a kingfisher balancing on a twig of hawthorn and as we came nearer there was a flash of turquoise as it darted into the shining water. Three heartbeats later it rose from the surface and flew back to its vantage point to gulp down a minnow.

At the river's side, I took off my boots and Simeon hoisted the skirt of his robe. He had on breeks which came to his knees and the water was no deeper than that—a pleasant, shallow river.

Later in the day we came to another, similar watercourse and we stopped by its side. Simeon scattered a few crumbs he had left in his pocket on the surface and dangled a length of fine twine from the end of a pole and pulled several fish from the water while I attended to a shelter. Using my sword, I cut long poles and leaned them against another supported by two trees. Leafy branches over the poles made a rough and ready thatch and a few branches from a conifer would keep us off the ground through the night. When I backed out of the lean-to Simeon had picked up my sword from where I'd left it and was looking at it.

"Roman," he said.

I nodded and held my hand out. Picking up someone else's weaponry was not an act of politeness, although a monk might not know that.

Simeon ran his finger along the design which had been etched into its surface. "This is antique, very old." He gave it back to me. "Where *do* you come from, Gerard?"

"From Germania, as I told you. Upper Germania."

"But you haven't told all, have you? Come, be as open as I have."

That seemed an open invitation to prevaricate as much as I might wish. "I lived on my parent's farm, then I left. I enlisted with the local army corps and was posted to the northern frontier, and then later, in the west."

"When was that?" he asked.

I frowned and shook my head. "Twenty years since?"

"You've still to see your thirtieth summer, from the looks of you. You're telling me you became a soldier at ten?"

I would not be bothered. "I have remarkable health," I shrugged, and made a joke of it. "No, I don't remember but you flatter me, I've certainly seen forty summers and winters."

"Your sword then—genuine army issue? Roman? Where did it come from?"

I decided to go along with it, as it wasn't all that important. "Genuine? It's real enough—this sword was forged by a master, have you ever heard of Weyland, a smith who lived in the far north?"

Simeon shook his head.

"Weyland's skill was consummate; he forged swords for the gods of the Northmmen. He forged this one for me, copying the Roman style. I watched him hammer the iron and twist it and fold it, I watched as he squeezed out the dross and made it into steel," I grinned. I could see he didn't believe it, but then *his* God didn't need mortals to make him a weapon.

"Why did he make this for you?"

"I became his friend. Friendship is the most important of virtues—he made it for the sake of friendship."

I had given him enough to think about and we baked the fish and ate them in silence. I brooded, too. I was as certain as I could be that our meeting had been an accident. I don't care to believe in predestined fate; however, I have led a life far stranger than most and indeed, significantly longer, too. Occasionally there have been things which gave me cause to wonder a little. Among those mighty wheels that turn the cosmos, could there be one small, insignificant cog that made me dance to the same grand tune?

It was not a thought I was comfortable with.

I dreamed that I was suddenly looking through a stranger's eyes once more, looking at the same group that had attacked the keep, gathered in a natural clearing in the forest. It was a place where layers of stone peered through the soil of the surrounding woodland and dared anything to grow. Their leader was a female not of this current world, but from an earlier time. Her sort had stalked the land when man was in his infancy and her long silver hair and darkly green eyes were testament to the fact. She shook her mane and made various signals, and while her accompanying speech seemed no more than grunts to me, in any language known to man they signified her anger at their ineptitude as she enjoined them to do better. She waved a hand at the sky, and beat it against her scabbard, emphasizing the need to find the prey quickly and recover that which they must. The bestial men grunted loudly, the wolves howled their approval, and the others grinned lasciviously with their long mouths.

The winds of time screamed through my mind, bearing change and shattering history as I slept and for a long time, Simeon sat beside me whispering, urging me to protect him and to follow him and his God.

VII

The following days were much the same. The road trended upward, evil did not threaten, and I earned my two derniers a day easily. However, there were times when I thought we were being followed or flanked: glimpses, the movement of a bush where there should have been none, silence where bird song would have been expected. There came a subliminal feeling of familiarity that put me in mind of a certain scheming member of my own Family, and if it were the truth, it was an even more uncomfortable thought to live with.

We passed through Nantes, stopping only for provisions. Considering it had once been a town of some substance, it was a disappointment—dusty and tumbledown. There had been warfare or pillaging in the recent past; I guessed the Vikings may have paid it more than an occasional visit.

We came to the edge of the town and started off, eager to leave the place behind us. But when wickedness reaches out and touches you on the shoulder, it is always unexpected; just when you think that all is right with the world, it turns round and bites you.

Thus, we had all but shaken the dust of Nantes from our boots and entered a small, prettily wooded gorge with the sun stabbing down through the leaves when we were confronted by three men—three men with swords drawn and ready for use. I might be able to handle three men but just to be sure, I looked behind us and, of course, there were three more.

"Can you fight six of them?" Simeon asked, trustingly.

"I can but I'd lose."

"So?"

"We do what they want."

Which was, of course, to search us for silver and gold after which they would almost certainly send us on our way to the Elysian Fields or, in Simeon's case, to his Heaven.

"You'd do better to seek our ransom," I muttered, as they searched me, relieving me of my recently earned pennies.

A few words were said in a language I did not follow; they might have been Gyptians.

"A ransom?" asked one of them in a remarkably high voice.

"My master is Bishop of Hypolita Keep," I told him… her, I realized. "He is travelling incognito to the Abbey at Mont Saint-Michel."

"And that place will pay for him?"

"For us."

The woman looked at Simeon and back at me, tapping her teeth and thinking. "It's an easy claim to make and would cause us much nuisance were we to believe you and no one at Mont Saint-Michel was interested."

I tried to buy us time. "Take a look in that precious case of his, it's filled with books the Abbey wants to buy."

Simeon heard me and became angry; whether he was play-acting or was indeed enraged, I hesitated to guess. "Look at them," he said, "there is no value, they're just antiques. Open and you'll see."

But none of them bothered as they were, after all, only footpads and illiterate. The woman came to a decision and gave orders. The bag was wrested from Simeon's arms while he protested vehemently and called me names that are not good for a Christian abbot to know. We were herded deeper into the woodlands and deeper still alongside a stream cascading over a shelf of rock. Here, a stockade had been built with a gate lashed tight and within, a rude but a quite large hut.

A complicated knot locked the gate. One of our captors undid the rope and we were taken through to be tied against wooden frames that had seen much use. Simeon's scroll case disappeared inside with the woman who, without doubt, was the chief of this little band of thieves.

I began straining at the bindings around my wrists; one of them seemed a little loose.

"Why did you tell them this rigmarole?" Simeon asked.

"To prolong our lives," I answered in a reasonable tone of voice. "It should give us more time. Did you want to be killed immediately?"

"I *did* hope they'd look at the writings. They often confuse and bring visions at first."

We listened in the hope of hearing something along these lines. When we didn't and the day was drawing on to dusk and we were becoming hungry, we shouted. Our shouting was ignored and I worked some more on loosening the cords at my wrists.

It was full dark, my wrists were as tightly bound as before and my fingers were sore from picking at the fibers; I was hungry, cold, and I was not in the best of tempers.

The door opened and light shone through the darkness. Someone came out and held a lantern to each of our faces. "This one." And another presence whom I had not seen with the light so close, came to my side and cut the cords at my wrists and ankles.

With a long knife against my windpipe, I was taken inside.

"Now, let me look at you, boy." The speaker was the woman, the leader, but—*boy*? "Let's see what you're made of." She gestured. "Take off your clothes."

"My clothes?"

"Off."

I pulled off my jerkin and then my shirt and stood there.

"Now the rest."

Feeling more and more ridiculous, I took off my belt with its empty knife and sword scabbards and let my breeches fall to the floor before stepping out of them.

She moved her hand in a small circle. "Turn around."

Which I did, until I was facing her again.

"In here." She took me to a corner which had been partitioned off with heavy blankets. A lantern hung from the ceiling and another stood on a shelf near a couch. A mirror leaned against the wall and reflected the standing lantern, adding more light to the bedroom.

She looked back at her band of five ferocious confederates and gave some orders. There was assent and what I took to be her name: Jaska. She closed off the space with another blanket.

As was common with most men and women in this age, Jaska preferred not to bathe too often. This became a little obvious as she took off her jacket and flung it into a corner. I would have preferred it otherwise but on this occasion—my life being involved—I was prepared to be a little less fastidious. I sat on the couch as she ran her fingers over my shoulders and torso. A little later, she noticed the pale silvery lines of the scars which crisscrossed my body, scars collected from a numberless list of wars and duels and battles.

"I have seen such as these in my time, but so many? How did you come to take so many... and survive?"

"It's a knack," I told her, "in both cases."

I undressed her a little further and kissed her where neck and shoulder met, she squirmed a little and I did it again. Jaska was not in the first flush of youth, nor in the second, but she was fit and very, very healthy.

Actually, I felt a little guilty. Quite apart from that single occasion when we had experienced a sudden passion for each other, there had been many evenings since when Morion and I had shared thoughts and a growing attachment for each other. Something was growing between us… yet it must be put aside for the time being. The continuance of life was more important. The drive to live was both a mental and a physical compulsion. Morion must be forgotten for the next few hours.

So we made love. I uncovered her body; hard, athletic, responsive; to all appearances, older than Morion though, of course, it could not be. Her breasts were as hard as wild pears and pressed against me. She moved, touching, counting the scars, caressing, stroking…

I watched. Somewhere there must be a knife, for I could not imagine that she would leave herself undefended. I waited, for I did not trust her even now; she might try to kill me as we neared the final moment. I was just a tool, after all—something with which to fulfill her needs.

We drew closer to that final moment. We joined, her eyes closed tightly and she panted and moaned and bucked beneath me, her back arched in ecstasy. I felt beneath the cushions, along the edges of couch. Even as I joined her in the climax I searched and found nothing. Had she assumed that someone younger than herself—a boy—would be too preoccupied with self-gratification to offer her harm at such a time? It did not seem in character to me.

Nor was it.

"Is this what you were looking for?" She asked. A wicked gleam of silver light appeared in her hand; small, but oh so sharp and so fast that I had not seen where it had come from. She stabbed and feinted and it went out of my sight and I felt it pricking against the skin beneath my chin, in the center of the hollow which lies at the base of the throat.

"Now you've found it," she said through teeth clamped together. "Now it's found you. And now, get out of me."

I was still buried deeply within and eased myself out a little and moved up and forward so that my pubis pressed against that place from which flow so many of a woman's sensations. She groaned quietly, the pressure of the knife point eased a little. There was an instant, a moment no longer than the space between heartbeats—but it was enough. I arched back a fraction and grabbed at her wrist and flung it down onto the cushion beside her head. It was easy then to fold her hand until the fingers opened and the knife was free. I took it and stabbed it into the wooden shelf next to the lamp.

"Get out," she hissed fiercely, "before I call my men."

"Call. You will be dead before the curtain is drawn."

I began to move slowly, a tight figure of eight, delicately grinding into her taut flesh.

"Mmm," she said, making the best of the situation. "Can you do that again?"

"I think it's likely." And I carried on, taking pleasure in the giving of pleasure rather than losing myself in the coupling. When at last it was over again, I wrenched the knife from the wooden shelf and looked at it. Plain, a boxwood handle, a blade as long as my hand and very sharp. I held it up and reflected light from the lantern into Jaska's eyes. "Get up," I ordered. "Get dressed."

"Now? It's the middle of the night."

"Now. The time is what I say it is—and I say it is time to get dressed." I slid the back of the knife blade across her throat and she shivered. She sat up and began to dress. When that was done, I tied her hands and dressed myself and took her to where the curtain still maintained her privacy. "Who's your right hand man?"

"Right hand man?"

"Your main man, your second-in-command?"

"That would be Leemish."

"Call him."

"Leemish," she called, her voice low. "Leemish." A little louder. There was a stirring in the darkness and presently, Leemish came to us. Jaska held up her hands to show him the binding on her wrists. I held my hand up to show him the little knife.

"Oh," he said, then "Ah." Jaska turned to look at me.

"Go and free my friend, bring him here." And Jaska translated.

When he had gone: "What now?" she asked.

"You'll be going with us for the time being. I want my weapons, Simeon wants his scroll bag and we both want our money."

These were brought and my companion checked that all was as it should be. It was a nice send off. The little band of less-than-ept brigands assembled to watch us depart; gloomy faces, every one of them.

Jaska led the way, a length of rope knotted round her neck; I even cut her hands free so she could push through the brush more easily. We walked for something like half an hour and then I stopped. Perforce, Jaska stopped and behind me, Simeon stopped as well. Behind *him*, like an echo, there were several muffled footfalls.

"Did you hear those boots just then?" I asked Jaska.

"Hmm?"

I closed the distance, the tether lying on the ground. "Jaska. I told you leave your friends behind. Did I not make this clear?"

She nodded and swung her hand in a tight arc, a narrow bladed knife came at my eyes out of the gloom but I was still the faster and caught her wrist before harm was done. Where had she got it from? One of her men probably, as we made ready. I had been careless and I was annoyed—with myself as much as her.

"I think you wondered how I had collected all those scars?" I put a threatening note into my voice, took hold of her collar, and pulled her across to me. "I will tell you something that you won't believe. When your ancestors crossed the Southern Ocean I was already a young man. I will still be alive when you are dead and rotting in the ground."

I whispered in her ear. "Your lives are a like a mayfly's; I do not give a fig for such as you. Now tell your lads to go home—or your corpse will be rotting right here, now."

"Leemish," she called and there was more than a tiny quaver in her voice.

"Leemish…" There followed several sentences which I hoped said what I had said.

We hurried north and once Nantes was well and truly behind us, we trod the country roads as before. Simeon thought a great deal and occasionally made a nuisance of himself by asking what had happened to me in the thieves' shelter while he had been freezing his sweetbreads off. I told him the incident had been too distressing, and I preferred not to discuss it.

Fish and game were plentiful; we bought bread at the occasional cottage and slept rough or with oxen and horses. I slept with Morion once in my dreams and wondered if I had disturbed Simeon at all—not that he said anything nor even gave a sign. I let her think I was on my way south and told her I travelled in the company of an old monk who made herbal tea every night.

We saw the lights of Vannes late on the seventh day as we crested the final pass, and we were now faced with the steep road down to the coast. We were later than usual since it had been agreed that one way or another, we would sleep in civilized beds this night. The light had gone entirely by the time we reached the harbor—still loud with town life. Shops were lit with strings of oil lamps suspended from the ceiling, standing lanterns, or the naked flames of flambeaux.

Here was a town which had overcome the envy of the Northmmen and prospered. There were dozens of smells in the air, most of them from eating places: cuts of meat, savory pastries, sausages, cakes, sweets. Mixed in were the odors of incense wafting from shrines, wine and ale from taverns, women's perfumes. The sound was compounded of street hawkers' cries, late-scavenging seagulls, fishing boats leaving for the night, the roar of surf and a thousand conversations—each pitched to carry over the rest. And the sights; there are always fresh things to see in a newly visited place; live a thousand years and you will still be surprised. Believe me.

Above us, a row of terracotta heads was mortared into the stonework between the floors of a rather grand house. They looked down at us with a variety of expressions—one with a squint, another with an overlong nose, and a third was sticking out its tongue. We passed a sad-looking scarecrow made of straw and sacking sitting with its feet locked into a set of stocks at the edge of the market square: *here, but for the grace of the Gods go you...* he seemed to say. A line of mortar squares sunk into the plaza in front of the church; each one imprinted, so a sign said, with the footprints of babies born on the day of dedication.

Whimsy, warning, and commemoration.

Although the hour was late by our reckoning, taverns were still trading briskly and in one of these a number of tables were set apart for eating. We entered here and ordered a meal of shrimp and fried seaweed, two loaves of crusted brown bread and a flagon of ale. I could not remember eating a finer meal, though hunger and four or five days of bland river fish may have prejudiced my judgment. Simeon broke open the shrimp shells, sliced the pale meat with his knife, and then took out his fork to spear the flesh.

We ate and talked. Simeon said, "It's been a pleasant journey this past few days. What of you? Have you enjoyed it?"

"Indeed I have. Actually, there has been no danger since the robbers released us. It would be wrong of me to continue taking money for protection you don't need."

"I still wonder how you made that happen. Mont Saint-Michel is two days away, only then I shall be going on to Britain. Why not keep me company as far as the monastery, anyway? Another dernier..."

He had not spoken loudly, yet I saw someone at a nearby table sit up and glance our way when he mentioned the Mont. I watched them surreptitiously as I took in my meal. They spoke to one another and looked ever and again at us from deep, dark eye sockets. These two were remarkably like the guards who had escorted me from Mandor though far more... sub-human. It was the only word that came to mind, though there was a passing shrewdness in their manner, and both wore overlarge hats, which hid their skulls.

There were three large shrimp left on my plate; I leaned low over the table as though I had found something wrong, poking at one of the shrimps and speaking to Simeon in a low voice.

"There are two men at a table to your left, a little behind you—no, don't look now," I warned. "They looked up when you mentioned Mont Saint-Michel." I picked apart the shell on my plate with slow thoroughness. "They are scrutinizing you again, now." I waited. "Now they are talking. Drop something on the floor and look at them while you pick it up."

He did this and put the knife back in the dish. He was agitated, though he covered it well enough. "They are the same ones—or the same sort. Note how alike they are, their dark coloring…"

I looked, nodding my head as though at some point we debated. "Rough, but not unintelligent. You say the same ones? Same as what?"

"Those who killed Ricard and stole my ring the other day. By now, they must know they have the wrong one."

"Hmm, I see. I had planned to walk along the quay tonight, up and down, just to pass the time. But if this place can offer us a bed then I suggest we stay inside."

Simeon nodded now, leaning back then forward again. "This may decide you to part company."

"On the contrary. I *will* come—not just to earn my pay, but…" I paused as I realized that I had come to like the fellow, even though he had short-changed me with the truth. "I will come because I want to see you safely to wherever you're going." I would press him for the rest of his story tonight. I wanted to know why two nasty-looking individuals with receding foreheads and black eyes under knobby brows were so interested in him.

Simeon ordered some more ale and at the same time, arranged for a bed-chamber, paying for the best place in the house. We took the ale with us and went to the highest room, up in the roof with the ridge pole running across the center of the small chamber. A narrow window looked out onto the harbor through the gable wall.

Simeon used his flint and iron to set a rush light burning, and as he straightened up, his shadow rose up the wall behind him like some hunchbacked black phantasm. I shivered and unbuckled my sword belt to sit down comfortably on a bed.

"Now. Tell me what this is all about," I said. "I need to know—it's part of providing effective protection. Why are they after you?"

Simeon cleaned his knife and fork. "I don't know for sure." He leaned his back against the wall and frowned. "I don't know what they are either, these men who set about us. Surely they've been born without God's Grace—so brutish and simian, unless there is a country where apes clever enough to eat at table are bred. They say the Moors in Lyonesse perform all manner of offensive rites; perhaps they are from there."

"Lyonesse?" I asked and shrugged. Lyonesse was a place I had never been to. Rumors were rife, and while they were probably wrong or exaggerated, there may have been some kernel of fact behind them. Still, I did not believe the teachings of Islam would allow such experiments—there or anywhere else. "Why would men from Lyonesse be interested in you?"

"Not me," he said. "It's the *scrolls* they are interested in." Simeon patted the leather case and dropped it on to the other bed. "They took my ring the other day purely to prove they had killed the right man. At least that's the only reason I can think of." He turned to lean a shoulder against the window's edge to look out into the night—and came face to face with a pair of glittering eyes.

He fell back with a cry of horror, but nowhere near fast enough; a hairy arm snaked through the narrow window and pulled him forward until his shoulders were jammed against either side of the opening. Simeon jabbed his meat fork into the creature's arm repeatedly until it stuck there immovably. I grabbed for my sword, stripping the scabbard away as I rushed across the room. By that time, a second hand had appeared. It tugged at the brick and plaster about the window and enlarged the hole as if the wall had been made of cheese.

This worked to my advantage, for it gave me more of a target than the single arm tightening around the back of Simeon's neck. I chopped at the wrist and as it withdrew from harm's way, stabbed at the exposed breast. The blade went in and a satisfying amount of blood leaked out as I pulled back, but it seemed not to discommode the creature in any way. I went for its face then, aiming for an eye. But it was too quick; with a jerk of its head to one side, it avoided my thrust— though not quite enough. The edge of my sword opened up a gash from its temple back over the ear and the sudden pain distracted it a moment. My next attack *did* connect with its eye and it let go of Simeon and fell silently back into the night.

Simeon could hardly speak, his face had been crushed against the wall or perhaps, against the creature's skull, it had given him a bloody nose and had almost throttled him. He turned about and suddenly mouthed something at me; massaging his throat, he pointed frantically.

I realized what he was trying to tell me as soon as another arm took *me* round the throat. It simply lifted me off my feet and slammed me up against the wall. The arm was bare, but it felt like an oak branch as it squeezed and I felt the other arm move behind me preparatory to plunging a knife into my back.

I was faster, though. Instinctively, I had already reversed my short Roman sword and drove it back along my right side. I felt it pierce something—my assailant's gut, I hoped. As the grip on my neck relaxed, I turned and it was as I had expected; the man—if I can call it that—was bent low, using his left hand to hold the gash in his belly closed but already coming back at me with a long knife extended.

I hacked at the knuckles and sent the knife flying, then followed through to the throat, which was exposed and taut as he looked up at me from his bent position. The blade entered and I pushed it up into the skull, making chopped meat of its brain. When I had ceased panting, I looked around and saw a hole torn in the thatch roof where he had come through. Had their timing been better—if the second had entered a dozen heartbeats earlier when I was fully involved with the first assailant, I would have lost my life—quite irrevocably.

The corpse was that of an exceedingly hirsute man, somewhat shorter than me, so of average height. Under a shock of wiry hair, a low forehead bulged with two great brow ridges and black eyes sunk into deep orbits, the skull was flattened and misshapen. I had ridden for a fortnight with sixteen men much like this one, though details were different and obviously their tribe was not the same. Although we might have strayed into the area of Max's operations, I did not believe that these two were connected with Max's undertaking. It felt more like an opportunistic attempt at theft to me.

I began to spell this out to Simeon as I urged him to help move the body. He frowned as we heaved it through the newly enlarged window and he saw the bare feet with toenails like claws and hands whose crooked digits would do duty as claws as well as fingers. We let go and I heard the corpse thud into the street below.

"What do we have worthy of theft?" he shivered in revulsion. "Those were vile, unnatural creatures."

I shrugged and recalled the creatures from my dreams of the other night. If these were throwbacks, then those other sorts must have come from nightmares. We cleaned ourselves up, I had some of their foul smelling blood on my shirt, which I washed off and wrung out as dry as I could before putting it back on again. I had also splashed the stuff over Simeon's hair when I'd cut the first one; he washed it thoroughly in water from the pitcher we had brought for morning ablutions.

"What do we do now?" he asked.

"First, we renegotiate my fee to three derniers a day," I said and laughed, trying to lighten his grim and frightened expression. Maybe it worked and maybe it didn't, but I was starting to have doubts. Was it worth it for a few coins?

"Whatever you think is fair," he said. "It's not safe here now; maybe we ought to go on tonight—now. Just walk out." He passed me a cup of what was becoming a customary nightcap.

As I drank I shook my head. "The money thing was a joke; isn't your order allowed to laugh? It's safe enough for the time being. Those two creatures from hell are too dead to report back on their failure. Perhaps you know every town around here, but I don't, and I don't like the idea of walking at random in the dark."

"No," he nodded and then shook his head. "I don't know the place either. I come from much further away."

"I'm going to get some sleep." I took off my boots and laid back.

"Sleep? After this?" Obviously, he thought it a lunatic idea.

"I'm tired. You keep watch if you like and I'll take over about midnight. All right?" And with that, I closed my eyes and oblivion took me until just before first light, and for once I slept without dreams or visions. Simeon, too, was asleep when I woke up, still propped up on his bed with his back against the wall. The second creature's knife lay across his knees as he snored robustly.

There was a cupful of water left in the pitcher. I dampened my kerchief with it and washed my face before waking Simeon.

"We'll leave before the place is properly awake. That way, there won't be recriminations about the damage."

He nodded and put the knife down on the bed as he went to wash. I picked it up and looked at it, the blade was longer than my forearm—almost a small sword and awkward for close fighting, which explained why it had taken so long for my assailant to plunge it between my ribs. It was one of those wiggly things, curving from side to side along the length of the blade, and the hand grip was made of copper wire with a brass pommel. Heavy, unwieldy, thank the gods. I lifted the blade and sniffed; a groove along the blade's centerline held an acrid smelling grease that left a sickly-sweet sensation behind it: *poison*. These were not the weapons that Morion's contingent had—which meant that there *were* other breeds about. These primitive men clearly kept to themselves, living concealed in the high forests in small groups within a tribe that rarely grew beyond a hundred or so.

We trod softly down the stairs and out through the tavern's back door. A sleepy boy was carrying kitchen rubbish out to a midden behind the tavern, but he was the only one to see us leave and would probably forget all about us within the hour.

We turned the corner and I looked up to confirm that this was the end of the building where our room had been. It was, there was the damaged window and here on the ground was the rubble. A stain of blood in the dust of the alley and a trace of that nauseous smell in the air. No bodies.

"How did they get up there?" Simeon asked. He had a point. The alley was quite wide—too wide to do a knees and back ascent. The window to our room looked out over the top of the next property, well out of reach of a cat burglar; that was why it was the landlord's most expensive room.

I pointed to marks in the wall. "Iron spikes in the wall, do you think?"

"Would they not be there still?" he asked, reasonably.

I chewed my lip. "Remember the creature's hands and toes?"

He nodded, "More like an animal's."

"I think they just hung on by their toe and fingernails."

"And the bodies—where have they gone?" Simeon had a way with questions.

"Maybe I didn't kill the first one after all, or maybe there was a third one out here." I stepped on something and looked down. "Simeon." Simeon's fork was there, I had trodden it into the dust, but the tines were still discolored with blood. He nodded and walked on.

"Don't you want it?"

He shook his head, "I don't wish to use it again—not after it's been stuck in one of those animals."

"You told me that you knew every town and village in these parts," I said when we were halfway through a brace of herring.

"Me? I'm a stranger here."

Which accorded with what I surmised. "You asked me about the village of Marcon, about the mayor—"

Simeon grinned a little shamefacedly. "I was making it up. I wanted to know what you were doing there, and where you'd come from. I just wanted to listen and see if you were telling the truth."

I chuckled and then and ate another mouthful. "And was I?"

The sun was dipping its lower edge into the far western sea as we reached the small town of Mont Saint-Michel. The mount was a black silhouette against the setting sun surrounded by shining sea. The tide rose and fell by more than the height of a two-story house in this bay, and it would remain high until well into the morning. We would have to wait to cross the half mile causeway on foot. Simeon and I quartered the town carefully and found nine taverns along the beach. We chose the smallest and darkest.

We dined. There was fish to be had, but I doubt it had swum within the past two days—we ate black bread instead and sour ale. I heard Simeon talking in my sleep, but it did not disturb me. I slept without incident... well, with only one small incident which rather pleased me. 'Twixt waking and dreaming, I felt the ghostly touch of Morion's lips upon my own.

Where are you? she seemed to ask in a whisper.

Old habits die hard, of course. I showed her mental pictures of snow-capped mountains in the distance, and a steep-sided valley with a tumbling river along its length. Her presence left me and I slept soundly.

After breakfast at a quite different establishment that was open to the wind, we walked along the quay. A pleasant springtime breeze surrounded us with that fresh, never-breathed-before feel to it, so rather than wait another hour to use the causeway, we hired a man to row us over the smooth and glistening waters. It was beautiful until we arrived; I stepped overboard into a patch of mud I swear would have swallowed me whole but for Simeon's quick reach. I made the steps barefoot, my boots under water and at the bottom of layers of mud.

"I may charge you for a pair of new boots," I said, by way of a joke.

Simeon missed the tone of voice. "Of course," he said but his attention was on the rocky spire ringed by military strength walls. "It's said that the Archangel Gabriel ordered the first church to be built here, but the Bishop ignored him until Gabriel burned a hole in his skull with his finger."

"Ouch." *Oh, excellent Gods!*

VIII

imeon described our destination. "There's a chapel at the top, the monastery is just beneath it. We may have to wait to get through the gate of course, I don't know what time it's opened."

We didn't have to wait long. The gateway was opened exactly as the sun lifted over the low inland hills, it glinted off spear points racked against the gate towers, crossbows wielded by guards, and from catapults mounted on the towers and turrets.

"To discourage pirates?" I asked, pointing. "What do they have that's so valuable?"

"It's said the monastery has more gold than most palaces," Simeon said. "I can believe it, too. The chapel dates from around the fourth century, but Abbot Hildebert plans a great abbey to replace it. He intends to have enough built in his life time to lay his bones beneath the altar in this place he calls home. And that takes gold."

Inside the wall, I had imagined there would be a maze of narrow streets lined with tall narrow buildings but it was not the case. A single broad roadway climbed the hill in a series of switchback curves; terraces ran off the main path with one- and two-story houses built on the upper side and the backs of the lower row forming a wall along the lower side.

Most of the buildings had shops or taverns on the ground floor with living accommodation above and doors opening onto the higher roadway. We looked along each of these until we came to a boot-maker. I chose, and Simeon paid for, a pair of fine leather boots made with iron studs in the heels and along the out-side of the soles. The pattern the boot maker embossed into the surface was made from a tracing of the interlocking lines engraved on my sword. These boots were infinitely better than the pair I had been wearing but, on reflection, I reckoned that Simeon owed me the extra in danger money. I presume he thought so too, he paid up when we collected them without a murmur, not even a hint of a haggle.

Further up we took breakfast. Very civilized: savory pastries and mulled wine in front of a shop selling all manner of weird paraphernalia. There was a pile of skulls in one corner—a notice said they were shrunken human skulls, I guessed them to be monkey heads; bundles of pungent herbs, glass globes both clear and

misty; mummified sea creatures; the shiny stone seashells that come from sift-
ing through shingle and the mysterious fish pictures which can be found in the
cracks between layers of rock.

We finished breakfast and threw crumbs to the ever-present seagulls. I put
my new boots on, trying them for comfort as we continued our climb up the
steep street. By the time we came to a stop, I was ready to pronounce my foot-
wear excellent, superb, unmatchable. We were before a small door of dusty oak
set between decaying sandstone pillars. The door was bound with thick bands of
iron and a spy window in its upper quarter was protected by a grille and an inner
trapdoor.

Simeon knocked and a minute or so later, the trap opened and an unpleasant
eye looked out at us. It was bloodshot and between the ruptured vessels, the sclera
was an unhealthy yellow; yet this proved to be the functional one.

The eyeball looked us over. A question was asked in an unknown language
to which Simeon gave answer in the same tongue. There was the dull rattle of
bolts being drawn, the lighter sound of a lock being released. The door opened.
The warden's other eye was a hollow empty socket partly filled with scar tissue
resembling a spoonful of old tripe.

He led us up wooden stairs paralleling the street outside, landings occurred
where the road leveled out for side turnings; whole streets had been roofed over
and made a part of the buildings on each side to create this mismatched maze.
From each landing, doors opened on to cross corridors on our left. Between, leading off the stairs, there were empty cells, store rooms, shrines; all of them seemingly added on without thought to the veritable warren in the making.

At the highest level was a transverse corridor with polished oak paneling and
carved posts to support the roof, a wool carpet of muted colors covered the floor,
painted traceries adorned the plaster ceiling: *upper rank country*. The ugly bent
old man led us along this corridor to the last door and knocked.

"Entrez."

The warden opened it and we *entrezed*. A waft of incense met us.

"Ah! Matthias."

My friend—whom I had known as Simeon until then—was recognized
immediately—without a second glance which was somewhat impressive. "Welcome to the abbey. One moment while I finish this…"

My immediate thought was how this clarified many things… the odd turn
of phrase, the things *Simeon-Matthias* had taken for granted. This was the Matthias who had been the thirteenth apostle. Should I query him about it or just call
him Matthias from now on? A second thought trailed the first: had I seen him in
centuries past? Perhaps, in Jerusalem?

The Abbot possessed a high domed skull which he kept shaved and polished—just to show off the impressive architecture. This was a man in which vanity had taken root and flourished like a flower tended with the utmost care and attention. He wore a cream-colored linen robe over a saffron undershirt, a plain ebony crucifix hung from a heavy gold chain around his neck. A multitude of gold rings adorned his fingers, and most of the rings carried gems. He also had an arrogant misunderstanding of time, the "moment" it took to finish his letter stretched out into minutes during which we were ignored completely. I used the time to take stock of how a high priest of the Christians furnished his work room.

The place was vast and where Hildebert sat, it was lit with the pink glow of sunlight entering through a most beautifully decorated roof light. The glass was cut and leaded to make a picture of the Christian God, the figure of a man nailed to a wooden cross in the Roman fashion. Having attended and officiated at such executions, I'm inclined to question a religion which has such an effigy of torture as its emblem. While the representation was grotesque to my eyes, the execution was exquisite; the colors were shades of pastel green and blue, many shades of ivory and the bright, bright red of blood. The central figure's flesh stood out pale and forlorn against the rich dark browns of timber.

Two walls were lined with laden book shelves stretching the length of the room and there were three large and heavy tables with pots of pens and inks. On the end wall there were no shelves; instead, a map of the world was fastened to the paneling and I wandered across to see it in detail. It extended from Cappadocia in the east to Lyonesse and from the lands of the Northmen to Tripolitania in the south. I leaned nearer so I could read the names of monasteries; there was Mont Saint-Michel, a tiny *almost-island* off the coast of Normandy.

"Curious, Gerard?" Simeon's or rather, Matthias's voice in my ear.

"Of course. You had better conclude your business with the Abbot first though."

My friend nodded. Presumably he had divined my meaning—I was more curious about Matthias than about geography. We turned back toward the cleric.

Already tall, the Abbot was seated at a writing lectern which put him a full head and several shoulders above us. He glanced once from Simeon to me and back again when he eventually laid down the quill. "And whom do we have here?" His tone of voice was affected; falsely world-weary, slow to the point of irritation, each syllable pronounced as though he spoke a foreign tongue.

"Hildebert, this is Gerard," said Matthias. "He is my protector, his trustworthiness is proven."

The Abbot tilted his head so he could really look down his long aristocratic nose at me: *a hired bodyguard? How vulgar,* the expression said. I folded my arms and conveyed my own dislike.

"Well, if you believe it necessary and you vouch for him."

"I do and I do."

"I expect you are weary, Matthias. Go and bathe, have something to eat and we will talk again in a little while. I dare say they can find something for your companion in the kitchen." He fluttered his fingers—a gesture of dismissal.

"If I have ever met a person more unpleasant than that one, it was so long ago that I have forgotten," I said as the door closed behind us. Our unsightly friend fixed me with his right eye and chortled, his teeth were as distasteful a sight as his mismatched eye sockets.

"He may possess qualities which are less obvious."

"It's unlikely, I usually tend to pick up on even the smallest good point." I turned to our companion. "While Matthias is bathing, you had better take me to the kitchen."

Simeon-Matthias put a restraining hand on my arm. "That will not be necessary. You will come with me; you will enjoy the same privileges that I do."

"Thank you," I said quietly. Matthias didn't answer though under cover of his beard, I saw his lips twitch into a smile.

We were taken to a communal bathing chamber although, at this particular hour, we had it to ourselves. Attendants filled two tubs with hot water. We disrobed and stepped in to the steaming water, it was so hot I had to bite my lip to stop myself from shouting. What luxury.

A boy rubbed my back with gritty soap and laved it with hot water. He would have attended to other regions of my body, but I took the soap and dealt with it myself. Then I shaved with a blade of Damascus steel and oiled my chin with an unguent scented with sandalwood, both steel and ointment I filched from a chest which made Matthias "tsk" at my effrontery and again when I put them neatly away, in my own bag.

Afterward, we were given a tour of the place. Matthias made obeisance in a small chapel and folded his hands in prayer. I stood at the back, fingering my sword and looking fierce so that my function would be obvious. We were shown our cells, that is, our sleeping accommodation; then, to a great hall where Abbot Hildebert was wont to address the brothers on occasion and finally, to the refectory. Our guide, not the abhorrent monk who had admitted us but a mostly silent and introverted man with an amazingly pink scalp shining through his tonsure, left us here after giving instructions to the two greasy-robed brothers who prepared the food.

We were hungry now, after what seemed the thirty or forty chains we had walked around the rambling monastery. We fell to, feasting on thick soup and warm crusty bread, sliced meats and juicy vegetables and a leathern beaker of ale where the kick was hidden by the sweetness on the tongue. My growing appetite thrust my questions temporarily to one side.

"Well," I spoke a little grudgingly with my mouth full. "Pathetic and unpleasant though undoubtedly he is, the Abbot of this place keeps a fine table."

"There you are, you see." Matthias too, spoke with difficulty through a full mouth. "Hidden qualities. Benedictines are noted for the quality of their table."

Then I remembered where I had first glimpsed my companion. "Matthias?"

"Hmm?"

"Are you named for the one who heads your order?"

He paused for quite a long time then: "Not exactly. More…"

"You *are* the head of your order?"

"Just so."

"I saw you once, on the way to an execution at Jerusalem."

"Jerusalem? That was…"

"A thousand years ago. Yes."

He nodded and when we had finished eating, Matthias began to speak. What he had said before was the truth—or I believe, it was the truth as far as he saw it, anyway.

We poured more ale and Matthias told me the whole tale, including the parts he had previously missed out.

The second manifestation of the Son aspect of his God had been expected almost every year since he had been killed. Signs and portents came thick and fast but there never was a second appearance. As the generations went by and the thousandth year after his incarnation drew closer, more and more of the Christian hierarchy became certain this would be the year of His return.

Sixteen years ago, the year in question arrived, the God did not.

Perversely, Christianity had spread like a plague but the Church had busied itself with irrelevant detail. It buried its God in meaningless ritual and set about gathering more wealth around its high priests than any king out of history. And they went to war with the Saracen to take Christian possession of Jerusalem and failed even to reach that city.

Matthias spoke fiercely and with authority. He spoke as though his God had been a friend and had confided in him. He spoke as though his God had grown ever more disheartened by the religion which had gathered such strength around the Jews' indifference. The world made their own image of Him, a ritual of ultimately meaningless activities and a set of rules that the wealthy circumvented every day.

God's interest waned.

To my mind, it was hardly surprising. Mankind is neither a pleasant species nor an amenable one and had I been seated on the divine throne, I too would have had second thoughts.

But Matthias's God seemed to have made no provision for the failure of His plan, and having failed, there was no alternative plan to go to.

As Matthias put it: "Men and women have grown evil and wayward, they refused to listen. God has abandoned the people He created and His thousand year plan. He has removed Himself rather than watch the evil and baseness passed on to generation after generation."

"And the twelve scrolls?"

"They are God's plan. I have collected them at Hypolita Keep over the generations. Now I have another from Hildebert and there is one more to collect in Britain. None of them can be read separately to any great effect, they all have to be together to bring about the complete rebuilding of the world. There is simply too much for one human brain to absorb but with enough people together, the entire meaning becomes clear. It can be put into effect even though He is no longer with us."

"It appears to be one tremendous job."

"Oh no. Not really. Once brought together, the plan will come to fruition as a matter of course. The physical assemblage comes first and then the reading which is what brings about God's will—a metaphysical process."

"There are copies of course?"

"Copies?" Matthias shook his head very slowly. "No. It would not be possible to copy them. Simply not possible."

I was taken aback. "And yet you—we—stroll around, unaccompanied, with these," I hesitated, trying to comprehend the thoughts which filled my brain, "these... priceless documents."

These were world-changing machines, hidden in a commonplace scroll case. I came to see their importance, a blinding insight, unique in all of history. "This is too great a responsibility for one man."

"You are accompanying me."

"You should have an army to protect you."

"In an ideal world..." Matthias thought some more. "You see Gerard, there are only a few of us who know of these relics, recognize their full import, and of those, even fewer who know as I do. And an army costs a lot of money, the Monastery of St. Hypolita has little."

"But it is not just the Monastery of St. Hypolita is it? There must be hundreds of monasteries and the like who would contribute."

"Sadly, that is not the case."

"What about our good Abbot Hildebert? You said yourself that there's a lot of gold here."

"All of it designated, though."

"But…" I frowned a moment. "Are there not priorities to consider?"

Matthias smiled a little sadly. "Priorities are already decided. To Hildebert, his tomb is of the highest, and his chantry of course. In any case, he has no belief in the destiny of the scrolls, nor is he alone in this."

"A small amount then, a small contingent of guards."

"Ha ha. You are that small contingent. No, the truth is that I, or at least, St. Hypolita's, have to pay Hildebert for the scroll. I have the final payment here."

"The final…? Is there no limit to the fellow's avarice?"

"I have no reason to believe he has limits of any kind. Did I not say there are hidden qualities."

"*Qualities?* "

"Qualities may be good or bad, Gerard." For once, his tone was bitter. He fell quiet for a few moments, then continued. "It is best to travel inconspicuously."

"But you haven't, Matthias. Someone knows about your scrolls."

"The situation is a little worrying. I pray to God every day, perhaps He will consider us a special case and give us his protection."

I leaned forward and refilled our cups. I leaned back again and looked at Matthias. "What is it like to speak with a God?"

"I cannot tell you that, Gerard. I do not have the words."

He fell silent again; silent for so long I thought he would not speak again. Perhaps I had offended him.

"Memories of love, of hope. Memories of worship," he said eventually. "The most beautiful place in this world pales into insignificance, it is rude, primitive against the fragmentary remembrances of His presence. The love of a mother or father, of a woman… they are nothing when I think of the smallest, most trivial of His concerns for us."

Again the silence and then almost in a whisper… "Even the self-loathing when I came to realize what an unworthy vessel I had become, was a wonder, a beauteous thing, something to cling to."

At the other end of the refectory, pans banged and kettles bubbled but the disturbance was far, far away. In *our* world, all was quiet.

And again, silence fell. I felt infinite compassion for this man who had spoken with his God, to be thrown crumbs which outweighed the whole world. Was pity misplaced, wrong?

Eventually I spoke. "I often wonder why a God would create a following of thousands of people, millions, for the purpose of abasing themselves and of worshipping Him. I know a God's intentions may well be inscrutable but it seems," I searched for a word, "it seems arrogant."

"God is God," Matthias said quietly. "Whatever His reasons they are not for us to question."

Which seemed no more than a get-out clause, I thought.

"I think that you think that God may come again to you if He sees his plan being worked out."

Matthias smiled a sad little smile. He shook his head. "God does not make decisions only to change them on a whim. He is not a capricious being."

It seemed to me that He very definitely did and He was. I changed the subject. "And was it this God who gifted you so long a life?"

"No. The long life is mine, it's a family trait."

I looked at him more closely. "A family trait? Where does your family come from?"

He shrugged. "From Euboea."

"Greece. I've heard of an Amaranthine family from there, the Family Cimon." I had the idea that perhaps Morion came from that family, too. *Coincidence?* I don't like coincidences; I'm suspicious of them.

Matthias nodded. "Cimon *is* my family, of course, though it has been a long, long time since I left there." He shook his head. "Too long when I think of it. Let us be truthful with one another, I was a physician in Jerusalem during the Roman occupation, I met Jesus there, shortly before He was put to death." He brooded for a moment or two. "I have never returned to Euboea since. In fact, for a long time they thought me truly dead."

He snorted with laughter, restored from the cruel recollections of his God. "I have heard from them, of course. I've had letters. They think I'm a fool perhaps, they think my beliefs are perverse. They gave me a derogatory name, called me Bishop when I was simply an Abbot." He shrugged, dismissing the matter. "Now," he said, turning on me suddenly, "it is your turn."

"Mine?"

"Yours. You have told me a pack of lies from beginning to end. Time for *you* to tell the truth."

I laughed a little. "Hmm. Where to start? At the beginning? That was where I told you, Upper Germania—that's where my Family lived and still do today. Myself, I was born when Crassus and Pompey ruled in Rome with Julius, that would be about…"

"I remember Julius Caesar announcing himself Dictator."

I shrugged. "It must have been a decade before that when I went south as a young man, over the mountains and enlisted in the Roman army—just to see the world." I thought back. "I saw a lot of frontiers without learning very much except how to fight and stay alive."

Matthias nodded. "You're Amaranthine, like me. It is surprising," he said, though he did not look surprised, "surprising how few we meet, of our sort I mean. What is your family?"

"Schonau."

"Schonau. Yes, I recall the name or something like it, probably the sound has changed since I was a part of the Families. I do remember marriage arrangements with a place in Germania. Some time, when we have the time, you must relate your life to me, so I can write it down."

I laughed. "I don't think so, Sim… Matthias. I don't think the Family would be happy about that at all."

"Hmm. Secretive."

"That's the word," I smiled.

"So what has brought you out this way, to where we met."

"Disgrace."

"Pardon?"

"Punishment. I'm in disgrace. I've been more or less banished from the Family estate until some trouble blows over."

"Would you care to tell me more?"

I laughed. "I had an escort from Uncle Max—I don't know what his real name is but he just called himself *Big* in the old words so we call him Maximus—Max." I stopped a moment, thinking of the men who had waylaid us at the inn. *Uncle's private army?* I was beginning to think of them as base and little more than wild animals… but it was not true. With an effort, I could admire them, living their own lives way up in the mountains. My head seemed bereft of its usual clarity since joining up with my friend.

"What were you being punished for?" Matthias asked, breaking the tenuous chain of thought.

"I told you that, remember?" I was about to continue when we were interrupted by a young boy rushing into the refectory.

"Brother Matthias?"

Matthias nodded. "I am Matthias. Am I needed?"

"Yes, yes. In the lower crypt, come quickly, the Prior is there, I will take you."

Matthias got up from his seat. I rose too, swinging my legs over the bench and away from the table.

"The Master said nothing about anyone else."

"That's all right," Matthias told him. "Where I go, so does my friend."

The boy lifted his shoulders. "Come then, this way."

He took us further into the warren of wood paneled corridors and while I maintained a certain feeling for my whereabouts, I soon lost the route we took through the man-made maze, plunging through a score of identical passages as we worked our way lower and lower. The timber floors and walls gave way to brick and then to native stone, and the ceilings were supported by heavily built pillars and archways. The ways were dim and lit with widely spaced oil lamps; the air smelt damp and smoky. Now the walls and ceilings were rounded and jagged with stalactites—caves, natural or cut by men into the bedrock.

At last we came to a vast, low-ceilinged room. It was filled with coffins: wooden, stone, bundled reeds and pottery urns. They dwindled into the distant shadows—hundreds of them, perhaps thousands.

Apart from a corner of relative brilliance, the place was swathed in shifting shadows and skeins of spider web burdened with the dust of ages. The boy took us to the lighted corner where a small brazier warmed and dried the immediate area. Two monks and the supercilious Hildebert were standing there, waiting. Somewhere in the darkness, water dripped steadily.

The Abbot looked at me once and then ignored me.

"The scroll has been stolen," he said, looking at Matthias then back to a slumped body half hidden in a monk's habit. "Brother Anselm was the guardian today. He has gone to his reward."

I turned the body over. Brother Anselm had been a very strong man, but probably neither fast nor aggressive. Of what use are great muscles against a single sword thrust through the left breast? I bent low and sniffed a faintly acrid smell with a sweet aftertaste. The same toxin was on the blade that Matthias now carried. "A poisoned knife."

"Where was the scroll kept?" Matthias asked.

"In this niche."

The niche which the Abbot had indicated had been closed off by a plain iron door with two separate locks to it. Both had been burst, the bolts bent and pulled clear of the sockets into which they had been driven; the door panel itself, though iron and as thick as my boot sole, was badly distorted.

"How long ago?" I asked.

The Abbot answered Matthias rather than me, "It occurred less than a half hour ago." "What is the state of the tide?" I asked

Again, the Abbot spoke to Matthias. "The tide is high. The causeway has been covered this past hour."

I tugged at Matthias's sleeve. "Tell this arrogant Christian to get as many patrols on to the walls as possible, in case they are still inside the town. We shall need some sort of authority to give orders to the militia and to have the gates opened for us."

Abbot Hildebert pressed his lips together but did, at last, deign to notice me. He took a ring from his finger and gave it to Matthias.

"You!" I caught hold of the boy who had brought us here by the shoulder. "Take us out to the street, the quickest way there is."

Outside of the crypt, rickety steps rose through a square hole in the ceiling; they went upwards as far as we could see. The youngster took us up three flights, which brought us to the timber-built section again—presumably above ground. A three minute run brought us to a small gate. I lifted the two bars out of their brackets and the door swung inwards with the protesting screams of long-disused hinges.

Beyond the door, the day was already over, the night dark; a slim crescent of moon and the few stars did little to light our way. We had exited far nearer the foot of the slope than I had realized and we came surprisingly quickly to the main gates which protected the settlement on the hill of Saint Michel.

Matthias found the Captain of the Guard inside the gatehouse sending squads of men along the wall to the east. We showed him the Prior's ring. "Has anything untoward been seen?"

"Untoward, you call it?" He hooked a thumb over his shoulder. "Three, four beast men and several wolves are killing off everything I send against them. Do you call that 'untoward'?"

"And? Progress?"

We're containing them but no more."

"Muster archers," I said. "These men are using poisoned swords. Shoot them; we do not need to take any of them alive."

The Officer looked at me once, nodded and went out to change the orders. We followed and as soon as he had his men organized, we asked where the engagement was. For answer he just pointed. The parapet was about the height of three men here, about a hundred paces along. Just before a tower where it turned a corner, a bunch of men-at-arms were gingerly probing the defenses of the force the Captain had mentioned. We approached and, even as we watched, a body flew off the walkway; others—dead or injured—lay in the street. However, archers were shooting up into the conflict now and the guard backed off a little more to give them room. A second force of bowmen had climbed to the roof of a nearby building and were loosing their arrows downward. A few successful shots killed several of the shambling creatures and brought one of the marauders tumbling down to the street, injured but alive. The creature walked on all fours and snapped at the guards who held it in a corner with spears. It died quickly, its body seeming to partly transform into a human being as it bled to death. I knew these half-beasts from my dreams and felt sick.

The other raiders had thrown caution to the winds and were climbing up between the crenulations. From there, they simply jumped outward.

"Open the gate," I shouted, "and bring lanterns."

There was a rattle of keys and the rumble of a heavy bar being drawn back as soon as the Captain of the Guard repeated my words. We ran out and along the foot of the wall where they must have landed.

They had lost a second of their number here. Clearly, both legs had been broken in the leap and he was dragging himself with his arms across the rocks and sand towards the waves; I dispatched him and watched the hairy legs of a wolf change back to a man's limbs. There were two others of that same ilk at least and in the deceiving light of the new moon, we could just make out movement close to where the causeway came up out of the sea. A boat was being rowed in towards shadowy figures running to the nearer end of the causeway.

"Catapults! Bring those catapults to bear," I bawled. "Sink the boat!"

Almost at once, something swished through the air above my head, glowing, leaving a trail of sparks. It hit the water just to one side of the causeway and erupted in flames—the flames spread out across the water while some were actually burning below the surface. The guard must have had the weapons on the wall already targeted on the causeway, primed and ready to fire at a moment's notice. I grinned in admiration of such efficiency; they had already been preparing the fire bombs, too. A second missile was released and would have hit the boat if it had not already backed off.

Greek fire, I suddenly realized—it burned underwater. The conflagration was spreading steadily, cutting off escape for the two who were capering about, outlined by the flames. What were they doing?

With a cry of dismay, I pelted out towards them, a distance of forty, fifty paces. I had my sword out and closed with the nearest of the brutes—as I expected, they were the primitives we had met with before. The nearest wheeled on me with his own weapon, incredibly fast but thankfully, with no skill at all. He shoved the point of his blade towards my face, I beat it aside and before he could overcome the inertia of the blow I had come in at his side and chopped at the wrist. The creature dropped the blade, its hand useless with half the tendons severed but, incredibly, it stooped and picked up the poisoned sword in its other hand, the left one. It swung around, the blade a wavering segment of bright steel illuminated by the baleful flare of the fire. I ducked and the sword hummed by over my head. I stood up and was about to stab into the kidneys when the beast-man crumpled.

An arrow had found its home in the great bull-neck. The sword rang repeatedly on the hard stone flags as the beast-man's arm spasmed. It was not proof but it was likely that these were from the group which had escorted me from Schonau—in which case, Max and Morion *were* involved.

I turned towards the other creature who had not taken part in the fighting. It was stripping the stolen record from the roller and casting it into the flames which floated in on every wave. I roared at the top of my voice, a wordless shriek of anger and went for it. I sank my short sword into the thing's throat and felt it cut through the vertebrae and exit behind. It fell and it twitched, its hand still spasmodically tearing at what was left of the long roll of papyrus. I pulled the precious document from its clutches and looked at it. The fragment was as long as my arm, a fraction of what must have been in the roll.

Back in the gatehouse, under the glare of a steady lamp, I looked at what I had retrieved. It was Latin, *"… hate vain thoughts but thy law…"* I read. A piece was torn out there but further along I read some more: *"… I have longed for thy salvation, Oh Lord…"*

"Matthias, what does this mean?"

Matthias looked at it, looked at me and took it nearer the lamp. "It's Latin."

"Yes I know."

"You read Latin?"

"Of course I do."

"This isn't what we came for. This piece is a psalm, a fairly recent copy."

"Well, I was sure it wasn't what we were expecting." I was still angry; why did I feel so tangled up with this business? I was here to protect Matthias, not some dusty archive. Matthias shook his head in mystification. "The real thing is not written in any language, or in any alphabet that can be recognized. It's universal, it speaks to everyone."

"Well, it doesn't speak to me."

Matthias handed the scrap to the Abbot Hildebert who had followed Matthias out to the gatehouse. He looked at it and screwed it up in one hand. "Yes. I know. The real one is safe." A smug little smile moved his lips for an instant.

"A dozen or more people have been killed and my friend and I might have died too for an unimportant roll of paper." Matthias could not keep the amazement out of his voice.

"No," said the Abbot, brandishing the wad of paper in his fist. "Those others died to protect the scroll which you are about to pay me for, which you believe to be the actual words of God as transcribed by his apostles. *That's* what they died for Matthias, and they died protecting it *successfully*. Now don't you, or your talking ape here, tell me how to carry out my duties. You want a certain scroll of paper, I have it. Pay me and take it, then it is *yours* to protect. Do you hear me?" His expression was a mixture of triumph and anger. He looked from Matthias to me, looking me full in the eye this time. "Do you?"

"I do," I said and then to Matthias: "He's right. Whatever value you place on the real record, it has been successfully safeguarded, we must admit that."

Odd, how we had to some extent, exchanged our feelings. Matthias nodded grudgingly.

"We had better leave as soon as we may then. We'll take the papyrus and go when the tide will let us. I had intended to sail tomorrow for Blalog."

The Abbot, who had also noted our changed positions, shook his head. "No. Tomorrow and the day after, a number of our brothers will leave here. They will be chosen to look as much like you two as possible; they will leave at odd intervals and will travel in pairs in many different directions so any future attacks will be thinned out. No one will know when you two leave here—somewhere in the last third of those others."

"But—but why are you doing this?" I asked clumsily, a churlish sounding question, even to my ears. "I mean, it isn't necessary." Perhaps Hildebert realized what I was trying to ask. "Matthias is a brother Abbot. If he puts such great store in a thousand-year old-treatise, why should I not send him on his way as safely as I can?"

"What do you think?" Matthias asked as we prepared for a much-delayed rest.

"I think the Abbot is a cleverer man than I gave him credit for," I told him. "Once you decide that the archives are all-important—worth more than human lives—using a substitute scroll and sending out sham couriers are clever ideas."

When I had laid myself down to sleep in my tiny cell, my brain would not settle. There were several unanswered questions whirling around my skull.

First and what was most important was this: what was the connection with my Uncle Max?

There was no denying that these *beast-men*, as the Captain of the watch had named them, were almost certainly those who had escorted me. Morion had talked about the *Bishop of Hypolita Keep* and Matthias had mentioned the same thing, so what was the connection?

Morion had been leading her own detachment in a search of someone when I had seen her—for Matthias? But why?

I could see no reason for Uncle or Morion to be interested in these religious writings; that left some third party to whom they had been hired out. Was Morion working for this other person? Were Matthias and his fellow Christians at odds?

A different question entirely was how the location of the substitute document had been known. For that matter, I wasn't certain how they had broken in—I would have to ask in the morning—but first impressions suggested they had gone straight to the hiding place in the crypt. An informer? I sat up; Abbot Hildebert should be warned of the possibility.

Third and not necessarily finally; why was I so interested in these twelve documents? I had always found Christians to be a bigoted lot who were liable to express their intolerance of non-believers in very physical and painful ways; Matthias was quite an exception.

Was it for Matthias, then, that I was putting myself in jeopardy? Had I taken so much to the man that I was prepared to stay with him, offering the one thing I held precious, my own life?

I valued friendship almost above anything else, but somehow I had not realized how much Matthias had become my friend. Although the journey was proving treacherous, how could I leave one who seemed as a brother to me to fight unknown forces alone? There were many more questions, but if this latest incident had done one thing it was to galvanize my will.

I would stay with my new-found friend until I had answers.

IX

ver the next two days nine pairs of men who had a superficial resemblance to Matthias and myself had been selected and instructed in what they were to do. Five of these couples had already departed the priory, some through the main entrance at the top of the Mount, some through the various small wicket gates about the place.

Matthias and I left at mid-afternoon, through the upper gateway, where the natural surface was being filled in with rubble and masonry to provide a level foundation for the new abbey. We descended the steep roadway; our instructions were to walk the road to Bayeux, the Prior there would arrange a boat across to Britain. I saw nothing wrong in these directions except that what went on in the Monastery seemed to be known by far too many people.

We walked in silence for quite some way, seagulls wheeled about in noisy clouds as they picked up small fish and crustaceans marooned in the shallow rock pools left on the causeway by the falling tide. As we drew nearer to the mainland I finally asked Matthias the question I had been meaning to ask for almost a day and a half.

"How do you think our enemies knew the whereabouts of that make-believe scroll?"

"One of the lay kitchen staff had been told very confidentially by Brother Ferris—the big one who supervises the cooking—where a very important scroll was being kept."

"How did Brother Ferris know?"

"He'd been told by someone further up the hierarchy, and then enjoined to keep the information secret. Could you think of a better way to spread information when you had a gossip to hand?"

"Stress its confidentiality, knowing that it would have the opposite effect. Hmm." I was struck silent for a while. *These are Christian people*, I thought, *supposedly full of loving kindness.* "Poor Brother Anselm, then, was an intended sacrifice to the greater plan."

"Indeed. I thought you had argued for its merit. Now you don't sound so sure."

"I said—and surely you remember this—that it had merit *only* if you agreed that the value of the scrolls is above life."

"So you did. So you did. I cannot stand with the Abbot on this. There must have been a better way."

"I hope you have the real scrolls, Matthias, and that our role is not that of a decoy."

Matthias's eyes opened a little wider. He said nothing until we had gone beyond the low sand dunes and were hidden from direct sight of the Mount. "As far as I know," he said, "Hildebert has no use at all for these—but we had better check all the same." He unbuckled the scroll case and pulled out one of the wrapped cylinders.

Carefully, he undid the wrapping and unwound a handbreadth of the yellowish paper filled with crabbed black characters. "Can you read it?"

"Me?" I glanced at the writing. "Is it Hebrew?"

But it wasn't. The effect was a little like standing too close to a large painting; it is not possible to see what it represents unless you half close your eyes, then the detail seems to become visible. Or perhaps it was like listening to a conversation at a party; once you get tuned into the sound of the other's voice, the rest of the noise recedes and the words become clear. As I looked, the meaning became slowly apparent. I concentrated on a phrase, two groups of characters.

"*...he who helps the cause is thrice blessed, he shall see all that is told come to pass and gain whatever he so desires for it is written...*"

With the words, there came pictures, visions. I saw myself dressed in purple and scarlet, I knew my head was filled with wisdom, I knew what God's holy will was and to help in bringing it about—however small my part—I would reap great reward. When I looked closely, the characters were squiggles with neither order nor sense: random marks. When I stopped trying to concentrate, I could read what was there. I became aware of something else, too. There was an obscure relationship between the few marks I had seen and all the rest of the record. There was a sort of tension between them all so the order of the marks and their shape across the whole of the document—even the major part that was still rolled up was important. There was no argument about the records, all of them together made a whole so powerful that real permanent change could be effected; I knew this beyond doubt. The scroll contained an energy, a million links with every particle in the cosmos.

I stepped back, stunned by the insight I was receiving. The effect faded and the visions grew filmy and transparent, the sights and the sounds of a late afternoon in Armorica gradually returned to me. I had gained a headache for my troubles.

Matthias was laughing. "Not Hebrew, no. So you can't read it then?"

"I can understand what I see there," I told him though I was not going to admit to the intuitive understanding I had been granted. "Is it real?"

"Oh yes. This is the original scroll."

"And the others?"

"You are suddenly very suspicious," he said. "Do you doubt Hildebert's honor?"

"I doubt everything to do with Hildebert," I replied, "and especially his honor."

Matthias checked each of the other ten scrolls before closing the case and making sure the buckle was fastened.

"Fine," I nodded. "As a precaution against the unknown, let us travel further before we look for a ship, we should be able to find something beyond Bayeux. I fear that the nearer boatyards could already be full of spies." I had to consider the importance of those rolls of paper, whatever it needed to preserve them must be achieved. Matthias thought about it for a while and nodded. "There is a small monastery near the coast beyond Rouen. We may well find passage from there."

"If the Abbot Hildebert disbelieves the potency of these scrolls, why has he caused such sacrifice to be made?" I asked.

"Hildebert may be a ruthless and driven man but he is still an honest one. He has received a great deal of money over the years for this scroll. Now he has received what he thinks is a fair and final payment, he has done his best to ensure that we have what was paid for and that we can safely take it away."

"But the cost in life…"

Matthias turned and started walking. "How long does an ordinary man live, Gerard?"

"Forty, fifty years."

"And his soul lives for all eternity. What are a few years lost against the rest of eternity?"

So we spent an extra day on the road, stopping at Bayeux only long enough to buy rations in the town and skirted the monastery there. In fact, the Abbot's plans seemed to have succeeded for we were not molested on the way, neither did I see anything to indicate an unwelcome presence.

I did wonder from time to time what was happening to those who were acting as decoys. Fortunately they were distant enough from us that my wondering was academic rather than emotional.

We stayed at the monastery of Saint Valery on the last night. Matthias obtained a linen bag and had it soaked in hot tallow to waterproof it. He put his scroll case inside this and laced the top up tightly. We took our customary drink and bedded down for the night. I suffered a fitful night filled with dreams and self-doubt yet woke up the next morning with few cares and looking forward to what the day held. At first light, we embarked on the *Petrel*, a sturdily built, small rounded tub of a ship with a high stern. Our destination was Pevensey, an anchorage east of where we might be expected to go ashore on the coast of Britain. Nor was our ship the only one leaving; a second—longer, narrower and owing some of its lines to the Danes who now ruled the Saxon shore—was also sailing for that port.

In fact, it was a busy time for shipping. Fishermen were leaving for their grounds and yet another trading vessel was waiting for them to clear the harbor so it could leave on its journey to Portchester beyond the island of Vectis.

The weather was clear as we headed east along the coast. Our captain would follow the coast for several hours and turn north—and a little west—but only when the lookout could see both Gaul on the starboard side and England to port. There were several passengers and toward mid-morning, most of us were on deck enjoying the sunshine and the salty air. The *Petrel* obviously took passengers regularly, since there were seats along the sides of the high after deck stepped so that people would not slide down the slope. Matthias smiled at a young serving girl holding her mistresses's bag; I smiled at the mistress who smiled back, blushed, and looked away.

Why would she do that? I wondered and admired the way her neck arched and how the breeze played with some strands of loose hair at her temple. A moment later she was looking my way again and we played the game a little longer. I was about to get up and buy a cup of ale and perhaps offer her some when my attention was distracted by loud voices from the stern where the steersman was looking back over his shoulder.

Almost on the horizon, a waterspout was visible; a long writhing tail of dark air descending from a bulbous blue-black cloud.

"The *Summer Hawk*," I heard someone say—that was the Viking ship which had sailed a little while before us. The men looking over the stern rail had a better view than those of us in the waist and I went back up the steep slope of the after deck which, at the stern, was quite high above the sea.

Looking back, it was now possible to see great waves breaking about the lean shape of the *Summer Hawk*. As I watched, lightning scratched a jagged line from the cloud to the single mast, rigging and spars flew skyward, snatched by that writhing funnel of air. The stern seemed to rise up and twist, the bows disappeared behind curtains of green and black water; the ship slid beneath the waves and was gone in a space of heartbeats. Gone, leaving only a wake to show she had ever been there.

The company was silent. A ship and her complement of lives had disappeared before our eyes in a matter of minutes, a tragedy which we dared not discuss for fear of drawing the attention of wrathful Gods or hungry sea-monsters. Yet the Captain slackened the pace; he gave the orders and we came about, sails were trimmed and we sailed first to the north for an hour and then south, tacking back to the place it had been.

Long before we got there, the waterspout had vanished, the clouds were still dark and low but the seas had gone down. Our vessel entered the area of strangely calm water, the surface greasy from a cargo of oil jars which had been smashed in the strange storm. Clouds pressed closely about us, grey, roiling; yet we could hear no wind beyond the lightest of breezes and that with scarcely enough strength to ghost us over the water. There were broken timbers floating on the unnaturally quiet surface, the split remains of boxes, bolts of cloth, oars… and bodies. There was nothing left alive, even the ship's cat was floating there; limp, broken like everything else. Bodies, bodies everywhere; corpses, death. The captain quartered the area which remained weirdly still and silent. We searched for two hours and found not even a seagull to relieve the scene of death. At length we left, quiet and melancholy, running with all sail before the prevailing breeze in an attempt to regain some of our lost time.

As we sailed, a dark foreboding came over me and some fear. I fought to put it to the back of my mind, not wishing to affect Matthias in the same way. When we came out into the sunshine once more all of our spirits lifted a little and men were talking of sea quakes and other unlikely things which fell just short of the supernatural. Probably their first experience of such an event but not mine, even the fear, though fast fading, was nothing new to me. An hour later though, the sun was losing its warmth and light; the sky was becoming brassy and overcast, the sun—nothing more than a cream-colored disk behind a saffron veil. There was discussion between the captain and his mate, gestures towards the west where the *Summer Hawk* had foundered. The discussion lengthened and eventually seemed to be resolved, for orders were shouted. Our prow turned away from the grey outline of Gaul to our south and made for the, still invisible, Saxon Shore to the north.

It was as if our change of course triggered events. Within minutes of taking the new course, the water became choppy and then turbulent, the waves growing until our ship wallowed into the troughs and tipped over the crests and sent anything loose sliding from one end of the ship to the other. Lightning—sometimes pink or white glares from within the gathering clouds, sometimes blue and white streaks which appeared like rents in the fabric separating us from the nether world. Thunder boomed around us so that the sailors had to bawl into each other's ears to be understood. The wind rose and blew randomly from all around, sheets of salt water sluiced across the decks knocking any of the crew without a handhold into the scuppers.

Of the half-dozen passengers, only Matthias and I remained on deck for neither of us relished the idea of being below if the *Petrel* was to sink. We made our preparations, Matthias strapped his scroll case tightly to his back, I took off my new boots and tied them around my neck. We took our station next to a barrel of drinking water and when opportunity offered, we emptied what was left, drove the bung tightly home then looped and tied some light rope around its girth.

The conditions continued to grow worse. The tubby *Petrel* spun down into the troughs between house-high waves, rolling onto her beam ends but somehow managing to stay afloat. The ship's survival seemed to anger the elements and the attacks grew ever stronger. The wind screamed around the ship enclosing us in a shrieking circle which gradually tightened into a force intent on plucking us out or the water. However, the *Petrel* was considerably heavier than the sleek *Summer Hawk*, it was simply too massive for such an attack to succeed.

This seemed no ordinary storm, there was sentience behind it. Matthias seemed to draw malevolence as a lone calf will draw predators, I began to wonder just what supernatural beings my friend had angered.

Now the heavens growled and black clouds descended, streams of witch fire writhed from our mastheads to light the lowering sky and there was a smell of dead fish and rotting seaweed in the air. The pale green flames crawled over everything, our flesh tingled and prickled and the flames rose from our heads and shoulders, from our hands when we lifted them. A succession of brilliant flashes blinded us and simultaneous detonations of sound deafened us over the space of a few heartbeats.

When our senses returned in some measure, it was to find the vessel burning around us, the end had come. Lightning had splintered the masts and the spars, sails had become heaped bonfires on the decks. More flames leaped from hatches, the decking was hot beneath my feet and the tarred caulking oozed from between the deck boards and ran in sluggish streams of fire into the bilges.

There were cracking sounds and shudders ran through the very structure of the vessel, the *Petrel* was breaking apart beneath our feet. Unable to make myself heard above the howling of the elements, I pointed to us and to the heaving water and our barrel, Matthias nodded and together, we pitched the barrel over the side and jumped after it.

The water was so cold that it simply stopped my breathing. Nothing worked; my muscles were locked, I thought my chest would burst and I panicked as my heart thumped madly. It seemed long minutes before the paralysis went away and even then it took a huge effort to splash towards the barrel and to simply hang on. Matthias had resisted the cold better than I and he pulled me close and wrapped the rope around my hands as we drifted slowly away from the stricken ship. As the gap between us and the *Petrel* grew wider, we could see through the ports along the side; the interior was an inferno; it was no wonder the decks were hot and the hatches belching flame. I thought then of the pretty woman who had blushed at my attention only a few hours ago—somewhere in there she and her maid, screaming with fear and pain, were dying. Suddenly, we were far enough from the hull for the waves to take us and we rose and fell with the breaking water. The violent sea thrashed at the barrel and it was torn from our grasp in moments and we clung to each other, buoyed up by Matthias's scroll case—still perfectly watertight in its waxed linen cover.

Time passed and the storm abated, the gloom of the dark clouds was replaced by the blackness of night. The wind, now steady rather than spiraling in from all directions, drove us through the water. I think we must have lost consciousness although, certain our grip on each other never slackened, we discovered later that there were great blanks in what we remembered.

Matthias told me of a great crashing of thunder and lightning far away—he had no idea what direction it had been in but I had no recollection of it. Nor did he remember the school of porpoises who had pushed and nudged us for an hour or more until we came to rest on a hard wet sandy beach where we woke up in the cold, clammy light of a new dawn. I don't know, I've heard such tales before—perhaps it was no more than a wishful dream.

I can't speak for Matthias, but my body was numb. There was a sense of cold, like that of a corpse in the grave but it was distant, my arms and legs were sluggish, it took forever to get them to move. We should have died there, an ephemeral would certainly have died and I doubt that many of my kind would have survived. Perhaps we two were hardier than most. Perhaps it was because there *were* the two of us—both helping the other or even, that our peculiar stubbornness in the face of death would not let one of us yield before the other. Or perhaps the *Him* that Matthias spoke of protected us, threw some sort of protective curtain around Matthias which also encompassed me. It didn't seem to matter but *something* drove me on. I levered myself up to my knees, from there to my feet. I swayed and moved a few steps, legs swinging awkwardly from the hips. It must have been the doggedness of my kind, the instinctive determination to live despite all. Little by little my muscles thawed out and I paid more attention to our surroundings. Matthias was recovering, too.

Debris lay everywhere, even a few items which might have come from the *Petrel,* but most of it was half buried in the sand, grey and weathered, matching the sky. We picked our way through the litter and climbed to the nearest high point, a thin cold wind flapped our wet clothes. Now we saw what a cruel joke had been played upon us.

The beach was no more than a large sand bar—soon to be swallowed by the rising tide; there was no sign of true land to be seen in any direction and sooner or later we would have to take to the sea again for there was no other choice open to us.

I sorted through the contents of my pouch and brought out a flint and striking iron. I looked around for something dry, some timber I could whittle flakes from, some old cloth trapped in the sand—there was nothing dry, nothing we could use. Plenty of damp salty drift wood but nothing to start a fire with. When I returned to Matthias, he had carefully torn a strip of papyrus from the edge of the scrolls; he held it out to me.

"Thanks," I said.

"That's all," he warned, "make it work."

But it didn't. Nothing I did would ignite it, sparks bounced away without effect as though it was a strip of brass. Shaking my head in despair, I split a hefty piece of drift wood with my sword and then shaved the inner wood so thinly that it was almost transparent and eventually, that did take light. I had been careful, gathering wood, grading it for size, I blew gently on the smoldering shavings until a tiny flame appeared; I fed it to others, splinters caught alight, sticks...

"It's a pity we didn't have the Angel Gabriel with us," I said as we began to warm up. "He would have got the fire burning in no time, just by pointing a finger at it."

Matthias corrected me. "*Arch*angel Gabriel." Matthias had less humor than a bad smell in a wine bottle, and I noticed how he looked up at the sky as he mentioned the name.

Well, we had a good fire, we felt warm for the first time in fifteen hours or so and although our clothes were stiff with salt, they were dry, and later, when the fire was a heap of hot embers, we circumnavigated our shrinking island.

"What's that?" asked Matthias, pointing. He was standing a little higher than I did and could see down to the encroaching water. "It looks like a boat. A small rowboat."

X

From disbelief, to relief, to despondency in a hundred heartbeats: it was a boat as Matthias had said; three quarters buried, grey enough to have been there for years. Despite its unpromising appearance, we began to dig it out of the sand with our cupped hands. It was bleached and weathered like the rest of the rubbish which had arrived here and with all the time in the world, it could not have been made seaworthy.

I stood up, straightened my back, and swore as I turned a full circle, seeing the sea already lapping around the far edge of our unfortunate boat.

"Matthias."

"Hmm?"

"Look."

Currents must shape and reshape sand banks every time they become submerged; at each low tide a new land is revealed with new miniature mountains and valleys, new forests of seaweed, new populations of fish marooned in small hollows for gulls to fight over. Here, a headland had been sculpted and as the tide rose, so rose what was unmistakably the keel of an upturned boat. Again neither of us believed what we were seeing until we had walked over to it and each of us had placed a hand on the rough wood.

We rolled it over, tipping out the water and setting it down again. On the stern, the wood had been carved with a single word: *Petrel*. It was the small skiff which had been lashed to the roof of the Captain's cabin. Naturally, it was no longer intact; part of the stern had been smashed and a long length of plank had been sprung and some of that had been torn away.

Cold water swirled around my calves, reminding me that time was not our friend. "Matthias," I shouted, shocked into action. "A gift from the sea. Can we wrench some planking from the old boat to repair this one?"

"The planks are much larger on that one. They won't fit."

But they could be made to fit, nearly enough. Using my sword to split the wood along the grain, we filled in the hole and braced it and the rest of the plank with cross pieces jammed against the far side. For caulking, we used seaweed; there were great, flat gelatinous ribbons of the stuff all over the sand bank.

Oars. We needed oars but had to rest content with two more planks pulled from the older boat. We tested the craft; it leaked—not unexpected, but neither was it uncontrollable. I prevailed on Matthias to transfer his scrolls into the linen bag so we could use the case itself for bailing and we left the rapidly diminishing sand bank behind. The substitute oars were useless as they were, as we needed a pair of pins on each gunwale to form a pivot for them. But there was no going back as our little island was already gone, so we cut pegs from each of the plank oars and whittled them to a size that would fit into the sockets. Even then, it was more than hard work; I think we went astern faster than we could row or paddle against the current.

Nevertheless, we heaved on the damned things until our hands were splintered and bloody. We wrapped them in strips torn from our clothing and carried on; sometimes we would both work the makeshift oars, at other times one of us paddled while the other bailed out the water that leaked in. We sailed northward because that was the direction of the prevailing wind, straining our eyes for some glimpse of shore—cliffs, breakers, sand—but there was nothing except a long, low bank of cloud along the horizon. Light faded gradually and before we realized it, night had fallen, a few stars shone for a time but these were rapidly blotted out as clouds swept in. We rested, wondering what the best course of action might be. Neither of us were seamen; we had been to sea only as passengers.

"There's a light over there," Matthias pointed. "Do you suppose it's another ship?"

I looked and he was right, though whether a ship or an onshore light or some sea-born will-o'-the-wisp, I couldn't say. "Can we make a light? We need something to burn. That waxed linen…"

"No," he said and stopped. "No," he added, a minute or so later, shaking his head, "I'm sorry." Then, after another long pause, he spoke again. "I don't think it is a ship. It's too steady. It's land—it has to be. It's a house, maybe."

The water was well over my ankles so I began to bail again, while Matthias pulled at the clumsy oars, looking over his shoulder every now and then to check his bearing. Once the water level in the boat was down, I shared the labor but we came no nearer to the light; in fact, it gradually became more distant as the ebb tide sucked us towards the west. We watched as the light faded into the distance, water slapping against the planking, while a steady trickle leaked through the gaps.

"Thirsty." Matthias was the first to voice the thought, and then lapsed into silence once more.

I don't think I paid any attention, as my eyes were on the flicker of lightning slicing the farther reaches of the night into crooked ribbons. Faintly came the sound of thunder, and rushing winds and the roar of hungry waves. We watched and said nothing, both of us certain that there was yet another ship as unfortunate as the *Petrel*.

How many ships had been attacked? I wondered. *How far does this evil extend?*

If there was any conversation that night, I don't recall it. The unnatural storm played itself out and we drifted until the first grey steaks of daylight tinged the clouds. We were drifting eastward again by this time, fast, for the tide was sweeping up the Gallic Narrows in full flood.

But there! A smudge of land to the north. In all probability, what we had taken for a cloud bank the previous afternoon had been the coast line. A line of white where land met the sea told us waves were breaking along the shore.

We put out the oars again and began pulling with more enthusiasm than before. We rowed for an hour until we were panting but seemed to get no closer. As we recovered and our gasps died away, a new sound came to our ears—surf, yet not from the shore, that was too far off to hear. We looked around, Matthias climbed wearily to his feet and looked again and finally pointed.

"An island. Not sand this time, it's a real one, a real island."

Now he had shown the direction, I could see it, too. Half a mile from us, low, rocky, a few trees and best of all, a hut built against one of the trees. We manned the oars again and pulled; we pulled and pulled, ignoring the rasp of breath in our lungs, ignoring the water which was almost to our knees, we pulled.

We were thirty paces from the shore when the boat sank beneath us, we didn't care, we stepped out into the hip-high water and waded ashore, Matthias holding on to his scrolls with a white-knuckled clutch.

Part way to the hut, we collapsed almost together. Later, we crawled the rest of the way and I summoned just enough strength to bang once upon the door.

Gutrun the hermit had lived there for three years, he told us. Nor was it a hut that he lived in. At first glance, it had seemed to be a rude hut supported by a tree trunk, but at closer quarters I saw it was a square stone-built building: the ground floor of an old lighthouse which at one time had stood at the edge of the salt marsh on the mainland. Now the sea had invaded the marsh and the structure occupied a minuscule island some one hundred paces long at its widest point. A corner of the upper story still stood and the wind whined around the old masonry. Our host lived on fish which he caught himself. He made bread when the mood took him from ingredients brought out to him by the people who lived along the seaward edge of Walland Marsh. A spring which bubbled out from the old lighthouse's foundations probably accounted for many of the visions he said he saw and the voices he heard, for it was more than just brackish. However, it assuaged our thirst for a while and Gutrun's indifferent cooking filled our hungry bellies until he was next visited by his provisioners a few days later.

We were still very weak from our ordeal and skinny—we looked like a couple of wicker effigies ready for the bonfire when we told our tale to the three men and a woman who had come to see Gutrun. They shook their heads and told us tales of at least seven ships sunk in the same way as the *Petrel*, flotsam had been picked up on beaches from Dymchurch to Pevensey, they said, and bodies. They listened gravely as we told them about the eerie calm around the place where the *Summer Hawk* had gone down and the cage of lightning which had set our *Petrel* alight.

"Bodies, bodies," they repeated. We were the only two who had been found living to tell the tale. If anything, this reassured me. If we were the only ones to survive, then surely, my friend was not the reason for these tragedies. How could he be?

Matthias left a silver coin with Gutrun and we bade him farewell as the visitors took us back across a knee-deep channel of water. Here was a small village, a score of small huts all but buried under sand dunes and shielded from the westerlies by a copse of conifers. Fisher folk; oyster pickers too, the shell fish had always proliferated along the south eastern shore and there were goats and a few scrawny hens. We stayed there another two days, gathering more strength than Gutrun's larder could have provided in a month. The following day was market day in Hastingas and a sled was loaded with goat cheese, pickled oysters and smoked fish.

We went with them to the market, taking our turn to pull the sled or retrieve the produce that fell off during its bumpy ride. It was only a dozen miles or so along the track which paralleled the sea shore; five or six houses appeared between us and the beach and signaled the start of the town. More houses appeared to either side of the rutted and muddy track way: huts, timber and wattle daubed with mud or plaster, a few stone and brick buildings which hemmed in the market place at the junction of two roads.

It had been a long time since I had seen so many people together. Two men bargaining for a brace of hares, three or four debating taxes, another two arguing about something quite obscure. There were goats with wickerwork panniers, donkeys with mounds of produce tied to their backs, one or two more sledges pulled by farmers piled with cheeses, animal skins, fish, adzes, axe heads… the noise was indescribable. The stench was almost as bad: raw meat, badly cured hides and spilt ale.

We inquired about transport to take us further west. There was little interest; no one came from any further away than we had journeyed that morning, no one was interested in our needs. Horses then, we searched for stables and found none, there would be a horse fair next month, on the last day of the month, they told us, no one here had a horse, all were too poor to own a horse. Still, next month we needed to be at Glastonbury, Matthias said. We needed to be there long before the next month was ended.

The captain of a small trader overheard us as we talked about our problem over leather cups of ale. He was taking oysters and a harsh liquor for his lunch in the low-ceilinged tavern at the side of the market. He was going to Pevensey and then on to Portchester if he could find the cargo. He offered us space if we cared to pay.

We were disturbed at the idea of putting to sea again, for a repeat of what we had been through haunted us, but we felt relieved that a solution to our problem had presented itself.

"We have heard sorry tales of disaster. How far from land will you go?"

The Captain leaned forward. "Sorry tales indeed." He held out his arms towards us with his palms a couple of spans apart. "Close enough to scrape every barnacle from my keel."

We accepted.

The captain was happy to take Matthias's money—a gold coin from Italy was as acceptable as those from Londinium or Winchester. In fact, he agreed to change some of my friend's derniers into silver pence and a fistful of smaller stuff, no doubt taking a goodly commission on the transaction. Where Matthias kept his seemingly endless supply of coins evaded me, robbed then shipwrecked, and he still managed to produce one from somewhere. He reminded me of a conjurer I had once seen at a fair.

There was a little rough weather but after what we had experienced, was of no consequence at all. It seemed very soon to us when we rounded the point at Selsey and slid gently into the lea of Vectis.

Between us and the coast, a shallow expanse of water spread, its surface glassy and smooth with deeper water clearly visible in the surface texture. As our steersman guided us along one of these deep water channels and into a wide lagoon, my mind did weird somersaults; I watched with a very real feeling of *déjà vu* as we took the eastern approach up to a line of quays where we made fast. What was the name of this place? Had I been here before, or had it been in one of my dreams or visions? Come to think of it, I had been dream free these past three days... what caused them to come and go like a zephyr?

It wouldn't come to my mind's eye but the line of low roofed taverns and workshops looked as though they might have been there for the past millennium. I had been here before; I knew the land even though the sea had encroached and what was now the harbor had once been a quay half a mile up the river.

"There's more bad weather on the way," Matthias observed, pointing to a roll of black cloud to the south and east.

A sea eagle rode the winds and, as we watched, plummeted down, catching the air in cupped wings, its white tail feathers spread. The bird rose again with something grasped in the claws of one foot. As it lifted, I saw another ship beyond the eagle, out to sea and driving before the wind which was hurrying the clouds over us. It was carrying a great deal of sail, an aggressive bow wave foamed up around her stem. I watched it nervously. Eventually though, it passed well to the west, disappearing into the waters between the mainland and Vectis.

Whatever had stalked the *Petrel* and those other ships that departed from Mont Saint-Michel seemed to have left the Narrows for the present.

We debarked and were accosted by a vaguely military person who followed the harbor master to the quay.

He wore a tattered surcoat with the seam of one arm burst open and a stiff hat with faded and worn gold braid sown on to it. He demanded a quite excessive fee from us. My sharp intake of breath drew his attention. "There is much to do, much to put right," he said. "With taxes and God's help, the new King will set the country to rights."

"The *new* King?" asked Matthias.

"Ethelred…" For a moment, I thought he was going to spit. "Ethelred is dead."

"Ah. We were shipwrecked a week or so ago. We have been without news since then."

"A week past? In one of those tempests?" The port official queried. "You are the first survivors I've seen. The ships that I've heard of sank with all hands."

"I suspect we were the only survivors of ours, too. So King Ethelred is dead?"

"Eight days since. Saint George's Day."

"Eight days?" Matthias looked concerned. "I must've lost a day in my reckoning. Today is?"

"The last day of April."

"The *last*? I am two days wrong. So then, the new King. Who is he?"

"Cnut. Or will be"

"Cnut? The Viking?"

"Just so. The Witan are sure to elect him; he'll be king by virtue of law."

"Well now. That's a surprise. And he's intent on putting things right…"

"You know a lot about this corner of the world, Matthias," I said when we had paid our dues and taken the receipt and were on our way.

"I was here eight years ago and again three years past, to make arrangements about these, as a matter of fact." Matthias patted his bag of scrolls. "The Vikings were being paid in silver to stay away. It didn't last, only until the money gave out, and it made a pauper of this land. I've kept up with the news since." He stared knowingly at me before adding, "Such events might be important to me."

The town was the better part of a mile inland and we talked a haulier into giving us a ride on his tailboard to save us the walk. Most of the way was lined with boat yards and chandler's shops, with a fair sprinkling of down-at-the-heel inns and taverns and insalubrious brothels. Noviomagus was larger than Mont Saint-Michel, though not by much. There might have been four hundred or so dwellings built within the old walls. Beside the little port we had arrived at, there were others at convenient inlets along the coast and most of the merchandise coming into the country or going out would come through Noviomagus. A cluster of large houses outside the town on the north and west showed where the wealth was.

The carter let us off in the town center where the buildings were substantial timber affairs with what seemed to be prosperous looking shops and one or two better class inns. However, I did not linger there, and took the lead, taking us off toward the East Gate, where Stane Street came into the town from Londinium. There was a huddle of houses, a blacksmith's and… I looked around, puzzled.

"Something the matter?" Matthias asked. He had not questioned why I had chosen this route or knew of it. "I thought we had decided on a meal before we'd choose a lodging."

"Ah." I had moved a few paces to the right and spotted it. Several newer buildings all but hid it. "A meal first indeed, and that's where we'll get it." I pointed to a long thatched roof structure.

"Hmm. Well." I could tell from his expression that my fellow traveler was not as impressed as he might have been.

I tugged him towards the tumble-down place. "The fish they serve here will… Um." I had pushed through the canvas curtain at the door.

He asked the question I had been expecting. "Been here before, then?"

"Oh yes," I answered and said no more. Three or four customers were inside, slouched at a long trestle table where a number of earthenware jugs were grouped at one end. The customers and the surly barman looked up from a deep discussion in low voices, sending suspicious glares and hostile expressions in our direction. A lantern on the table between them cast their shadows on the roof like grimy ghosts among the cobwebs. There was no welcome for us here, unlike the comfortable ale house we had visited across the Narrows. "I think we'll try that place back in the town."

We backed out and I spent a few moments looking northwest, along the road. "Yes," I repeated. "I've been here before, but it's changed."

"When were you here?"

I nodded to a crumbling pile of stone on the far side of Stane Street, the south side. "See the mound of stone down there?"

"I see it."

"That was an amphitheater. I saw to its building and carried a vine staff. I had joint charge of two thousand legionaries." I nodded at some fairly substantial buildings. "I'd guess the stone for half of these houses came from it."

Then he realized what I'd said. "Roman legionaries? And a vine staff, too? Well, so you *were* a centurion then?"

We had reached the central square again where the buildings looked a little less fine and a little more scruffy than at first glance. We turned in through the door of the first inn we came to.

"Tribune Valerius Gerrus something or other," I said when we were seated with a cup of ale each and waiting for bowls of stewed hare to reach us. "I forget. Tib… something, Tibullus."

"And is that your real name?"

I grinned and shook my head. "The owner of that name died when his detail was set upon by natives. I borrowed it and his uniform and used it for a while. Then, when I left the army, I left my uniform and name with another dead man. Did I tell you I joined as a legionary when I was younger?"

"You did."

"I served about twelve years, I think. I got myself missing, presumed dead, when I realized I still looked like a recruit when the others were into their thirties. I unofficially rejoined a few years later, when I had learned to look older."

"So, how long ago, really?"

I pursed my lips and thought back. "It was the year Severus came. Two hundred and ten, two eleven by your calendar, something like that."

"And you expected things to be the same after seven, eight hundred years?"

"No, obviously not. It just caught me unawares, so little seemed to have changed; I simply forgot how long it had been."

Matthias nodded. "Did you realize you'd been speaking in Latin?"

Since meeting, we had been speaking Gallic. "Latin? Really?"

He nodded again, smiling. "Odd accent."

I ventured a few words and listened to what I said. I shook my head. "Authentic. For then."

Britain was a byword for miserable weather, and the Roman legionary would often wear native-style trousers rather than his leather kilt. The following day, we shopped for clothes more suited to the climate. In fact, I paid for my own. My pay was good, three derniers a day—Matthias had insisted on the new rate and since I had no real interest in the stuff, I spared no expense. A soft, thin leather coat with overstitched seams, a hat of rather more substantial leather, two woolen shirts, linen breeches and some hose in fanciful colors. The weather, I thought, could do its worst—I was prepared. Matthias made similar purchases and parceled up his monkish habit for later. He also purchased food, a new case for his scrolls which he wrapped in the linen bag, and a pair of horses and a sack of oats.

We looked a very fine pair of gentlemen indeed when we took the Great West Road toward Venta. Not long after we had started, I pointed to the mounded remains of a large square building; bricks and roof tiles survived amongst the nettles and bushes, an odd piece of dressed stone. "Used to be a palace," I told him. "Belonged to... some local chief who admired the Roman way. There was a fire but we arrived too late to do anything useful, never got rebuilt... not enough money." I snapped my fingers as my thoughts crystallized. "The town *still* looks like that. Not enough money around to keep the place going."

"I told you," Matthias replied. "Yesterday. Ethelred bled the country white, paying off the Danes. Everywhere it is impoverished."

"As bad as that?"

"There *must* be places where it's better, but generally speaking it's bad."

We continued on along the track, which was covered with grass, and scrub, and small trees grew right up to the edges. Once there had been paving and rainwater drains, and the trees then had been cut back to the distance of a bow shot. It was all gone or hidden now, but the old foundations still provided a firm base, still ran as straight as they always did. Even after a thousand years, it was still a main thoroughfare.

"Venta, did you say?"

I nodded.

"Today we call it Winchester. A big place, perhaps the largest town in Britain."

"To Winchester, then."

resh horses, a pleasant morning's ride: great oak trees already bursting into green leaf and patches of yellow flowers along the road like pools of sunlight. Birds ignored us, dashing from branch to branch, the males showing off new spring finery in pursuit of the females.

The road crossed innumerable rivers by means of shallow fords and one had stepping stones so even a man on foot might cross dry shod. And then Winchester grew up around us. In spite of the financial problems Matthias had mentioned, this British town looked wealthy. Once inside the walls there were many prosperous houses built from stone or brick, quite a number had an upper floor and there were shops with all manner of goods for sale. We passed a street fogged with the smoke of smithy's furnaces; bundles of shovels and hoes, hay forks, sickles stood waiting for the next market day. Further along, wheelwrights made wheels for carts being built next door, leather workers cut harnesses and aprons and hats and… the list went on and on.

After passing alongside the quiet waters of a river and through the gate, we saw our destination ahead of us—a great abbey. Ever and again, Matthias smiled to himself. I knew from several remarks he had made that, so close to the final scroll and having survived several attacks, he was a man well pleased with life.

"Whom do we seek here?" I asked as the abbey walls began to rear above us.

Matthias ceased to smile, his words were abrupt. "Brother Britrig."

"A problem?"

"There should not be. Britrig wants to be rid of the scroll almost as much as I wish to possess it."

"So?"

"Britrig is not a likeable man. He has the scroll because he thought it would impress his superiors, that he would gain great office in return for donating such a sacred relic. It was written by Saint Peter, who is regarded as the first Pope of Christ's Church."

"And his plans did not prosper?"

"The Bishop Aelfsige declared it to be unholy, a work of the Devil."

"Ah. Yet he still has it?"

"He had looked on it, like you. Once he had done that, it was not possible for him to destroy it. It is difficult even to order it destroyed."

I was a little nonplussed at this. I examined my feelings, why should I not throw the scrolls into the river, or onto a fire? I felt no revulsion at the idea. It seemed to me that I would do so if it was ever necessary. Perhaps I would have to be a believer—a Christian—before it would affect me like that. I made no reply; I felt it better not to discuss the subject.

At the main gateway, an entrance wide enough for three horses to pass through abreast, Matthias inquired of the gatekeeper about Britrig. The gatekeeper shook his head and suggested we should find the Hospitaller and ask him.

We entered the abbey, leading our horses along a path of broken chalk. The wall to our left supported gnarled old apple trees which had been pruned and trained to spread along the brickwork. Beneath the trees were beds of herbs and smaller bushes which would bear fruit later in the year. On our right, the earth was tilled but not yet sown with seed. A young boy went to find the Hospitaller who made us welcome in a very civilized manner, very unlike our treatment at Mont Saint-Michel. Our horses were taken to stables, we were shown where we could wash the dust of travel from our persons—this when bathing was considered bad for the health. Afterwards, Brother Aethan, the hospitaller, returned and asked how the abbey could be of help.

Matthias introduced himself and leaned forward. "We are seeking a man whom I met here three years ago," he said. "A brother Britrig. I understand that he is principally, an archivist."

"Brother Britrig?" Aethan frowned, thought a moment. "The name is that of our Abbot, Sir. Do you think he was the person you spoke to?"

Matthias raised his considerable eyebrows. "Not unless your Abbot is an exceedingly modest man."

I know of no other, let me inquire. What was it you came to see him about?"

"I have corresponded with him several times about very old writings which he had in his keeping. I was interested in seeing them for myself."

"Can you tell me the nature of the writings?"

"I believed them to be contemporary with Christ's apostles."

Aethan smiled. "I am no expert in the field you understand but I thought such a thing would be known to all."

Matthias chewed his bottom lip for a moment. "I'd have thought so too but I suppose they are valuable and therefore known to only a few?"

"There is that possibility, especially if they were contentious in any way?"

Matthias frowned "By God's grace, as far as I am aware, there is nothing farther from the truth. At the time we wrote to each other, we had a shared interest in how God was worshipped in the long ago."

"Perhaps you could ask if we can see the Abbot though. I would at least appreciate a word or two with him before continuing my journey."

"Of course, of course."

Aethan left us to sit in the sun outside the hospitium and returned quite a long time later and somewhat ill at ease. "I have spoken with our Abbot, he is indeed the one you corresponded with and the documents you mentioned—presumably it is these you wish to discuss with him?"

"Well yes, that's so."

Aethan's brow furrowed. "I will tell you this then but please, I beg of you, have a care. These documents have been declared heretical."

Matthias put on a shocked expression. "With God's help I shall be on my guard, constantly. I thank you for the warning."

Reassured, Aethan nodded. "Very well. I will take you to him—your companion too, Sir Gerard?"

The hospitaller took us along gravel pathways and around the outside of a cloister, leaving us at the steps of a small church.

"The Abbot is at prayer just now, he will be out in due course."

We waited and waited then waited some more. I stood up. "Abbot Britrig must have a lot to say to his God. I'll see how much longer he might be." Before Matthias could lift a restraining hand, I went inside.

For me, it was unexpectedly plain. I had been into Christian churches in the east where fine gold leaf and brilliant paint cling to every surface. Here, the statues were painted with umbers, with dark reds and blues and maroons; these were set against pale lime-washed walls. Then I saw the window at the east end and gasped: it was beautiful in its simplicity. The Christ pointing to an entry in a book, the God's Mother to one side, her robe stained a most lovely blue, the same blue as that of the Southern Ocean in sunlight.

There was movement there beneath the window: a boy was clearing a plate and a goblet from a small table.

"Boy," I spoke quietly and gently but the lad had been so engrossed in his task, he jumped as though he had stepped on a hot ember.

"Master!" He gasped and then looked past me where Matthias had followed me in.

"I am sorry to startle you," I spoke carefully in the as-yet unfamiliar dialect, "We seek Abbot Britrig. We've come a long way."

"The Abbot is over in the big hall, Master."

"The big hall?"

"Yes. He took communion with the priest and has gone back to his work."

"Can you direct us?"

"Certainly."

We thanked the boy and did as he suggested, going across to the great hall and seeking a side door to enter. A series of extra rooms were built along the eastern side, one of them—towards the front—was furnished with a pair of weathered timber doors. We knocked on the carved oak panels and finding the door unlocked, we pushed it open and entered.

"Well, well, a brother, now an Abbot," Matthias said quietly.

"Perhaps he has friends among the elite?" I suggested.

There was no one in sight but there were sounds of work and we followed these to their source: a kitchen to one side where pots were being scraped and huge sides of sheep already spitted and racked above slow fires; the smell of meat cooking made juices run down my chin.

"We seek Britrig, um—the Abbot," Matthias said and the pot scourer, a woman with forearms like legs of ham protruding from her sleeves, peered up at us. She smeared back locks of greasy hair at either temple and looked from Matthias to me.

"Abbot? Of what, eh? An unimportant Abbey with no holy things and a tiny church with a leaky font? A jumped up monk is what he is." This last was said in low tones. "You'll find him beyond, within the hall there. He'll be writing something or other, he does nothing else all day."

Inside, looking to right and left we saw several doorways set into the wall. We entered the body of the hall, a space which must have been all of ten yards across and three times that in length with a roof high enough to remain in shadow. Wide beams spanned the space to support the roof with a complicated tracery of joists and lesser beams joined and pegged high above our heads. Seven or eight long tables were set in two lines and another crosswise at one end of the hall. The floor was freshly strewn with rushes that crackled beneath our boots.

The noise drew the attention of the grey-robed cleric who sat by a window where the light fell on the work he was doing. "Yes?" He said a trifle imperiously, I thought. "What business do you have here?"

"Abbot Britrig?"

"I am he." The Abbot bowed his head briefly—mock humility. "What do you want?"

"I am the Abbot Matthias, from…"

The other frowned, held up his hand to stop Matthias speaking. "Ah yes, from the monastery of St. Hypolita," Britrig finished for him; he carefully replaced his pen on a stand and closed the ink pot before rising ponderously from his seat. "I remember clearly, it is some time since we met."

"Three years," Matthias agreed. "Though we have corresponded since then of course."

Several expressions chased each other across Britrig's face as they spoke, many of them too fleeting to be certain of what I saw. There was a sort of satisfaction there and cunning—a narrowing of the eyes; no friendship though, no good will.

"I remember, the Scroll of Simon Peter—that is what you want, right?" Britrig put his head on one side.

"Just so."

Brother Britrig got to his feet and faced Matthias. "It will take a little time to retrieve, I don't keep it close. It is hidden away."

"Oh? And why is that?" Matthias asked.

I glanced at the papers on his desk—plans, building plans. A church with a bell tower which might have been those outside had they been larger, this was marked in red ink. Roundabout it lay other buildings, a quadrangle perhaps, and a line of cells. A new monastery in the making?

"Ah. I feel it exudes a dangerous humor, I keep it in a secret place."

Matthias shrugged. "I know you want to be rid of it, I shall be happy to take it away as soon as you can arrange it."

Britrig nodded and eyed the bag which swung from my friend's shoulder. "And these are the others, I'd warrant."

Matthias smiled. "Indeed."

"Bring the bag with you and we'll put the twelfth with them after the feast tonight."

"A feast?" I asked, hardly a surprise after coming through the kitchen.

"Saint Peter's and Saint Paul's day. The villagers have fasted and tonight they celebrate."

"Very well then. Tonight," Matthias nodded.

"Good, come to the feasting then. And for now, go with God."

There was a firm note to the last three words which made us consider ourselves dismissed, we turned about and headed back past the kitchen. Britrig also left, going into a room further down the hall. He looked back at us once, a quick glance, an unreadable expression and then he was gone.

"I'm not sure I trust that one," I told Matthias. "Not sure at all. You seem to be the only Christian cleric I've met with a civil tongue in his head."

Matthias wore a pained expression. "I know you're hired to protect me but there's no need to suspect everyone we meet."

"There was no welcome, no friendliness at all."

"He invited us to the feast."

"I practically asked," I pointed out.

"Well, it may be he does not count me a friend."

"Oh? Why not?" I persisted.

"Britrig obviously doesn't care to be near the scroll—'a dangerous humor'."

"Frightened of it?"

Matthias shrugged.

We asked at the kitchen again where we could find something to eat and were *tsked* at by the woman. "It's late in the day. What do you expect at this time, near three hours past midday?" She looked us both up and down. "Come far?"

"With God's protection, from Chichester."

"Today?"

We nodded.

"Cold pig? A slice or two? I may have some bread left."

We told her that would be welcome. She fetched the food and gestured to a bench. "Ale?"

"Ah, thank you. God's blessings upon you."

"You'll be at the feast tonight?" We nodded between bites. "Come back this way and I'll see you get a seat in the hall itself."

"Thank you again. We had best see to our horses; we'll be back in a quarter hour."

We found the place our horses had been taken to and were assured that our saddles and harness would be safely looked after. We stripped them, brushed them down, left a few coins as reward for those who would keep them, and returned to the refectory.

I wondered about Britrig's attitude to the scroll. "Why does Britrig consider the scroll so bad?"

"Britrig? Because he was told so by his Bishop, I fancy."

"And why should *he* feel that way?"

Matthias lifted his shoulders and let them fall in a long, slow shrug "Perhaps six months ago, Britrig said it had been concluded that the scrolls were not holy objects at all. I cannot tell you the reasons; I can only tell you he was wrong."

"So perhaps he thinks some devil created them?"

"The Devil, Gerard. *Satan.* There is only the one."

"Not in my belief. But a bad God?"

"Not a God." Matthias turned to me and stood still. "Satan is an angel who turned against his Creator."

I scratched my head. "An angel? Can an angel be a threat to your God?"

"Oh yes, indeed so, as can anyone who works against Him."

"But in your creed, God created all of us, everything, didn't He? According to *your* beliefs. Surely one who was made by your God cannot be a threat to Him?"

"But he can, a *real* threat. You see, Gerard, my God has allowed free will, He has not prevented such malice."

We put the empty dishes together. "Until now?"

"Now?" asked Matthias and stopped again.

"Until your scrolls are read?"

Matthias frowned. "The scrolls are the work of men, of the Apostles, not of God."

"So you will prevent this… this Devil's machinations."

"That's so. Exactly."

"Ah…" I was suddenly aware of connections, meanings, of layers of purpose within those twelve scrolls. "Your God has lost interest, there's no longer a power that will control your evil angel."

"Until the scrolls are read."

"Until the scrolls have been read." I had felt before that Matthias's intentions were really a supplication to his God to return to His worshippers. But, perhaps for the first time my mind did harbor doubts as to why I was accompanying Matthias. I carried the platters to the table where the woman had been at work.

I continued. "Suppose he really does want to get rid of the scroll and his reward is the rank of Abbot. Suppose Britrig convinced Bishop Aelfsige he could dispose of the scroll? Hmm? The Bishop rewards him by lifting a mere archivist to the rank of Abbot? "

Matthias frowned.

"If he and his Bishop really believe as we do, that the scrolls will change the world," I rapped the dishes with a knife, " They may fear the changes that will come about."

He turned and looked at me for some time before answering. Clearly, he was thinking hard.

"There were plans on his work table today," I told him. "They looked like building plans to me, for cloisters, for sleeping cells. A bigger abbey, a much bigger, a much richer abbey."

"Well now. If you're right... what if you're right? What will happen?"

"I don't know. He certainly won't want your strategy to succeed; all his hopes and dreams would become very flimsy. We are going to have to be careful after the merry making tonight."

"Don't drink too much ale."

We went outside and walked around the abbey, watching the gardeners planting fruit trees, masons building new dovecots, laborers raising dams to make fish ponds. Britrig had a vision and it was not like those I had been having.

The nearby alehouse was as different again from the last one we'd visited. Here the patrons sat around tables facing one another whilst serving girls brought the tankards out on huge wooden trays. I marveled at the skill and dexterity required to maneuver such heavy articles in and around legs, bodies and groping hands. Unlike the earlier one, this place heaved with people all of whom seemed happy; I felt the pressures of the road and standing guard for so many nights leaving me.

There was a competition of insults in full flow...

"His name's Forrester but it should be Ale-supper," offered a merry red-faced soul.

"Well they call you Shepherd but it should be Sheepsbum, 'cos that's what your face looks like," Came the reply. And the populace erupted with laughter.

"Better that than Elric Bottoms, he should have been called Soggy because his holding has only soggy bottoms."

I turned to the man I sat next to. "Are all the people named after their work or living place?"

"More or less," he replied jovially, "I'm called Hill, my friend is Townsend and that noisy pair over there are named Fletcher and Carpenter. You must be travelers. See, it makes sense to us for there are three Elrics and four Harulds who drink in here daily and the only way to tell them apart is to name them in such a manner."

It made sense to me and I could have stayed in there all evening soaking in the atmosphere of happy people, but my empty stomach and Matthias convinced me we should head back to the abbey.

Part way back, we sat on a knoll to rest and massage our legs which, along with our nether regions, still ached from the unaccustomed jarring of solid roads and hard saddles. I was looking at a leaf, following the tracery when it faded from my gaze to be replaced by the view over a horse's head.

I was astride a small gelding; I could feel the wind rushing through my hair as we galloped along a grassy lane. In front, someone dashed ahead; for some reason, I assumed it was Morion and I wondered why we were both in such a big hurry.

A glance back answered that question; behind were wolves obviously in pursuit; a pack, a whole host of them. Unlike other packs I had come into contact with these were not of one color: black, brown, white; these were mixed and at their head was one I had heard of but never before seen. It was twice the size of its companions and passed me by as close as was possible without colliding with my mount. As the wolf passed, it turned and grinned with exposed teeth drooling spittle and in an evil and all but human sort of way. An intelligent malevolence shone in its eyes, I knew this one, the stuff of nightmares: a werewolf.

Matthias broke me out of my vision by stating loudly that it was time to go. I gathered my thoughts and stood, fully aware that this time, the memory of the vision—because this had to have been a vision, I had not been asleep—lingered with me. Unlike many dreams that disappear within seconds this one was going to remain to torture my mind.

When we returned, fires had been built outside and the villagers and local farmers were sitting around them, awaiting their share of the feast.

Inside, the kitchen was even thicker with the odors of meat being turned on the spits by youngsters, fat dripped and splashed onto the embers, bursting into sudden flame on the glowing charcoal.

The place was now a-bustle with cooks and skivvies. Pots hung above fire grates and bubbled and hissed mouth-watering smells into the air, steam hung in diffuse clouds everywhere as though the big room had its own weather. A pile of bread leaned against the wall in one corner and big earthenware crocks of ale gave off fumes strong enough to make my eyes water.

We caught the attention of the woman we had seen earlier and busy though she was, she found a boy to take us through and find places for us at the tables inside. Others were already sitting so we too took our seats, about halfway along the hall, conveniently near to the kitchens so we might be served first after the top table.

Before it grew dark, a pair of lads came through and lit flambeaux set in sconces high up on the walls. The Duke of Winchester—a broad shouldered man of average height entered through the main doors at the head of a short procession of minor nobles—brothers, sons and nephews judging by the squat nose and beetling brows which adorned most of them. Most of them wore green and red clothing too—no doubt, the colors of Percy, Lord Winchester.

Following our neighbors, we rose as they entered, sat again after they had been seated and watched as roughly carved meat was brought in on thick slabs of bread and placed before them; our mouths watered as the smells of roast meat permeated every nook and cranny of the huge dining area. Despite eating halfway through the afternoon, we were starving. Ale followed; earthenware jugs with pewter goblets. Soon the top table had their knives out and were greedily digging into the food while those of us at the lower tables waited for ours with rumbling stomachs. Once our betters had been served, a handful of young boys eventually brought planks of wood piled with the less choice cuts of meat; loaves of bread were piled on the table and then more ale in leather cups was served to us.

We took out our knives and split the loaves to make our own trenchers and skewered what meat we could in the general reaching and shoving. Sweet cakes were served later for the lord and his family, while we of humbler birth watched and drank ale. When the sweetmeats were finished, our host called for silence and the Abbot, our erstwhile Brother Britrig, in a robe of fine grey fabric and wide-brimmed hat, stood up and recited various prayers in exceedingly bad Latin. Finally, he blessed those in the hall and the others who were eating outside.

"My Lord," said Britrig, taking his hat off with a flourish and making a sweeping bow to the senior figures at the transverse table. "Those two of whom I spoke are with us. For your amusement and for the instruction of the commoners, it may please you to give your judgment now."

The Lord raised his eyebrows and considered Britrig's suggestion while he picked pieces of meat from his teeth. Long before he had come to a conclusion Matthias and I had realized Britrig had planned far more than we had expected— we were the two who were going to be the recipients of that judgment. We were out of our seats and halfway to the kitchens by the time he began to nod. Our dash was in vain, we discovered a body of militia blocking the doorway solidly, grinning at us in an unfriendly way. The men with whom we'd shared the feast were also chuckling as they saw how we had been duped. There was no way out, we had been out-maneuvered by a master.

"Piers Archer, bring in the bag of blasphemous writings." Although we could no longer see him behind the many that were standing, we knew it to be Britrig's voice.

"If they do look at the scrolls to judge for themselves, they are lost," Matthias whispered.

"Be ready."

"Let my scribe read it," said Lord Percy.

"Percy's illiterate," I muttered to Matthias. "So no gain there." There was the rustling sound of fine papyrus being straightened out.

"He can still read those scrolls though... oh." Matthias saw the point. "He won't since he'll be expecting Latin or English."

"Ah!" The voice was old and querulous. "My God, you are come."

Heads had turned from us and we could see an old cleric, presumably Lord Percy's scribe, in threadbare habit staring at one of Matthias's opened scrolls.

"Judge these creatures Oh Lord..." and his sweeping gestures took in all of his employers and the Abbot, too. "Judge them and consign them to the lowest pits of Hell for they are not fit..."

Britrig, keeping his eyes averted, rolled the scroll up and slammed it down on to the table but the old man went on with his castigation and list of accusations and too, he was obviously scoring hits with some of what he was saying.

"This rapist and despoiler of young girls is he who judged Martin the Fowler last week and his son..."

"Enough, said the Duke. Enough I say." But the man would not be stopped until Britrig put his hand over the scribe's mouth and got someone else to tie a gag around his face. Percy turned his attention to us. "Take them away, all three of them, lock them away until morning and we shall have a beheading..." This raised a cheer, not only a feast but a beheading on the following morn—what an entertainer was their Lord.

I missed anything else that was said but what it amounted to was our being dragged by the heels across to the church and thrown into the crypt. The door slammed shut and there was the sound of a pair of bars being slid into brackets outside.

"Hmm," I ventured after a suitably long silence. "Told you I didn't trust him."

Matthias said nothing for some time. Then, mildly: "Yes, Gerard. You did."

"They didn't bring the old man with us."

Matthias did not reply.

The darkness of the crypt was not absolute and as my eyes accommodated themselves I traced the glimmer of dim light to a pair of iron barred windows set just above eye level—ground level from the outside. By feel, I found a box or something to stand on and was able to look across to the fire pits which still glowed out there in the darkness. I stepped down and waited for my eyes to readjust then made a circuit of the walls dragging the box I had found. I was searching for loose stones in the part of the structure which was above ground but found nothing, even when I did it again and for the third time; every joint was tight, every stone was mortared firmly into place. The four iron bound windows were just as strong as the walls and the door did not budge the thickness of a fingernail when I pressed against it.

It was disheartening. I found a place among the rubbish that had accumulated down here over the years and lying down, I went to sleep.

Matthias woke me some time later. "There's commotion outside, I think you need to take a look."

I crossed to a window. Matthias, who had also found something to stand on, did the same. Figures were congregating around one of the fires and logs were being thrown onto the embers until presently, flames were leaping and lighting the score of men who were crowding round at one end.

One figure was conspicuous—the Abbot who stood next to a small pile of logs. He was holding one of these in his hands and made to throw it onto the flames. At the last moment he changed his mind and gestured wildly to another man—the old scribe who had presumably recovered somewhat from his visions. Now he took up one of the logs and was about to toss it into the pit when he too put it back again.

"Those are the scrolls," Matthias cried out. "They're trying to destroy them. I told you it can't be done once you've read them. Remember? I told you Britrig wouldn't get rid of them once he'd seen the writing. Wouldn't destroy them."

"He's just experimenting, Matthias. There are plenty of others there who can."

And so it proved. Britrig shouted something to the small crowd and each one of the scrolls was picked up and the miraculous things were cast onto the fire; great sheets of flame erupted.

Matthias cried wordlessly at the wanton destruction and I think that I did so, too. Certainly, I could see Britrig and the scribe wringing their hands in their own anguish at the desecration. Matthias could bear to watch no longer and went towards the east end of the crypt and prayed to the God who had abandoned him.

I stayed there and watched as some of the men stirred the embers with long poles. There were hot words up there as well as hot flames; arguments with exaggerated gestures which lasted more than a half hour. Eventually, the pokers were put into use again and stuff pulled out of the pit.

"Matthias," I whispered. "Matthias, come here," I shouted. "Matthias, they haven't burned."

Matthias joined me and awkwardly, we both looked out of the tiny window at the pile of scrolls which had been recovered. The distance was considerable but to me, it looked as though none of them had been touched by the flames. Matthias too watched with disbelief.

"You didn't know they wouldn't burn?" I asked. He shook his head.

Britrig tried to have them cut with an axe. One of the men swung the axe and the blade bounced. The shaft slid straight out of the man's numbed hand and flew through the massed onlookers. It knocked two of them down and ended its flight stuck in a third. Afterwards, the pile of mysterious papyrus was skirted at a respectable distance.

Further into the night there were sounds above us. Light gleamed between the flagstones which formed our roof and the floor to the church above us. The footsteps we heard belonged to six or seven people, they progressed steadily from the west to the east of the church and I estimated they stopped around the table under the eastern window. There were prayers, chanting and more prayers to which Matthias listened intently while I mentally marked those slabs of stone which were smallest and which had the widest margins of flickering light.

The activity went on interminably, finishing at last only just before the dawn. Exhausted, I slept until hunger woke me well into the morning. Matthias too had clearly slept heavily when the noise had stopped and we looked at each other blearily, trying to wake up properly before our execution party visited us.

"What do we do, Gerard?" Matthias asked at last. "They promised to execute us today. Do we try and run?"

I got to my feet and paced stiffly around the small underground room, looking at the ceiling. It was not as easy as it had seemed in the dark. The ceiling slabs were supported by pillars, each of which branched in four directions to make a series of shallow arches. Finally I was satisfied. "I watched where the light came through last night and I think they are loosest just here," I pointed upward. "I believe I saw these two move when people walked on them."

We dragged a dusty chest over to the spot I had indicated and piled another smaller one, a coffin, on top. Matthias supported me as I climbed up and put my back against one of the flagstones. I pushed and felt the tiniest of movements. I pushed again, harder this time and raised the stone by the breadth of two or three fingers. It was just enough to shift it to one side and let it down on top of its neighbor.

Encouraged, we changed places and Matthias—now fresher than me—pushed and slid the stone aside little by little.

"Wide enough now, I think." Matthias put his arms up through the gap and then his head and shoulders, he went up and his feet vanished through the opening. I waited a moment but he didn't look back down again.

I shrugged and carefully scrambled onto the coffin lid and pushed myself through the hole. Matthias put his hands under my armpits and lifted me through as though I weighed no more than a mouse.

Only it wasn't Matthias.

Two guards with identical grins stretched across their faces stood in front of me, two more—the pair who had hauled me up—were behind me and to one side two more held Matthias with a sword blade at his throat and a hand like a slab of meat across his mouth.

"God be with you," chuckled one as another slid the stone back into place.

Abbot Britrig was not in such a jovial mood. He scowled at us and paced from one side to the other of the hall where we had been arrested the night before.

It still smelled of cooked meat though it was a stale smell now, truly unappetizing. Dogs snuffled through the rushes searching out gobbets of meat and bolting them down before one of the other animals could challenge them for it.

"You knew the accursed things cannot be destroyed?" Britrig accused.

"Perhaps you have not tried hard enough," I said and his pale washed-out blue eyes swiveled from Matthias to me. I wished I could learn to keep my mouth closed.

"How *can* they be destroyed then?"

I shrugged and shook my head. I had no idea and that was unfortunate for judging by Britrig's narrowing eyes, I could guess what was to come next.

"I can take the secret from you," he said, not bothering with the smile which often accompanies such remarks. "Torture will make your tongue wag whether you will or no."

I sweated a bit and he saw it. Now he smiled. He really was a very unpleasant character.

"Guards, take him to the smithy and tell young Haag to make the fire good and hot." He turned to Matthias. "Now, this bauble that shines day and night..." He placed Matthias's silver ring on the table. "What is it?"

Matthias shrugged. "A finger ring."

"Hit him."

The guards stopped propelling my unwilling feet across the hall and one went back. He boxed Matthias's ears so roundly that I doubt he could hear for a space of several breaths.

"Answer me," Britrig said angrily.

Matthias spoke quietly but every word was audible, chopped off, and separate: "It is the ring from the hand of Jesus Christ when he was taken to be crucified."

"What makes it shine?"

"The very Grace of God. It has shone from the very instant that Christ died upon the cross."

"So fitting for our new Abbey, a relic so recognizable. It will draw the pilgrims as no other holy relic could possibly do." Britrig gave a real smile then, beatific, and nodded to the guards. "Take them."

The pair of us were pushed and pulled across the compound. Matthias's face was grey and I knew mine was no better. "Have you gone through this sort of thing before?" I asked him. Matthias shook his head.

"Once the pain reaches a threshold, when you think you cannot stand another moment of it, you can turn it off; make believe it's not really happening to you," I said.

He nodded but didn't believe me.

It is true, but even I didn't believe me just then.

In the smithy, they tied us to roof trees and showed us the irons which were just beginning to glow. Young Haag—I assumed the youth with the bulging muscles was he—licked his lips nervously as he inspected the pokers and replaced the tools in the fire.

"This is your first and only chance to absolve yourselves," Britrig told us. "Tell me how to get rid of those unholy scrolls and I promise you will be executed quickly."

"There is only one way," said Matthias quietly. I looked round at him but he didn't look at me. "Give them to me and send us on our way."

"That still leaves these writings of the Devil in the world, Abbot. They have to be destroyed utterly."

"It cannot be done. They are God's work, not the Devil's. They cannot be destroyed, ever."

"Haag." He called.

The human frame is rich in senses, the brain is a marvel of imagination. Both work so intimately with the crafts of the torturer that often, it takes no more than the word itself to make cowards of strong men. While I do not count myself a coward, I do admit the threat of torture turns my bowels to water; the thought of my body being deliberately mutilated, my flesh being violated by knives or red hot instruments—so different from the wounds of combat and war.

Haag, the young smith took out a poker and came towards us. Slowly and with a shaking hand, he pushed the poker nearer and nearer to my face. He stopped when my left eyebrow began to singe—at first I thought it was for effect but he could not bring himself to do the deed. After all, he was a blacksmith, torture is a skill which needs to be learned.

A sudden shadow blocked the daylight at the doorway.

XII

ord Percy asked, "What is happening here?" I breathed a sigh of relief as the immediate threat was delayed while Britrig explained and Percy came round in front to look at us.

At length, shook Percy head. "It's not going work, is it? He cannot do it." He turned towards Britrig. "Could *you* do it?" he asked the Abbot.

Britrig opened his mouth to speak and then thought better of it. Percy rubbed his chin thoughtfully; he did not take his heavy lidded eyes off us. "I told you, these were for the chopping block. However" He stood there looking at us for a long time, long enough for me to wonder if he had forgotten what he was going to say. At length he spoke again, slowly. "You intended the scrolls to be the holy relics that would make your abbey famous—until Bishop Aelfsige pronounced them the work of Satan."

"Yes, yes. This water has already run." Britrig was testy and no doubt, he wondered: had he overstepped the mark with his lord?

Not at all, apparently.

"But now we have something better—the ring. Renown will bring money. Also…" He put his hand on the Abbot's arm and took him out of earshot. They turned and looked back at us while Percy spoke quietly into the other's ear. The frown on Britrig's face deepened for several long heart beats and then faded away.

Percy continued, gesturing towards us repeatedly. Britrig didn't smile but the effort to avoid doing so was evident; his expression was anticipatory, almost lascivious. On another, it would have been sexual.

We were taken out of the dark smithy with its smells of burning metal and singed leather. Back across the village again and we were chained to the very posts to which we had tied our horses yesterday, when we first arrived.

"Can you guess what he has in store for us?"

Matthias shook his head. "Nothing pleasant. These two men are the basest. I suspect there will be some sort of depravity."

He was right of course, though neither of us would have guessed what was to come.

A week or two ago, the Christian world had celebrated the death and resurrection of their God: with unmistakable glee in his voice, Britrig told us we would re-enact the crucifixion for the enlightenment of all. Matthias was outraged. He did not seem to care about our fate, what mattered to him was the sense of blasphemy, of sacrilege even. Eventually, he was speechless, he spluttered, he could find nothing coherent to say.

I was no better, though for different reasons. I had been in charge of such occasions, I knew what it was like to be a spectator, knew what it was like to drive the spikes and watch men hung up to die.

Right up to the point when they forced me back against the timber ready to hammer the nails into the palms of my hands, I could say nothing intelligible.

I wasn't speechless. As they stripped me naked in every sense of the word, I used every vile expression I had learned in over a thousand years in nine different languages at the top of my voice. Until they drove the nails home and my mind seemed to shut down.

Britrig and Percy enjoyed it immensely. The good humor did not leave their faces even when they found the carpenter's nails they had were not long enough to go all the way through my crossed ankles. They did not try to find longer nails; there was to be no pause in the fun.

The guards nailed a crosspiece to the log and lashed my feet in place against it while a dozen willing helpers hoisted me upright—I passed out then, the pain of the weight suddenly being taken by my hands and my shoulders was indescribable.

They brought me round with a bucketful of cold water thrown in my face. When I came to, I saw they had done the same to Matthias and placed a plaited circlet of thorns around his head. I have to admit that the Roman method of execution was one of their more barbaric practices, it first robbed a man of dignity and only then of his life. Those events were quite terrible and it does not do to think about them for too long; when I *do* talk about them, even when I think about them; I try to keep it light—and quick. It was not quick at the time of course, time passed agonizingly slowly. Blood ran in thickening streams down our arms and sides and flies buzzed around the wounds, breathing was difficult and to make it easier, we had to fight to stand up straight on the little supports beneath our feet.

It was during what I had thought was a lucid moment that Uncle Max came to me, whether in a dream or a vision I was unsure because I was in and out of consciousness a lot. His face was less expressive than humankind's today and the look he gave me might have been benign, or despairing; I could not tell. He spoke and the words rattled around between my ears. "I told you, go Cordova." It was definitely an admonishment of a sort but the tone was one of "I told you so."

When my vision was working again, I saw we were surrounded by a crowd of onlookers: young men and women looking interested but hardly shocked, a few families with fathers pointing out things to their children. No one looked as if their faith was being strengthened.

Britrig came by occasionally to ask us about destroying the scrolls and went away each time shaking his head when we had nothing to say. He tried four times over the course of the afternoon. When dusk arrived tardily, I was wishing for death or at least, for unconsciousness and at the very, very least, for our spectators to leave us to our pain and degradation.

As the night air sucked the heat from our bodies, it helped to revive us a little. Our hands and wrists were more or less numb and as they grew colder, the pain receded just a little.

Fortunately—for there was a *fortunately* in this sorry business—Britrig had made the same mistake everyone else had done over the past thousand or so years. You only have to look at those pathetic pictures of their crucified God, the nails are driven through the hands instead of the wrists. And in our case too, the nails were made for carpentry, they had small heads. A hair's breadth at a time, I pulled the nails through the palms of my hands.

It was an excruciating task. It is not easy to inflict injury on oneself, it took more willpower than I had supposed. When even the small support of the nails through the flesh of my palms was gone I crumpled in a dead faint. It was probably only a minute or so. I came to lying on my back with arms spread out in a crazy imitation of the cross above me. My ankles were still tied to the upright two feet or so above the ground and wriggling free from the lashings took nearly as long as getting free of the nails.

Eventually it was done and I talked Matthias through the pain of pulling the nails through his hands, then I let him down as gently as I could and unknotted the cords around his ankles. We had no idea what to do; our minds were reeling from the extra hurt we had inflicted on ourselves and thinking was not an easy task for an hour or more. Not that there was much we could do at the moment with our crop of injuries.

Matthias had the idea that he wanted to find out what had happened to the scrolls straight away.

"We have to hide for the time being," I insisted. "We are hurt, we have to give ourselves time to heal; even an hour or so will help. We also need some clothing if we're not to freeze to death instead of bleeding."

At length he saw reason. "Mm. We can probably hide in the church."

"Or even the crypt."

"The church will be warmer."

There were some wall hangings in the church which we pulled down and wrapped around ourselves. We sat on a bench near the rear of the building and tried to ignore the pain and the cold.

Max's earlier visitation had reminded me how long it had been since Morion had visited me in dream time. Perhaps she knew I had been lying about going south to Terraconensis and was not happy with me. I shrugged, I was engaged on something more important.

Over the next hour or more, Matthias did a lot of muttering under his breath. "No," he said at last. "This is no good, it won't get us anywhere. We have to take advantage of these wounds, use them as weapons."

I didn't understand.

"Trust me," he said. "It's symbolic."

He spent some time looking for the wreath of thorns they had made him wear and which he had removed very carefully. Then with me following him, Matthias discarded the woolen tapestries and left the church. Clad in nothing but the circlet of thorn twigs, he crossed to the guest house; I followed in a similar state of dress. We went up to the big oak doors where ornate carvings stood out in the moonlight like skulls nailed to the door.

Matthias made certain his crown of thorns was on straight and suddenly I realized what he was about to do. If Britrig and his Lord could re-enact the crucifixion, Matthias was going to take it one step beyond, to the Resurrection. With the mutilations making him awkward, he picked up a stone and held it in both hands; he held it over his head and brought it forward to strike the door panel with a resounding crash. In the silence of the night, the blow echoed through the house and back from the walls of the church and the great hall.

"Will that not awaken the dead?"

"Most of them, I think."

It woke someone inside, we could hear steps beyond the door, steps and any amount of uncouth blasphemy.

"Copy me." Matthias dropped the stone and held his hands up, palms forward so that the still bleeding wounds were clearly visible.

The door opened.

"Bless you, my son," said Matthias.

The door stayed open, but there was no sign of the guard who had briefly stood there except for the rapidly fading sounds of running feet.

"I think we'd better try again." Matthias repeated the knocking. In fact, he repeated it several times before an irritated and cursing master-at-arms came to the door. The man looked at us blearily for ten or twelve heartbeats and then blanched. Even in the silver light of the moon, we could see his face turn several shades paler. "What...?" he managed to say and almost fainted away.

"May God bless you and keep you my son. Bring your Lord out here."

The thoroughly shaken man nodded. He turned and tottered unsteadily back into the house and before long; Lord Percy came to the door and looked us over. Britrig, who had followed, said nothing, his upper teeth were firmly embedded in his bottom lip and blood ran down his chin, it was the only reason his teeth did not chatter with fright. When Percy saw us properly, his ponderous aplomb faded as quickly as Britrig's color.

"God withholds His anger, my son," Matthias said gently, lowering his arms and clasping his hands in front of him. Thankfully, I did the same, my shoulder joints ached fiercely. "He seeks to enlighten you and your household, not to punish."

Percy croaked something and cleared his throat, tried again with no better result.

"God requires that you hide our nakedness, that you fill our bellies and that you give those holy objects into our keeping. You may also include the finger ring of our Lord, Jesus Christ."

Matthias paused and Percy nodded eagerly but my friend had not yet finished. "We shall be given beds with fresh linen and food for our journey. Our horses will be groomed and saddled for our departure at noon."

All this was said in the most patient of tones with just a touch of sadness at the other's lack of civility. And as Matthias proposed, so it came to pass.

Well out of sight of the cursed place, we stopped and Matthias unbuckled the scroll case to inspect the contents. Apart from some ash and smudges of charcoal, there was no sign of fire on any of them, one did show a deep cut—from the axe blow, the blade had bitten cleanly through the paper and struck the ebony roller at the center . The silver ring was there, glowing faintly, even in the light of day.

"I never thought that would work." I said.

Matthias smiled, thin lipped. "Oh ye of little faith. Lord Percy and Britig may well have their doubts as they think about it, but they will feel they had no choice. They are at least rid of the devilish scrolls and two unwelcome visitors."

Matthias paused and chuckled. "Word will get 'round to the villagers, the story of our resurrection will be exaggerated... mark my words, people will pay the abbey so they might stand on the site of the miracle and be blessed."

We headed south again, to roads I knew from my memories of long ago; and our wounds healed as they do for our kind.

XIII

 little before mid-afternoon, after one of his frequent backward glances as we rode silently along, Matthias shook his head slowly and cleared his throat. "We're being followed."

I nodded. "Yes. By one of our snaggle-toothed friends." After all this time, I had thought they would have presumed us drowned with all the other poor souls and gone home.

"You knew? How long has he been there?"

"About an hour." I turned in the saddle and shot a glance behind me and considered the one following: big, blocky, dark mop of untidy hair.

"What do you suggest we do?"

"I don't know," I said. I had been trying to find an answer to that ever since I had seen him. "I suppose we have to kill him but I've been wondering where his friends are."

"Perhaps he's alone."

"There were two the first time you were attacked, two at the inn. And," I thought back, "a small horde of them and other things at Mont Saint-Michel."

"Hmm. But with Prior Hildebert sending decoys out, can we not assume they are spread quite thinly, even if there were a dozen or two?"

I raised my eyebrows; here was something I had not considered.

And Matthias spoke thoughtfully again. "In any case, at the Mont, you and the garrison killed many; only one survived, I think. Only one got away."

"I think you're right," I said, but I chose not to tell him about the ones in my visions.

"We're in Wessex now, England. Has there been time for our enemies to get a detail together?"

I shook my head slowly, in time to the horse's gait. "I don't know. I think that whoever is sending them after us would rather have had the business finished on the other side of the Narrows. You could be right though, Matthias. This one could be the only one left."

"For the time being."

I didn't reply but I had to agree; there *had* to be more of them but I knew not where.

We rode onward while other considerations filled my skull. Once they had left me back in Brittany, what then? Max already had business there; escorting me into exile had been a coincidence, hadn't it? Could it be *Max* who wanted Matthias dead? Just to lay hands on his scroll bag, they had presumably followed Matthias into Armorica and… could Max do things like that? Command the winds and the lightning? Could he? Did he have a pact with elementals? It was not something he had ever mentioned to me.

"Does that get us any closer to deciding what to do about our pursuer?"

"No. It doesn't. Suppose we were to ambush him and kill him? That would prevent him joining up with any others later and letting them know where we are."

"But he doesn't know whether we're the ones they want or not," Matthias frowned. "If they've been waiting here in Britain for someone to come over from Armorican Gaul, they have no idea who it would be. For all they know, their quarry has been drowned in one of those storms." He stopped abruptly and I wondered if he was thinking along the same lines I had. "Can we put him off the scent somehow?"

"Now that's a good idea because he would report back and tell the rest to ignore us. Let me think."

I thought about it at length. So did Matthias.

"Suppose we let him catch up… we'll hide the scrolls first." He ran out of ideas.

"Yes. We put something else in your scroll case instead."

"He may decide to kill us before he leaves."

"He might try, yes, but why should he? It's the scrolls that are important—and your ring—although they *did* kill your comrade." I thought about that. "Why did they take your ring?"

My remark had started Matthias thinking about the monk who had been killed. I could see his thoughts backtrack to what I had said as he considered the question.

"They thought it was the real one."

"The real what?"

"The ring. It was—as I said to Britrig—the ring worn by Christ, Jesus Christ. I was the last disciple. I took it from His hand when he was stripped at Golgotha."

I looked at Matthias. Even though I'd mentioned it to him, did he really not recognize me from those far-off days when I was a young centurion? I no longer lived in that body but mannerisms continued on—certainly enough for my Mother to recognize me.

"As well as assembling all these documents, the ring is my last connection with Him and it does help with identification; it is known by many."

"The last connection with your God?" I queried.

"Exactly so."

We passed another half mile in silence and then Matthias thought of something else. "You know, it's on foot. Can't we just gallop the horses and leave it far behind?"

I shook my head. "We can try if you like, but I wouldn't lay many wagers on it."

"You think it can outrun a galloping horse?"

"That I *would* lay a wager on." It was a wager I *knew* I would win.

"We'll wait until we're out of sight and then try, hmm? Just to get a bit of a lead."

"Fine."

And that is what we did. We crested a hill with our follower still half a mile behind us and then kicked the horses up to a gallop. We reached the foot of the hill and there was a slight bend with enough trees to put us out of sight for a little longer.

"Hold," Matthias called and I pulled on the reins a few moments afterwards. "I've another idea as well," he said and dismounted. "No, stay on your horse." He took off his scroll case and I trotted my mount into the woodland after him.

"Care to explain what you're doing?"

"Of course." He took the case from its linen bag, undid the buckles and spilled its contents into the bag; which he left under a spreading alder. "I'm hiding the important stuff as we decided and I'll fill the case with other things." He sorted through, pulled out the small bundle which held the all-important ring. "Keep this yourself." He passed it up and I put it in my belt pouch; my fingers shook a little, it is not every day that I handle something once worn by a God.

"Need help?" I asked as he covered the rest up.

"No. Ride into the woods and hide your horse." He went back to his own horse and started to transfer food and drink from one of the saddlebags to the case.

"Come back here but stay hidden. Right? Don't come too close, just in case it can smell you, that's why I suggested you don't dismount. Do it now and hurry, I still have things I need to say."

I hastened off the road, dismounted and wound the reins around a tree limb some distance into the woods. I returned, staying out of sight. Our pursuer was charging along at a great speed until he saw Matthias sitting by the side of the road chewing a grass stalk. The creature quickly slowed back down to a walk.

"Matthias, I'm back. Talk," I whispered as loud as I dared.

"If I get killed, take the scrolls and the ring to Glastonbury. I should have told you this before. Seek out Fergal, the prior at the monastery there, and show him what you have. Explain the circumstances."

"Right. Now what are we doing here?"

"If I can persuade this creature that I'm an innocent traveler, it will go on its way and leave us alone. They don't seem to have a lot of initiative, do they?"

"No, not many of them. But they may have been told just to kill you anyway."

"That's why you're there. By the way, there are several rolls of derniers among the papers, enough for expenses and to pay you."

"Matthias, this stopped being a hired labor thing some time ago, this is friendship, all right?"

Matthias paused for six or seven heart beats. "Thank you," he said with a curiously embarrassed sort of expression.

Our pursuer arrived. He came abreast of Matthias, stopped and looked closely at him. Matthias looked right back. The beast-man didn't speak. He approached, pulled the scroll case from Matthias's hands and pushed him back. He opened the case, upended it and scrabbled through the pile of bread and meat and the two bottles of wine. He looked at Matthias, back in the case, and back at Matthias again.

Dropping the case, he pulled my comrade to his feet. I tensed, my sword arm tensed, there was a knife in my left hand too, ready to throw. He pulled open Matthias's coat and searched him, thoroughly and vigorously—I could hear the seams coming apart. When he found nothing, he turned his attention to the horse and searched the saddle bags. He came back. "Other one," he growled in a guttural voice.

"What?" asked Matthias.

"The other man, where?"

"He left me behind." Matthias pointed up the road. "That way."

Clearly in difficulty, the beast-man thought about things for some minutes, looking from Matthias to the road. Eventually he released his grip on Matthias's clothing and went back to the road. I breathed a sigh of relief.

Changing his mind, the beast man returned and took hold of Matthias by the throat. He sniffed at Matthias's face.

Matthias struggled but the grip remained unbroken. The beast man slowly and deliberately drew his knife, swung it back above his left shoulder and then forward to take my friend's head off at ear level.

My knife blade entered the creature's ear just as the forward stroke was gaining momentum. The beast-man's blade dropped from nerveless fingers but for some reason, the clawed fingers did not relax their grasp on Matthias's neck. I ran forward from my hiding place, I retrieved my knife and cut away the dead thumb to break the death hold. It... he, crumpled to the ground.

"Thanks, I thought I was going to die then. I thought that whoever is directing these creatures wouldn't want every traveler they accosted to be killed but I was wrong." Matthias wiped his forehead which was running with sweat. "At the moment, we're in relatively populated country. We've passed three or perhaps four villages this morning, and farms, churches. If word goes round that there are murderers on the loose, footpads; the local militia might be roused."

"What you say may be true," I said, looking at the empty eye-socket. I tore the sleeve from the creature's shirt along the seam. "But this was revenge, look." I pointed to two purple wounds on the arm.

"What're those?"

"I think you'd find they'd match up with the blades on that fork of yours, if you still had it."

"God's Blood. The one who grabbed me round the neck at the inn?"

"Do you remember it smelling you just now," I asked. "It remembered your scent. The question now is where do we go from here? By killing this one, we've left a signpost. They will guess this road is the one we're following."

"Mm. We can strike off the main road, follow byways and forest paths," Matthias suggested.

I had known this part of Britain quite well almost eight centuries ago and most of the memories would still be in my skull somewhere. I tried to visualize the maps we had had in those days; they had been reasonably accurate, put together by army surveyors who knew what they were about.

"We can go back as far as Noviomagus, take the road north to Caleva and then strike out west again, it won't make much difference in the long run."

"Noviomagus, that's Chichester, right?"

I grinned. "How did it get to be Chichester from Noviomagus?"

"Perhaps it was called that, or something like it, before your armies tramped over everything and made your own names up."

"Ah." I considered what he said and nodded. "I suppose you might be right. Anyway, whatever it's called, I think you mentioned there was an important date.

How much time do we actually have to reach Glastonbury?" As I was talking I was absentmindedly going through the dead creature's purse. Apart from a few copper coins which I retained, there was nothing there.

Matthias picked a leather-bound note case out of the litter the beast-man had left behind and looked at a column of numbers and words written on a small sheet of vellum. Quite a lot had been crossed out. He counted the uncrossed-out ones.

I pulled open the quilted shirt and found a linen bag on a string around the short neck.

"Six days. Prior Fergal estimated it would take us six days to get there."

I carefully brought the old maps into my mind's eye. "I would reckon on a hundred and twenty Roman miles, a four-day march."

"I'm not as fit as one of your legionaries. Let's say eight."

"But we're on horseback. Four days. Now, how long do we have before this celestial event of yours?"

"Sixteen days."

I recovered my horse while Matthias repacked the scrolls. Then, after dragging the rank-smelling corpse well into the woodland, we retraced yesterday's travel to Chichester, a safer course of action than trying to find our way along hunting trails. It was fortunate we had indeed returned to Chichester. Once we had ridden a few miles to the north, the forest closed in around us. The road was still there but great oaks and beeches with hazel and alder between them grew ever closer and higher until we travelled some great leafy tunnel. Sometimes, a narrow, irregular line of blue sky or white cloud could be glimpsed through the leafy canopy. Birds made the afternoon raucous with their cries and occasionally the sound of some larger beast—a bear or a boar—could be heard off in the underbrush. Without a travelled road to guide us, we would certainly have lost our way more than a time or two.

We travelled steadily north and west to a place the Saxons had called the City in the Woodland, passing small villages of rounded timber huts and sometimes a stone-built church. Occasionally, it was possible to see a grander house set back where trees had been thinned or even cleared entirely. These were mostly of timber with thatched roofs and a lot more care and effort had gone into their building; trees had been cleared for crops or grazing.

In the early afternoon we came to a place where a long fragment of Roman wall stood alongside the ancient roadway we followed. *Caleva Atrebatum*, the City in the Woodland. Caleva had been a sprawling place. Once the meeting place of five or six roads and a city as grand as any built in these islands, there was now only a single major road and one or two trails which came out of the forest of the Great Weald and continued westward. I remembered lines of shops and villas, a forum, a public baths, temples, but all that was left today were three woodsmen's huts clustered around one of the junctions.

We looked at each other, up at the sun and continued on without stopping. Cunetio was next and I thought the road had vanished altogether as we left Caleva behind. However, we came across a small hamlet at which there was, unexpectedly, a prosperous inn. It must have been at just the right place to thrive. When we entered, an hour before sunset, the room which comprised most of the building was filled with woodcutters and farmers. Without doubt they were wait-ing for nightfall to set clandestine traps or dig boar pits in the forest.

Matthias sat down in a corner while I went to get some ale and ask for accom-modation. The accommodation was the upper floor of a stable behind the main building; in spite of the size of the place, there were no rooms to let—not an inn but a tavern. We took what was offered and after rubbing the horses down, went back into the tavern to get something to eat. Afterwards, we did not bother to keep watch; we spread our coats out across the hay, a comfortable enough bed, laid our swords beside us and trusted the horses to wake us if anything intruded.

A long time after I had drunk my nightcap I saw a tiny red dot of smoldering ash burning at the end of the rush light. As the light departed so Morion's mind touched mine. Together, we dreamed of warm sand and blue seas.

Later, she sought information—that was obvious. Probing tendrils of energy searched hither and thither inside my head whilst at the same time she was mak-ing reassuring sounds, noises on the primeval level like an animal comforting its cub. This was a new Morion, serious and insistent so I think my duplicity was discovered. She left me only after our ethereal bodies had joined once more, promising to meet me at this place of sunlight and water that she pretended to believe existed—a swirl of thoughts within my own skull. I longed to reach out for her, to touch her, draw her close to me but noises were reverberating in my skull. Loud they seemed and guttural, filled with clicks and rasps and then, just like that, I felt refreshed; filled with love for Matthias and our cause. The journey was all—I must protect the scrolls at all and any costs.

The following morning I felt invigorated and for several hours afterwards, we fought. That is to say, we practiced fighting. Matthias still clung to the wavy bladed weapon he had taken from the beast-man and with this he defended him-self against my gentle attacks. They started out softly enough as did Matthias's defensive moves but it was self-evident that he had once fought with a sword of much the same size and weight as the one he now wielded. His skills were merely neglected and the third time we practiced, he began to attack and my gentle lunges had to become sharper and stronger. It quickly became obvious that Mat-thias had done far more than wander around listening to Jesus Christ's sermons, there was a military precision behind his fighting style and because the blade he used was envenomed, I worked carefully and vigilantly when we practiced.

Matthias's new-found confidence in his ability wrought other changes, too. He held himself straighter than before; he lost the hunched-shoulder posture, the partial bow and the hands perpetually clasped went away. When we begged food or shelter, he seemed to don the monkish pose like a suit of clothes. Other things too—his ability to deceive grew by leaps and bounds; from fighting strictly by the book he went to attacking before we had saluted each other at the start of a session, his feints became increasingly subtle, he would pretend to be hurt when my blade slapped his wrist and then stab at me unexpectedly. Yet I knew he would not harm me because we were brothers. He needed me; I was sure he did.

Our journey turned up more missing places. After Cunetio there should have been Verlucio but again, nothing but a woodsman's hut and a pile of weed-covered stones remained to mark the fort which had once stood there. Once bustling centers of trade, markets, big farm holdings—all were gone or transformed into hovels.

Change.

It is the only constant for Amaranthine people such as Matthias and myself. Fortresses, cities, temples; they all fall down eventually. Harbors silt up, the sea moves away or drowns them, rivers change course. Survive long enough, I've been told, and you'll see the pole star move.

Change.

Everything changes except people. In every age you meet the same individuals; they change their names and their lineages, they forget their former lives but they are the same. Sometimes the change is skin deep; other times, the likeness is exact.

Occasionally, when I think along these lines, I wonder how Matthias can maintain his faith—looking forward to a day when the graves give up all their dead, even though his God has lost interest. It seems self-evident to me; the Ephemerals live their lives over and over again. If there is reason to it, then surely it is to do it better each time?

XIV

In this way we came to Akemanchester, the town that had been Aqua Sulis in my younger days. An exhibition town, built to show the Britons what really civilized living was about. While the Roman stations I had known were gone and forgotten or at best, replaced by scruffy little hamlets, Aqua Sulis had prospered.

We came on it from the northeast, having spent the night at a small monastery a mile or two from the city. At first, just a few huts along each side of the road but then we came to a great ditch, the water covered with bright green duckweed. Beyond the bridge which carried us across, the houses were larger and more crowded. Behind them were vegetable patches and, once or twice, pens of plaited withies holding geese or chickens.

The road led us deeper into the city. One or two stone-built residences—stone I'd wager had once been a part of the walls of the old colonia, for I saw Latin inscriptions and acanthus leaves here and there. I smiled. If I hadn't, I would have cried. Half a mile more and we came upon the remnants of those same walls, much of them still there. A lot of the dressed stonework had been taken leaving the rubble core and here and there even that had gone to be replaced by brick or old, heavy timbers for it had obviously still been a defensive barrier until recently and perhaps, was still maintained as such. We came to a gateway, the old guardhouse still largely as it had been and here we were inspected and passed through when Matthias spoke his pious words: "Bless you my son. We are wandering monks of the Order of St. Hypolita."

The huge vaulted roof over the great bath had collapsed and the temple to Sulis Minerva was no more than a flattened mound covered in grass and wild flowers with an occasional carving pushing through the surface. A small chapel had been built over it, dedicated—of course—to Matthias's ubiquitous God. We had arrived in the late afternoon and found a comfortable hostelry where we rented a room for two nights. The interior was huge, the roof supported by a dozen or more pillars, each cut from a whole tree trunk. There was a partial upper floor which had been added at some later date by laying stout boards across the beams which supported the roof trestles.

Thus, the inn was now on two floors and our room, a sort of rude solar, was close under the thatch, just high enough to walk upright. The window gave on to the front and we had a good view of the bustling street along which we had come.

The evening was given over to rest and refreshment, as Matthias put it. We rested with a tall pitcher of ale to hand so we did not have to go far for refreshment; we felt an ever-present concern that eyes were watching us. The more we showed ourselves in public the more chance our whereabouts could be broadcast. Food was available in the main room; the bread was somewhat stale but soaked up the gravy from our platters readily enough.

Later, it was a fine spring evening and with capes pulled over our heads we walked to the town center by the light of the moon peering over sway-backed roofs. A fire had been built in the square and two spits of chickens were being roasted by a local butcher. When the aroma became unbearable and our mouths ran wet with saliva, I bought one and got the fellow to cut it in half. Matthias and I ate our way through them with grease running down our chins and up our sleeves. We drank quite a lot too, before turning to go back to the inn.

As we walked around the square, a short obese fellow bumped into us. He hadn't been looking where he was going and was drunk enough to be truculent about the encounter. Matthias snarled at the man and reaching back over his shoulder, he drew his short sword and brandished it. The tipsy villain waddled off as fast as his little legs would move. A drunk Matthias was a quite different character to the one with whom I had travelled all the way from Brittany.

We returned to our lodgings to clean up and get some sleep. It had been a very pleasant evening despite our encounter with the drunk, apart from this, the covering up seemed to have worked pretty well—I was not certain I liked the new self-confident Matthias but I tried to put this from my mind for I had enjoyed the evening otherwise. What had really made it so enjoyable however, was the fact that we had seen nothing of the beast-men who had pursued us from Brittany. And there had been no more of the strange storms which now seemed as much imagined as real.

Matthias had lugged his heavy scroll case around the whole time and was worried about its safety while we slept. I tended to agree with him, in a place this size there were too many opportunist thieves around and it would be considered that a container so large must contain something worth stealing. He was quite prepared to sleep with the thing in his bed until I found a void behind the plaster under the window. With the case in there, out of sight, we went to bed.

I was sitting in a circle of happy laughing faces, a cup in my hand, enjoying the jokes being made about one another. I was enjoying the mead but looking forward more to the feast and the expected entertainment to follow. Uncle Max sat almost opposite me with Morion to his right, my left, and I thought how incredibly fortunate I was to have a companion like her; she was trying her best not to look at me from under her long eyelashes.

The food was brought out in heavy iron pots, carried on boards with a cut-out for each of the vessels. The smell of roast meat was overpowering and my mouth was not the only one dribbling juices in anticipation.

Not bothering to wait for a trencher, I reached forward and rescued a meat wrapped bone from the pot nearest to me and sank my teeth into the hot flesh. The smell of the meat hit me at the same time as the flavor: sweet, heady, more-ish. One taste was sufficient to assuage hunger, swallowing was an effort, yet I longed for more. I looked questioningly across at Max, then at Morion; neither one would meet my gaze. Looking into the pot again I saw bones and meat swimming in the gravy, bobbing in and out of the juices with first one part showing, then another until I saw just what was in the stew, I felt sick to the pit of my stomach, though quite why, I don't know. What I saw was a head, not that of a pig or a sheep or a goat; this one had long jaws and an ear sill clung to the bone.

I recognized it then, it was the skull of a wolf—not that much different from dog which I had eaten in the past but somehow, I knew beyond doubt this was not wolf but werewolf and therefore more than partly human.

Then Max did look at me, and slowly winked before he too, changed his shape to a great shambling, furred thing.

I awoke with a start, in a cold sweat, to find Matthias shaking me. I needed to blurt it all out to him, to tell him about the meal I had dreamed, and all the other things I had so far kept to myself because as yet, I had no ready explanation.

Which of my dreams and visions and nightmares were connected to reality? Even those brief connections with Morion seemed suspect this morning. No, I could say nothing, I found I still did not trust my friend sufficiently to tell him the full truth about Max or Morion, perhaps it was my natural wariness. I did not know.

I sat up with a lurch, mumbled apologies and made to rise. I pulled on a jerkin to hide my face and thoughts and stumbled from the room.

Downstairs, we both crossed to the privies. Matthias had followed me—probably because he was ready sooner, rather than out of an inbuilt need to care for me. As a Greek, Matthias liked to be clean; and, thoroughly Romanized myself, I felt the same way. Although an onlooker would certainly have found our actions odd, we washed as much travel muck off as we could in the stone water trough just outside the stables. Afterwards, we found Sarah, the landlord's daughter, sweeping out the ground floor. She would not listen to our entreaties for breakfast until she was finished. Finally she was done and consented to making us porridge and bringing each of us a mug of weak beer.

Later, after seeing to our horses, we toured the town by daylight and replenished our supplies. I had lost my whetstone and looked for an armorer while Matthias found a tailor to re-sew the seams of his clothing pulled apart by the beast-man. The streets were narrow and rarely ran straight for more than twenty paces. Any street wide enough for a cart to pass along had a stinking drain down the center and this morning, in the frosty air, pestilential vapors rose from the murky liquid like plumes of steam. I asked a passer-by where I might find an armorer and was directed along a narrow lane. Pushing past a saddler who was hanging his wares outside the shop, I squeezed around a small horse cart where a wheelwright was fitting a new axle. And there was my armorer, all on his own at the end of a street which otherwise saw to horse tackle.

I told him what I wanted. A small whetstone.

"Small? To carry with you?"

I nodded and he showed me three, small, medium and medium large. The smallest fitted in a box, the lid of which carried a picture burned into it with a red hot wire. There were only a half dozen quick strokes, enough to render a horse's head with extraordinary élan, it persuaded me to buy the thing for the sketch was delicate and appealed to me. We thanked each other for the purchase and I set off again, meandering from main thoroughfares to narrow alleyways and back again. I passed a dozen trades in as many minutes; tapestry and embroidery, fine metalwork, a street of carpenters and another of bowyers. Shops by the dozen: lace, wool, work clothes; a shambles, a street full of jewelers; close by there were cages of twittering finches and one with a silent raven with a curiously knowing expression in its eyes. I carried on around a corner and collided with someone coming the opposite way.

"My apologies," I said and helped the other to stand up.

"My fault," he said and picked up the little box with its whetstone which I had dropped. He was about to return it to me when he saw the sketch and looked at it a little longer. "Fine piece of work."

"Hmm? Isn't it? Yes." I was distracted. Over his shoulder, which fortunately was a broad one, I saw Morion marching along the narrow street. Morion knew I was not on my way to Terraconensis, probably by now, Max did, too. I could not face her, however much I desired it.

I bent over, rubbed my finger over the poker work. "Just bought it this morning, actually," I said, moving a little, contriving to keep him between myself and Morion.

"A lucky purchase."

I agreed, nodded madly and watched her stop at a stall selling spices and herbs. She reached out and squeezed a leaf between her fingers then brought them back to her face, sniffing the aroma. She smiled, bought a small bunch and tucked it into the fold of her collar to shield her from the less pleasant smells of the city.

To be so near my love and unable to speak to her for fear of discovery by her companions, to be unable to touch her face, was maddening. I was like a young boy suddenly confronted by the girl with whom he was secretly infatuated. When she had passed from sight, I turned and ran and reached the inn just as the midday chimes were striking from a nearby bell tower. Matthias was inside, a plate already set before him.

"Let's go over there, in the corner. I'll join you as soon as I get something to eat."

How was I going to tell him? I wondered. *What was I going to tell him?*

Matthias spoke as I was sitting down, before I had a chance to say anything. "I thought I saw one of our beast-men, this morning," he said between gulps as though he was talking about a hunting dog.

I looked up. "We'd better move on quickly, then."

He laid a calming hand on my arm. "I said I *thought* I saw one. In fact, I was wrong but the fellow I'd mistaken for one still gave that…" Matthias paused, seeking an apt word, "that sense of primitive, you know?"

I nodded. "There are such. So, a false alarm. What was it made you think of the beast-men?" I asked.

Matthias finished his mouthful. "The same sort of build perhaps, although he was rather shorter. Same shaped head, that was it; low forehead; large, deep eye sockets. Big—huge—hands. Everyone he passed gave him a plenty of room."

It had to be Maximus.

Morion and Uncle Max, what were they doing here? Had my earlier dream not been a dream? Was it some parallel reality I had experienced? Could they be after the scrolls? Had they been following us all the time? And did those beast-men I had assumed to be some other group give their allegiance to Max?

I had no answers. I ate some bread to delay having to say anything. Whatever the reason, I was worried. I was going to have to lie.

"I saw three of the real thing today."

"Real what?"

"Real beast-men. I was in a shop, buying a whetstone when they went past."

Matthias started to look worried. "They didn't see you then?"

I shook my head. "No. I took care as I came back here. I didn't see them again."

"What do we do?"

"We hide. We'll take the evening meal to our room and then go to bed early," I suggested. *What could there possibly be that was of interest to Max around here? Surely it could only be Matthias or his scrolls?* "We'll get up early, before it's light, we'll be at the gate ready to leave as soon as it opens and breakfast on the way."

"Why not go tonight, we could leave just before they close the gate."

Which was a good idea if my lie had been the truth. "That's a good idea, so long as we go carefully as soon as it's dark. I'll find out when the gates are shut, may well be sunset in which case we'll have to risk going in the light."

We prepared to leave, packing the saddle bags and taking them down to the stables for when we saddled the horses. I asked the landlord about the gates and it turned out they shut about an hour after sunset, which was good fortune.

We napped for the remainder of the afternoon but were awakened just as the sun was leaving the sky. Not by the landlord, who had agreed to call us, but by his daughter screaming at the top of her voice. I got up and looked down from our window. Young Sarah was squirming in the grip of one of four beast-men standing outside the main door; Uncle Max was looking on with a benign smile while Morion put her to the question. Now her father stepped out.

"What's going on out here?" he roared, and when he saw Sarah being man-handled, he roared louder still. What he said, I couldn't make out. He rushed forward but two of the beast-men took him as if he were a ten-year-old and held him fast. Morion produced a knife.

Our good fortune had turned sour very quickly

"That's the man I saw this morning," Matthias whispered. "What do we do?"

"We go, now." We went, creeping down the stairs and passing into the kitchen at the rear. I opened the door just a crack and looked out.

I put a finger to my lips and pointed at Matthias's second-hand knife which tonight, he wore over his surcoat. He passed it to me; I could just detect the bittersweet smell of the poison. I pulled the door open until there was enough room to get my fist through and stabbed the beast-man who guarded the door in the back of the neck. He collapsed instantly; I was pleased to note the blade had not lost its potency. Another look round outside assured me he was the only one guarding the back door. I cleaned the knife perfunctorily on the fellow's clothes and we crossed to the stable as silently as we could. All was quiet inside. The horses would have been moving uneasily if any of the creatures were inside. I stepped into the gloom, Matthias followed and we saddled the horses, we were about to walk outside, down to the main road when I had second thoughts. "I don't think we can get by them without being seen."

Matthias frowned. "We had better go and see."

We went to the corner of the inn, looked along the frontage. Max and Morion had gone inside with their hostages but two of the beast men were visible, left outside to discourage customers.

"The other way?" Matthias whispered, eyebrows raised.

I shook my head. "It goes nowhere, just behind the two shops further along."

"What's behind the stables?"

"A fence," I breathed.

"I'll take a look." While he was away, what was left of the evening light dropped out of the sky.

He was back quickly. He shook his head. "Another row of houses, and I think there are gardens or something between the houses and fence."

"It's the only way. We'll get the saddle bags but we are going to have to leave the horses."

We went back to the stables, treading on the grass at the edge of the pathway so our steps were silent. I took the saddle bags off the horses and we left. Seconds later, there was an urgent shout. Someone had found the dead guard.

We ran, found a stunted tree and flung our bags over the man-high fence. There was a burst of shouting behind us and the sound of feet, Matthias scrambled over the fence with the aid of the tree and I leaped for the top and pulled myself up and over by brute force. Matthias found his scroll case and I picked up the saddle bags and we crossed the open area towards the buildings beyond. It was now almost pitch dark and we blundered through the remains of last year's crops and here and there, the soft earth of newly dug plots. Near the houses, the ground was hard and firm and we pushed on until a patch of light revealed a gap between the buildings. There were sounds behind us but we did not stop to investigate, we pushed through the narrow alleyway and came out on another street, the last stains of the sunset showed where the west was, we turned in that direction and ran as hard as we could. There was definite pursuit now and it was gaining on us. Not only were the beast-men faster than we were but I fancied they could see better in the dark and as Matthias had said days before, they might well be able to follow our scent.

All these things went through my mind as we ran.

As with most streets in towns, there was a runnel of noisome water down the middle of the street, I ran into it to fuddle any sense of smell that the beast-men might have and Matthias, guessing my reasoning followed me. We went on, scattering splatters of smelly liquid at each step until the shallow ditch deepened and ran into what, outside the town walls, would probably have been an idyllic little stream with water cress and sticklebacks. Here, the only water life that managed to exist was likely to be rats and water beetles. We stayed with the waterway, moving more slowly as it became deeper. Both Matthias and I had the skirts of our coats hiked up well above the knees and I was thankful that I wore boots rather than sandals. Especially when the channel disappeared into a black hole just ahead. Above us, the town wall heaved skyward, making it even darker, the waterway ran through the foundations of the wall. It was a safe wager that there would be bars preventing egress but as a hidy-hole, we were not going to find anything better. We waded on, stopping six or seven paces into the culvert.

The turgid water ran almost silently around our legs, and after a while, we could hear the thud of running feet. Matthias touched my shoulder. "Deeper," he whispered and slowly, to avoid splashing, we moved further in until we did indeed come up against a barrier of metal bars. We stopped again and listened, the sounds grew louder although the thump of my heartbeat seemed as though it might drown them out.

The footsteps were muffled, difficult to hear; the entrance to the culvert was now twenty feet away or perhaps, more; a small oval of blackness slightly paler than the surrounding darkness. I watched it steadfastly until it seemed to waver in and out of visibility. Then all was quiet.

We retraced our steps; I crept out of the culvert and immediately took a stunning blow to the side of my head. The night lit up with a hundred flashes of brilliant white light and then turned blacker than before. It was unfortunate that I did not remain unconscious longer; when I came too; I was hanging over someone's shoulder like a dead boar and the someone was jogging along at a pace that did my aching brain no good at all. Only one of Max's beast-men could have kept this pace up for as long. The jouncing went on for a half hour. I became aware of illumination. I saw that Matthias was being treated the same way although he had had the sense to stay unconscious for a while.

They realized we were awake and set us down, marching at the usual double time right back to the inn we had recently left.

Inside, there was no sign of anything unusual. Daniel was serving his special customers, the ones who came late and stayed later and Sarah was carrying around platters of food. Apart from a surreptitious glance from both father and daughter, no one paid any attention to us as we were herded upstairs. I even thought we were going to be put in our old room but we were pushed on to the end of the landing where an empty space was used to store all sorts of rubbish that should have been thrown out long ago: broken tables and chairs, barrels, a box full of old cups.

They tied Matthias's wrists together behind one of the big poles that held up the roof then did the same with me; we were back to back with the pole between us. They searched us perfunctorily, took my sword and dagger and Matthias's sword, they exclaimed once or twice when they discovered it to be one of theirs. There was a thump as our saddle bags and the scroll case were tossed into a nearby chamber,

"Well, I suppose that's it now?" asked Matthias, sliding his hands down so he could sit and lean back against the pole.

I shrugged and sat down too, thinking. In hindsight, this meeting was always inevitable. Max or Morion was going to recognize me and I was going to have to come clean with them and with Matthias. All my earlier thoughts of keeping things secret from him had blown out of the window. I shook my head. "At least we may find out what all the fuss has been about, what they want of you and why."

For a long period we waited for someone to come. I for one could not imagine why my kinsman had not burst in and unmasked me, revealed my relationship to one and all but no one came and after a while I must have dropped off.

"Gerard." Waking from a doze—an uneventful one this time—took several heartbeats longer than usual. "Gerard, what are we waiting for? Why haven't we been marched in front of these beast-men's commanders?" Matthias echoed my thoughts.

"Is that what you woke me for?" I thought about it as my mind slowly came awake. "I suppose they aren't here at the moment. Some of the party may still be searching—not informed of our capture."

"So we're left with a bunch of not very bright guards."

"Very strong not very bright guards."

"Yes, I know that."

"Guards who can follow our scent and see in the dark a lot better than we can," I pointed out.

"That too but to me they still seem rather stupid."

"Well." It was true, of course. There were two of them sitting on a pair of boxes drinking steadily and talking in slow sentences. The brighter ones will be downstairs, enjoying themselves so, if we were going to get out of this, then the time was now—or at least, when one or other of the guards went to refill their cups. "They've taken my weapons, my knife—"

"There's a knife in my left hand pocket."

"Right."

Matthias moved his hands to one side and I pushed my own backward but it was not easy.

"Gerard. That's my left side."

"Ah!" I tried again and this time I eventually found the lip of his coat pocket and worked my hands down inside. I could not find a knife. "Are you sure it's there?"

"Certainly it's there; and take care, it's sharp."

I eventually located something knife shaped but hardly big enough to do any damage with. "I've got something, how big is it?"

"About the size of your finger, a pen knife."

"Oh, right. Hold on, they're looking at us."

The two guards had stopped talking and were staring at us. When I stopped squirming, they eventually returned to their conversation and slowly, I drew Matthias's pen knife from his pocket. Its small size actually made it a little easier to maneuver and I started to saw at my bonds; one by one I felt the several strands part. Then, when I was almost through, perhaps a little too enthusiastic, I dropped the tiny knife with what seemed a terrible clatter.

One of our guards looked across at us again then back at his obviously empty cup. He picked up a pitcher which I had not noticed before and found that it too was empty. He rose and—walking carefully, I thought, which suggested he was drunk—went back to the stairs. I strained at the last cord around my wrist and broke it. Just discernible in the dark was a pile of broom handles—not really stout enough to do much harm but they were all that I could see.

I sprang to my feet. At least, that was my intention but after sitting there so long, my buttocks were numb and my legs gave me all the support of two pieces of rope—I sprawled forward on my belly. The guard came to his feet and grabbed the first weapon he saw, it happened to be *my* sword. Some feeling returned to my lower limbs and I lurched forward again, just far enough to grab a broom pole.

He came at me with my sword held high above my head. I waited and down it came, I jabbed the end of the pole into his stomach—the pole snapped off a span from the end. The sword was still on its way down. I rolled to one side and as the beast-man came within reach I dug the broken end into his throat and that gave him pause, a bloody one. The sword blade fell beside me and I swept it up, the handle falling comfortably into my palm. The neck wound would probably have killed the thing eventually but it was still crawling towards me as I rolled further away. I killed it off, with a single thrust into the side of its neck and got to my knees, then to my feet. Apart from the thud of feet and my sword falling to the floor, there had been no sound, no shouts, no voices at all.

I picked up the knife I had dropped and sliced the bonds on Matthias's wrists, a plan forming in my mind. I cut a hole into the thatch, just above the eaves. Next, I arranged the dead guard at the hole with his head and arm thrust through.

"Quick," I said in a loud whisper. "The other's coming back." I slid my sword into its empty scabbard. "We go over the edge of the floor, hang onto the edge of the boards."

"What?"

"Do it!"

We did. Both of us. Hanging literally by our fingertips from the edge of the upper floor. The dead guard's partner returned with a brimming jug and we imagined the creature looking round, finding us gone, seeing the other apparently crawling into the hole in the roof.

There was a thud, a muffled exclamation. The killing had been discovered. More sounds, perhaps the guard was looking through the hole. The sound of feet running, a shout. While the guard went down the stairs, we pulled ourselves up and rolled in two ungainly heaps onto the floor boards.

There was no time to lay there, though. "Come on, they'll probably all come up for a look."

The best hiding place we could find was the triangular space between the roof and the outer wall of the guest bedrooms, barely shoulder width at the base. Still, on our sides, we could squeeze along between the inner and outer walls. Just before I backed all the way in, I pulled a bundle of smelly leather across the opening. Then we waited. No one came. We heard boots thud across the ground floor and outside the room. Shouted orders, boots again, running around the house, others marching double-time into the distance.

"Now it's our turn to go, come on."

"There may still be some left here."

"Almost certainly, my friend. I'm open to suggestions."

Matthias did not make any. I pointed to one of the long knives that the beast-men used; it had been left embedded point-first in the floor. "You might as well take that with you."

Reconnaissance showed that two guards had been left behind. They were not used to their fellows being killed on a simple guard duty and they were obviously jittery, perhaps suspecting some third party was leagued with us against them.

We drew back into the shadows at the far end of the main room and sat down on a bench.

"If you were our enemies, what would you expect us to do?" I asked in a low voice.

"Find another way out of the city?"

I nodded in the dark. "Right," I replied, realizing he couldn't see the gesture. "What else?"

"Go to ground? Go to ground at the abbey."

"Yes, but the abbey is outside the gates—the southern gates, and—"

"The scrolls?" Matthias whispered fiercely. "What have they done with them?" We stopped speaking, wondering, thinking furiously. A bundle of leather, it had smelled rotten—or of sewage.

"You remember when we hid just now?" I asked, and Matthias grunted. "I think I pulled the case across the opening."

I had; we retrieved it along with the saddlebags and my companion, looking somewhat relieved, went back to our debate.

"Where do you suppose that woman and the gross old man have got to?" Matthias asked.

"I don't know. Another inn, perhaps. Checking the gates in case we got away from their guards? I've no idea."

"I wonder if there are any other gates—small ones, secret ones."

"I don't know. And if *we* don't, it's unlikely that they do."

We were silent for a space. We were tired and ideas were not coming quickly.

"You know, we don't really need a gate or a tunnel to get out."

"We fly?"

"We climb down from a suitable place with a length of rope."

"Well, it's different. What about the city guard?"

"They'll be tucked up in the guard house in front of a nice hot brazier with jugs full of ale."

"Are you suggesting that these noble fellows don't take their duties seriously?"

"What do they have to guard against? We're a long way from the sea here. No more marauders—the Danes are in control, they'll have a Danish king soon. They open the gates at dawn, close them at sunset—that will be the total of their duty."

"A nice warm brazier, now that's quite a thought. Rope? I wonder where we can find some."

"There's probably some out at the back, near the stables."

"That means killing one or both of the guards. I'd prefer not to advertise the fact that we were here all along, they'll know that we can't be too far away."

"Mm."

"Besides, it might get me killed this time. I prefer to keep the odds as long as possible on that."

"Upstairs? Where they were keeping us?"

"Perhaps. You go and look while I keep an eye on the guards."

Matthias went and I looked carefully through the few windows until I had located them both. My comrade returned with some of the rather thin line they had tied us up with, not exactly rope. I put two lengths together and tried them in my fists for size, I was not happy. Eventually we went to ask the innkeeper. We found his bedroom; I clamped a hand over his mouth and held his nose. He woke up terrified. I let him breathe through his nose.

"It's all right. We're about to leave. Stay quiet, all right?" He nodded and I took my hand from his mouth, ready to replace it if necessary.

"We want some rope. Is there any about?"

He nodded. "You—"

"Whisper."

"You stink."

I ignored the remark. "Where's the rope?"

"Back of the pantry, where the meat's hung."

"Have you seen a man like these others but larger? With a woman?"

Daniel nodded. "They're not here."

"I know that. Do you know where they are?"

"Someone came to claim a reward. For a sighting, I think." Thoughts worked through his slowly waking brain. "Maybe for you two?"

The pantry was a smallish room, knee-deep in the ground to help keep it cool. I couldn't see any rope so I returned to his bedside. "Get up. Show me."

I held on to his arm as he got up off his bed and padded through to the kitchen. He reached for the lamp which had been turned down low; apart from the fire's embers, it was the only thing left burning all night to provide a flame in the morning. I pulled his hand away. "No, no light."

We continued on through the door into the pantry, stepping down the steps—one, two, three. The landlord felt his way along the side wall until we came to a side of beef and half a pig hanging on hooks suspended from the rafters. We passed between them; he bent down and felt around, straightened up and thrust something at me. It felt like a coil of rope, with one or two tangles. "Thank you," I whispered. We retraced our steps and in the kitchen, I used the dim light to check what I had. It *was* what it seemed to be. As the landlord padded silently back to his bed, I stepped into the pantry again and took some food—yesterday's bread, two cuts of meat and what I thought was some cheese. I found a bag and stole that too, to put the provisions in and dropped it into a saddlebag. Evading the guards was not difficult. They paced slowly from front to rear, one around the east side, the other to the west. When they met, they paused for a few words before returning and repeating the whole thing at the front.

When they were outside the main door, we quietly dropped out of the kitchen window and followed our previous escape route from the dark back lane across vegetable plots and through the line of buildings. Leaving the horses was a wrench but it had to be done.

"Where to, Gerard? Which part of the wall?"

"Wherever's nearest, I think." Then I thought again. "No. Let's go east, back the way we came. It's almost as though we made a mistake in coming here at all."

We turned and stumbled along the street towards the north east and turned into another which seemed to go more easterly. It took us less than an hour, even in the dark, to find ourselves at the wall. Several dwellings had been built, lean-to style, against the mixture of old Roman masonry and modern repairs. It was simple to climb up the angle between one house and the rough walling to gain the walkway.

I looked both ways carefully; I could see no zealous guards making the rounds. I crossed, hid in the corner made by a buttress which still had most of its facing stone intact and began to pay the rope out. When I felt it touch the ground, I tried to judge what was left.

"What's the matter?" Matthias whispered. "Isn't there enough?"

"More than enough but I want to drop a double length over and hook the middle round something up here. Then I can pull it down after us. That way we leave no clues and it might be useful to us. It's too short though."

"Here," Matthias held out his hand and tied the end around the nearest crenulations. The knot was not one I had seen before. "Trust me. Get yourself down there and I'll follow."

I shrugged and let myself over the edge and went down hand over hand and when my feet touched the ground, I gave the rope a little shake. The rope began to move as Matthias followed me, I hung on to the end to make his descent easier.

"And now?" I asked as Matthias reached ground level. He smiled at me, gave the rope a shake, sending a loop snaking up into the darkness. Twenty feet or so above, there was a small sound and the rope fell down in untidy loops. "Yes," I said gathering it up and coiling it, "I like it." Even after a thousand years, you can learn something new.

Well away from our pursuers we stopped to rest, I was having deep thoughts as to whether we should split up, go our separate ways to put our followers off and I said as much. Matthias said nothing but as I closed my eyes and dropped off he knelt over me and chanted.

XV

e chewed on the cold meat as we made our way to the abbey at which we had briefly stayed before reaching Akemanchester. Without waking anyone, we broke very gently and carefully into the stables and slept an hour or more until the bell woke us for first prayers. Matthias attended these while I purchased two donkeys—using Matthias's money—from the monk who seemed to be in charge of transport. Matthias's attendance apparently bought us a quick but uninspiring breakfast of salty porridge and beer and we were away before the dawn was more than a hazy line of grey in the eastern sky.

We headed east once more over marshy ground and hummocky terrain until we were within the confines of some light woodland. We turned south and made as much speed as we could, avoiding farms and the occasional hamlets until late afternoon. We had come to the edge of a good sized pond which filled a wide forest glade and a grey heron stood guard at its edge—a sure sign that fish swam beneath its still surface. We had thoughts of staying the night among the trees nearby.

Matthias took out his twine and a few of the crumbs of bread which remained. The cheese we had carried for days turned out to be even better when Matthias the fisherman placed some of the smelly green stuff on a hook by way of an experiment and hooked us three small silvery fish without disturbing the heron.

"I know," he said, when I pointed out the unmoving bird to him. "Quite remarkable." He left me to clean the fish while he crept slowly up to the stilt-legged bird. He came back a few minutes later chuckling so much he could hardly breathe. "It's to scare other herons off. Made of cloth and a pair of sticks."

I smiled. "Unfortunately it means someone has stocked the pool and I'd rather not meet anyone who could recognize our description."

"Mm. You're right, hadn't thought of that, we'd better move on; maybe deeper into the trees."

"We should go along a water course to kill our scent and perhaps we can wash some of this stink off us."

There were no streams, but sheets of shallow water and green slime lay between the trees. We moved the slime to one side and managed to remove much of the stench of the sewers from our bodies though a residue remained on our clothes. Wherever there were slight hollows in the ground, we drove the animals along these areas. Just before it became too dark to see, we found a rise in the land to take us above the water table: a small copse of willows surrounding a round knob of land. Alders grew in a thick inner ring on the drier, rising ground leaving a small stony area at the middle almost devoid of grass.

We hobbled the donkeys and withdrew to the central clearing. Between two slabs of stone, we hollowed a small fire pit and cooked our fish over handfuls of alder twigs. Over the meal, made more pleasant by having to work for it, we discussed our situation while our clothes dried.

"Why do you think those beast-creatures took us prisoner?" asked Matthias.

"Probably because they were told to, but I would have thought they'd have taken the scrolls," I shrugged. "They seemed to have no interest in those."

"No, nor for the ring. I find it most puzzling."

"Perhaps it's as you said: they are creatures of limited intelligence and they were only told to follow our smell and hold us until someone else got there."

"That has the ring of truth to it," sighed Matthias. "Someone else in charge? Someone more powerful that we aren't aware of, with bigger fish to bake?"

I told Matthias about Max and Morion—not everything. I could not understand why neither Morion nor Uncle Max had returned and come to see us sooner.

I was beginning to hate the fact that I was running away from that person who was the dearest thing in my heart, and I was beginning to wonder why I dared not tell Morion the truth and seek her and Max's aid in this endeavor.

I expected Matthias to prepare a nightcap but there was no water to hand. It was odd, we'd missed it last night too and I was disappointed; I guess I was coming to rely on its restorative properties.

We slept, far more soundly than we should have done, but we were truly near exhaustion and neither of us could command the willpower to stay on watch.

The following day was much the same, we travelled on more urgently through the fringes of woodland. Towards the day's end, when we had to stop to rest our mounts, Matthias astonished me by fashioning a sling from strands of rope and a piece of leather cut from his coat and bringing down a hare for our evening repast. He *did* need about twenty casts before a lucky shot stunned the creature but fortunately, the whizzing stones did not seem to frighten it away, it merely looked up and went back to eating until a pebble finally bounced off its skull.

We skinned, cooked and ate the foolish thing and again lay down to sleep, this time in turns though the precautions were not needed.

Since leaving Akemanchester, we had been circling the city at a distance. On the third day, we were to the west once again and about midday, at the woodland's edge, I climbed the tallest tree I could find. Glastonbury's hill was just visible in the haze, near enough to reach that evening perhaps. We crossed the road which ran from Akemanchester to Ilchester, it was still there but no more than a firm footing through the marshes which abounded in this area and became steadily more brackish as we progressed west. The warmth from the spring sun was still drawing spirals of vapors from the pools and wet ground; the whole area was misty, slightly unreal, dreamlike. Even sounds were deadened or distorted in the air, thick with the stench of decay.

The noise must have been going on for some time without our really being aware of it. As it grew louder and we suddenly became conscious of it, we stopped. The sound was that of marching feet from the road which was a half mile behind us. We slid off the donkeys and crouched as still as boulders between the low tufts of reed and cane. There was two score, at least, of them. Slightly stooped, long arms, thick bowed legs, untidy mops of hair, marching at double time.

"May God keep and protect us," breathed Matthias.

I thought of many things, nothing along the lines that Matthias had mentioned though. Compared with those we had seen before these seemed inferior somehow—even their marching was more of a stumble.

"They're going straight north," I pointed out. "The road goes only to Aqua Sulis."

Matthias nodded. "Akemanchester," he corrected me mildly. "To join up with the others and whomsoever commands them."

"Reinforcements. For us? We must be a mightier army than I'd realized."

When they were out of sight, we remounted and pushed on. Darkness fell, we continued carefully along the just discernible path, heading for the never-failing *Light of Grace* which shone from the top of the Tor. It had led wanderers such as ourselves across the marshes for almost a century. The slopes glistened silver white with ghostly coils of haze around them in the thin orange light of the old moon; now more than ever, the Tor looked like an island, the Island of Glass as it had been called, with the pale beams from the mysterious lantern stronger when the moon was hidden by drifting cloud. We left the animals to pick their own way, guiding them only gently towards the beacon.

It was a great black bulk against the sky, blotting out the stars and seeming to be forever falling on us as the cloud streamed across the wild sky. The hill was like a giant tumulus with its ancient diggings and ditches all around it. The tomb of some giant god upon which the abbey had been built.

Five hundred feet is a long way when it is all uphill. We were puffing like old men before we reached the great doors set into solid frames; the donkeys, even without burdens, were little better. Between the cloud cover, the moon cast shadows across the carvings on the door frames. Harsh black and silver-grey relief from which the blind eyes of elongated animals looked out between the woven stems of improbable plants.

The first and the greatest abbey in Britain, Matthias said. Raised by an ancient king and then enlarged by Saint Dunstan less than eighty years ago. I nodded; I had heard it all at least once every day since leaving Akemanchester as well as the legends which related how the original mud and wattle church had been built by the young Jesus Christ and his uncle, Joseph of Harimathea, whom, I remembered suddenly, I had once met at an ill-favored place of execution.

The sun had been set all of two hours when Matthias finally struck his newly cut staff against the great doors barricading the abbey against the night. Great they might have been; quick to open up to wayfarers they most certainly were not. We thumped and shouted for a quarter hour before there was the sound of someone coming.

Bolts were drawn and a face looked out. Not some ravaged face this time, the face of a young boy with moonlight on it so that his hair seemed white as dried grass and oddly pale eyes, like the painted eyes of an alabaster statue.

Matthias explained who he was, told the boy that he was expected by Fergal, his Prior.

"My lord Prior is dead, Sir. Laid to rest in the earth before the altar two months gone."

"Oh?" Matthias was nonplussed. "I had a letter from him not six weeks ago, his hand was firm with the letters; he did not mention that he was ill."

"He was as hale as you or I, sir, but he died of a lance wound taken when he was returning from Winchester."

"Terrible news my son but pray, let us in, out here we shall die of ague and pestilent vapors."

"I cannot grant you entrance by myself, Sir Abbot of Hypolita. I must seek out Brother Michael, our Hospitaller."

Matthias rolled his eyes heavenwards. "Then be quick, we pray you. These miasmas from the marshes are scarcely healthy."

"I shall be quick Sir, as fast as a mouse taking cheese."

Quickness was relative. We were standing still with the night airs clinging close, cold and damp, and we were soon shivering ever more violently before the Hospitaller finally arrived.

Brother Michael was a man of generous proportions with great sad eyes and a drooping moustache. He listened to Matthias's entreaties with ponderous nods and when my friend was silent, he nodded once more. "I fear to wake the Abbot before the last of Vigils, he sometimes wakes with a most unreasonable temper Sir."

"Then let us in, I beg of you. Let us await the Abbot's pleasure inside."

Brother Michael drew in a great breath and held it for a dozen heartbeats while he looked through the grille at us. He shook his head. "It cannot be done. Cannot. It will be midnight directly, sit you down on the steps and I will bring him to you immediately his prayers are done."

"Midnight directly?" I said. "There are two, three hours to go yet."

"My friend is right," added Matthias. "This is a poor welcome for an emissary of Jesus Christ yet I suppose, no worse a welcome than was given our blessed Virgin."

"An Emissary? How can this be, my Lord? Is the Christ risen again and news not yet come to us? Surely not."

Matthias was searching his pockets in vain, he was about to undo the straps on his scroll case when he suddenly looked at me. "The ring, Gerard. Christ's ring."

"Ah!" The ring, which was—somewhere. My fingers were blue with cold and too stiff to work properly. I felt through various pockets, through my pouch, back to the pockets. "I gave it back to you after we had been to Winchester."

Matthias expelled an audible sigh. "So you did." He began again and finally found the relic. He held it up. "Christ's ring."

"Ah…" Brother Michael managed to frown and look surprised at the same time, his eyebrows becoming lost among the furrows on his forehead. For a moment his expression became beatific. "I *have* been told to expect this ring." Then his face showed suspicion. "But how am I to know that this is the ring of Jesus Christ?"

"Look at it Brother. Look at the flame which burns at the heart of the stone. It is akin to that which keeps your lantern burning."

Brother Michael the Hospitaller stared at the stone for a long time and then he sighed.

"Enter my Lord Emissary. Enter and be welcome."

Slow as they had been to let us enter, they were commendably swift in making amends. A blaze was blown up from embers in the refectory fire place and logs put on, hot soup was brought to us and warm woolen gowns to wrap ourselves in while our own clothes were washed and dried.

"Is the matter urgent enough to bring the Abbot here?" asked the Hospitaller, a worried expression creasing his ample face into anxious lines once again.

"No, no indeed," Matthias reassured him. "There is ample time left to us, the morning will be soon enough. We have slept in wild places for the past two nights; a dry mattress would seem but a step from heaven to us."

The Hospitaller was appalled at our story. "At once, my Lord. At once. Brother Mark!" he called.

And as good as his word, he drew a monk to one side and gave him instructions. Brother Mark bustled off to perform whatever duties had been laid upon him and when we had taken our soup, the young boy was told to show us the way.

Now that we saw him by good candlelight rather than by that of the moon, the boy's hair was yellow and his eyes were a pale sea blue. He brought us along rough wood-paneled corridors lined with doors, down staircases and more corridors until he stopped and pushed at a door, peering inside before he entered with his candle held high. The boy lit a rush light from his candle and pointed into a very narrow room with a straw filled tick on a wooden base filling the space. He gestured Matthias to enter. Matthias nodded, thanked him and turned to me. "We shall be woken at midnight and early morning for prayers," he said. "Try not to become too annoyed."

Our guide showed me to another identical cell and left me there. The waking and the prayers went exactly as Matthias had said; in between, I slept badly at first. For a dozen unknown reasons I was beginning to have doubts about this mission yet I knew not why. I eventually dropped off and slept as soundly as the late members of Uncle Max's guard. Except once; I half woke to smell the scent of Morion's hair close by, her lips were on mine, an unseen fingertip touched my forehead. *Where are you now?* Came the whisper and I was aware that it had been a while since her last visit inside my head but due to the events of the past few days I was reluctant to part with even a whisper of thought about that. For some reason every time I became tempted to tell her anything Matthias's grim visage filled my visions.

So close to sleeping, it was easier to dream pictures of blue seas and the dark glossy leaves of orange trees. I watched an ocean swell come toward me, watched the top begin to curl over, saw the light strike through the water. White froth, green translucence, crashing, tumbling, rushing, reaching up the beach, hissing across the sand. This was silly. Both of us knew I was lying, neither of us dared to say anything. I lifted the cup of wine to my lips and tasted it as the water retreated again and the next wave labored over the last, broke and scattered.

Morion left me, with sadness filling both our thoughts. I slept again and woke wondering, how a Prior came to die from a lance wound on the way back from Winchester.

Brother Michael shivered and shook his head sadly when I asked him the question as we broke our fast the next morning. "An evil beast attacked him; conjured straight from Hell it was, an animal bent to stand on its hind legs like a person, covered in dark hair and wearing clothes like a natural man." He ate two or three large spoonfuls of oatmeal porridge into which he had stirred some honey. "There were two, leaping from bushes at either hand, one with a spear, one with a dagger."

"You were there, then?"

"I, Sir? No, Sir. My duty is here, to welcome pilgrims and… and emissaries and their protectors. No. I had it from Brother Patrick who died soon after they got him back here. The Prior died in the instant, Brother Patrick took longer."

"These two creatures that Brother Michael has described were beast-men," I stated. Matthias nodded, knowing it to be true. "Here long before you or I met up, perhaps before you left Hypolita Keep."

"All along, my plans have been known to whoever my enemies are." He shook his head sadly. "There are so few of us, Gerard. Less than a dozen men are party to this scheme. There has been betrayal or careless talk at the least."

Betrayal or careless talk that had come to Uncle Max's ears. "Why would these people be so interested in that, Matthias? Interested enough to chase us across half the world?" By all the Gods I longed to know the truth.

"Can't you see, Gerard? These scrolls are anathema to those who are in league with Satan."

Max or Morion, in league with Matthias's God of Evil? I wanted to laugh.

"You can smile all you like, Gerard. It is up to us. *We* are the last chance of putting things right."

So I wiped the smirk off my face. It didn't help. Max would have no pact with a god of good or evil, he was contemptuous of those he had had dealings with through the ages.

"And how is it done?" asked Beorhtred, Abbot of the great Dominican abbey at Glastonbury. Matthias had opened one of the scrolls, peeling back the oiled silk and then splitting the wax covering and unrolling it a span—enough to expose no more than a character or two of the actual text. It was mid-morning; we were in the Abbot's room which had windows facing each of the cardinal points and high enough to see over the roof of the cloisters. From here, the near-island aspect of Glastonbury was even more plain; the land to the west was an expanse of marshland stretching as far as could be seen. The wetland spread both to the north and south and east as far as the ridge along which the roadway passed.

Within, there were several couches—old, overstuffed and comfortable. Thick hangings hung all over the walls and mats of woven straw covered the rough wood of the floor.

"The scrolls need to be read," Matthias was saying, tapping the paper with the silver ring."

"And that is the very ring from Our Lord's finger?"

Matthias held it up and nodded. "The one and true."

Beorhtred crossed himself and muttered a number of incantations. "To think that I am here at such a time. At such a privileged time."

"Indeed. We are all of us privileged. As I said, the scrolls must be read."

"That is all?" asked the Abbot, astounded.

"Almost. The reading must be in a place of power—such as this—and there are certain difficulties."

"Of course there are, tell me what they are." Beorhtred took a swallow of a herbal infusion which even from my distance, smelled pungent to say the least. He grimaced and put the small pot back on the table beside his couch.

"The process will need some time and reading the scrolls causes visions. They grow less intense with time and familiarity, but they make the task impossible until the readers become seasoned. Even then, there are twelve scrolls, each of them twenty to forty feet in length, a yard in width."

"And then? After the reading?"

"Then it begins, or so I believe. The words which were written by Our Lord's disciples will come to pass, become reality."

"And what of these who pursue you? Surely they will not dare to trespass in such a holy place as this?"

"Surely they will, my Lord Abbot. Surely they will. However, Gerard, my companion here was formerly an officer in the military, he has the knowledge to defend this place."

This was fresh news to my ears. Matthias was making plans extempore. He continued, "We can hold them at bay while the holy work is carried out. Afterwards it will not matter, for then, all things will be as God has willed."

"Amen."

"Amen," I said. "And how and with what am I to defend this place?"

"What do you need," Matthias asked.

"About a thousand men to start with—with mattocks, with timber. Seven days…"

Matthias was looking at me with a tight smile on his face, as though I was making a poor joke. Beorhtred nodded gravely. "A thousand—I don't see how…"

The situation was discussed. I was to get five hundred men, two hundred and fifty now if they could be spared from the farms, and another two hundred and fifty who would cut enough wood for each man to erect six feet of stockade. Beorhtred's monks would begin the following dawn to recruit them. It seemed for the first time on our quest Matthias had found someone else who believed in him and what he was doing.

I had paced out the length and width of the great hall of the abbey which was fifty paces long and twenty wide. There was a range of cells along the north wall and one or two buildings beyond the bell tower at the west end. A cloister was built against the southern wall of the Abbey. I could build a stockade around the top of the more or less oval hill and given time, another just below it.

Actually, the week I had asked for was far longer than I needed. Each of the two hundred and fifty men would build a fence as wide as his outstretched arms, a matter of half a day considering that most would be unskilled at the work. Then they had to do the same again on a level below but on a wider front.

When the first contingent started arriving around the following midday, I had examined the slopes of the hill which were quite steep and convoluted with what had once been protective ditches. I instructed the farmers as to what I wanted—the terraces which had once been ditches around a hill fort to be dug out again.

Time was in short supply but it was four days before the sentinels I had set to watch from the roof of the abbey reported anything which might have been reconnaissance and we had most of the work done. In that time I had also set those men who were able to do so to fletching and to the making of throwing brands—arm-length branches wrapped with sheep's wool and dipped in tar.

I climbed the makeshift rope ladder to the roof and stared out in the direction of the lookout's pointed finger. I watched for half an hour before glimpsing anything and I believed the fellow had been right. There were things out there among the reeds and muddy waterways which looked like beast-men and their allies, the wolves. So they had arrived and were busy surveying our defenses or looking for a way in.

Below me, on the slopes, a steep-sided ditch had been cut twice around the hill on the southern side and another half on the north side. To the west, starting between two of the outbuildings, a narrow cut had been made down the nearly vertical slope. The cut was shored up beneath the two stockade fences and closed off by traps of thick timbers which slid down grooves in the shoring.

We were as ready as we could be. The five hundred farmers had exchanged their mattocks for bundles of sharpened sticks to do duty as spears and those who had experience of hunting with bow and arrow, were equipped with bow staves and the hastily fletched arrows their brethren had made or brought in from the surrounding villages.

I breathed a great sigh and descended to the ground, going in search of Matthias and the monks who were working on the scrolls. I had not seen my companion for almost two days, both of us had been working every moment we could stay awake.

"They are here," I told him. "They're sizing us up. I'd guess they will attack during the darkness which will give them an advantage."

Matthias shook his head. "We have begun but the process is very much slower than I had foreseen. It takes far longer than I had expected to become used to the visions, we have barely touched the first scroll. Come and see."

He led me up a narrow staircase which brought us out on to an equally narrow gallery running the length of the great hall. Above us, the roof creaked in the wind which blew constantly at this height; the main timbers were just above our heads: beams a hand span in width and two in breadth bore the weight of the thatch and the square poles to which it was tied. Large transverse beams carried the long ones and these were held up from below by oak crooks and the joints fastened together with wooden pins. Tall timbers squared from single tree trunks rose from circular foundations to hold the whole roof in place twenty-five feet above the flagstone floor. Below us, a scroll had been partly unrolled along the floor; a monk was just about to kneel at the edge of the sheet of papyrus while another was led away, his footsteps uncertain.

"What's the matter with him?"

"He has to rest while the visions dim."

I remembered the disorientation I had experienced when I had looked at one of them. Below, the kneeling monk stretched his arm out and touched a finger to a line of symbols. He began to read aloud.

"He seems to manage quite well."

"He has had several sessions, it will take longer for the visions to have an effect on him," Matthias explained.

"And is there any consequence?" I asked. "Other than the visions, I mean. Can you feel anything happening?"

"I don't think so but this is all history. What is happening here is that the prophesies are being made real…"

I was lost immediately. Matthias may have understood what he was saying but I didn't. I put a hand on his arm. "We simply don't have the time, my friend. The beast-men will be on us before it can be finished."

"But you said the place could be made defensible."

"And you said it would take less time. The place is defensible but that is relative. Instead of overrunning us immediately, it will take a few days to break in. This is going to take longer than a few days, isn't it?"

"If we had room to spread more than one or two scrolls…"

"But you don't have the men to even read two. How many have you got reading this scroll?"

"Six. But every day, the number will increase."

"Three days."

"That is all?"

I nodded. "Three." I pointed up through a roof light at the sky. "The moon?" I was about to ask if the moon's phase made the timetable but I fell silent. It looked like a cloud to begin with, a great circular cloud of iridescent vapor.

We hurried outside and stared upward. The cloud had thickened and it was alive, a cloud of individual creatures. They gathered above Glastonbury Tor, swooping and climbing on wings the color of burning embers; their bodies were human-like, they left trails of burning sparks as they leaped and capered.

"Angels!" Matthias exclaimed lifting his arms in ecstatic greeting. "God has sent his…"

"Not Angels, *elementals*," I said in disgust. "Fire elementals, kin to those that were marshaled above the Gallic Narrows when our ship was sunk. As they were then, these will be directed by Max. You know, the one you saw, the one with the big hands I told you about."

Matthias merely nodded his head, his mind on the celestial activities above.

Now we had a supernatural threat literally hanging above our heads. Both Matthias's work and mine went ahead though we labored with heavy hearts. The monks lined up to be familiarized with the visions—some got used to them quickly, others never did. The stockade was strengthened, platforms for watchmen were made with protective walls to the front and weapons and armament were stacked ready for use.

The beast-men attacked us at midnight. They must have seen the preparations I had arranged, yet they took no notice. These primitives from central Germania knew hunting and weapons and following orders but except for a few, they had little ability to understand more than this. They crawled over the lower ramparts and skidded into the ditches where they impaled themselves on the stakes and those who followed behind used the bodies of the dying as bridges across the traps.

We had five makeshift catapults. I had wanted to make Greek fire but could find no one who knew how to go about it, so we threw bundles of straw into the ditches along with the fire brands I had instructed the men to make, these ignited both the pitch and the oil we had poured along the ditch bottoms. By the light of the flames we saw that the beast-men numbered many more than the two-score that Matthias and I had seen on the road from Ilchester; there was easily twice that number and perhaps more but they died—often from their own folly and at no time did I experience fear.

The attack petered out within two hours with only a single beast-man reaching the lower palisade and the fiery beings above us had not yet attacked. Our farmers strutted about proudly, talking bravely about putting down the attack and how cowardly were these creatures both above and below.

When daylight came—a single bar of yellow light along the eastern horizon—we saw them bunched in several places along the lowest of the earthen ramparts. The wind brought us the acrid smell of the blood they had spilt on the ramparts mingled with the odor of burning meat from the still smoldering bodies.

There were more, far more than the day before. These new arrivals were different, they stood more upright, their movements were less of a shamble. We could see pointing and gesticulating, even some argument by the look of it. We waited, as, for the moment, did they. We watched each other across the fortifications and gazed at the dull red of the flying army above us. We wondered what to do next. I ate a sweet wrinkled apple and walked along the stockade fence, making a complete circuit. And then an astonishing thing happened.

It was as if, as I blinked, something changed and it took a moment or two to see what it was. The flock of fire elementals above us were falling; fluttering down like ragged sheets of parchment. As they fell, the creatures grew insubstantial. None of them reached the ground except as a fine powder, like ash.

I went inside to find out what Matthias and the Abbot were doing. Along narrow, stone flagged corridors up a flight of steps and into the hall. Both were sitting at the back of the great hall, wearing glum faces.

"Well?" asked Matthias, his voice tired and leaden. "Have we been invaded yet?"

"No. And the fire beings have gone, faded and gone. Do you think…"

"The readings?" Matthias was suddenly galvanized. "Definitely, there can be no other explanation. It's working Gerard, it is working!"

I made no reply to that. Maybe it was, maybe not. "We've held the beast-men at bay although they seem pretty disorganized at the moment," I went on. "You look as though you've had a hard time of it."

Matthias nodded and leaned back against the wooden seat. "It may even be why you've had so little trouble with the beast-men themselves but it is so slow that we cannot hope to finish it in the time we have."

I nodded. "It's something that needs planning."

"We have two who have come through their visions, more or less. They can read for an hour before needing to rest. It's unbelievably slow."

"Besides the elementals, how do you know that it works? That something is actually happening?"

"We can feel it. We can feel the world change."

"I didn't…"

"Lord Gerard…"

One of my so-called militia had come to the door.

"Yes?" I got up and crossed to him so he would not have to raise his voice.

"There's more movement down there on the plain. The beast-men are making something."

I followed him along the passageways out into the open where I realized I was still holding the core of the apple I had been eating; I tossed it over the rampart. The beast men had come together and were building something from roughly trimmed trees and rope at the foot of the eastern slope. With the brightening day, it was now clearly illuminated. Matthias had also stepped outside and had come up behind me without my realizing.

"May God defend us!"

I agreed with the sentiment for what they were working on had suddenly become plain to see. A great crossbow with power coming from a thick bow of green wood. They labored on it until midday and then began to refine their weapon. Bolts were fired, overshooting and undershooting until finally, a pole as thick as my arm smashed against the side of the Great Hall.

"May the Gods curse the lot of you," I said, keeping my voice low. The beast-men had loaded a great bolt against the rope which did duty as a bowstring. Rags soaked in oil stolen from our own trenches were bound around the forward end and they set these alight as we watched. With their winged fire-beings gone, the beast-men were taking the initiative.

One of them tripped the firing mechanism and the bolt screamed through sundered air trailing smoke and flames from the oil-soaked fabric. The bolt flew true; up, up, curving down a little just beyond midpoint. Down, down and lodged with a great thump in the ancient dirty grey thatch which roofed the Abbey's Great Hall.

I rushed into the hall where Beorhtred was standing over a monk on his knees at the edge of an opened scroll.

"Fire!" I yelled as soon as I was inside. "The roof's on fire. Get these people out and the scrolls." Something obliged me to rush to the rescue of the scrolls. I pulled the kneeling monk out of the way, rolling up the scroll and looking round for others, gathering them up. Matthias had followed me in and was doing the same. "Matthias, where's the case? Quickly."

Sparks were falling from the burning roof, lending weight to my urgency. Matthias found the case and helped me slide the other scrolls into it. We went outside and looked up at the burning building. There was no hope of saving it; it was too high to throw water at and already the fire was too advanced to do anything but watch. Another and then more of the fire bolts were fired; more hit the already burning roof, while others found smaller buildings.

The burning roof fell inwards in a shower of sparks and leaping flames. Fire caught hold inside, smoke poured from the windows and quickly turned to flames, a huge pall of smoke billowed up, darkening the pale spring sunlight. Monks ran in and out in a frenzy; saving scrolls and effigies, a box of relics, altar cloths—all sorts of things.

Saint Mary's Abbey burned to the ground in two hours. The great lantern tower which had cast its pure and constant light across the water meadows for almost a hundred years crashed to the earth. The coldly glowing glass was broken into a myriad shining fragments.

Every once in a while something collapsed a little further and a fountain of sparks and flames would burst into the air but mostly, the fires ate steadily at the timbers until they were blackened charcoal or heaps of grey, smoldering ash.

Beorhtred and Matthias watched grimly, many of the brothers wept openly, others were angry and picked up pikes or slings and went to stand by the ramparts. A watch was still being kept on the beast-men, who, now their purpose had been achieved, wandered about aimlessly once more.

A shout arose on the northern side just as light was beginning to fail, I went across and Matthias followed me. Below, a great wagon was drawn up just beyond the range of our arbalests. On the seat stood Morion, her whip coiled in her left hand. Uncle Max was on the ground, gesticulating fiercely. One of his hands caught a beast-man on the side of the head, the creature fell and did not get up. For some reason, Max was not pleased with what they had done. Whatever his plan had been, setting fire to the Abbey had not been a part of it. Morion reached down and put her hand on his shoulder, she pointed up towards us. At that moment I felt the touch of her mind. *Gerard?* And a moment later, a darker, simpler, more massive inquiry which must have been Max, perhaps making use of Morion's link to me. *GERARD.*

My limbs stopped working.

COME.

My foot began to move forward, try as I might, I could not stop it.

"Hold me." I grunted at Matthias as I fought. "Stop my legs from moving."

"What?"

"Don't ask, I'll explain later. Just hold me still."

Matthias did as I asked and when my feet still moved, he motioned to one of the men to help him. After an age of straining against the summons, it weakened and stopped.

"All right. Thanks, it's fine now."

"What was happening?" asked a mystified Matthias.

"Wait. Just a little longer." I walked, carefully, so those who were looking up would detect nothing strange in the way I moved. Once I was out of sight, I sat down on a sack, as weak as a kitten and drenched in cold sweat.

"Somehow they laid a compulsion on me," I stated but did not explain and stopped again with my hand up to forestall questions.

I felt her presence once more. *Gerard. Where are you? You know I love you and only want the best for you. Why are you fighting against us? What Max is trying to do is to save life as we know it—your Christian companion has been lying to you. Come, come back to your own before it's too late. Back where your heart beats against mine.*

I had no answer for Morion for in truth, I did not know. I even wondered if my obstinacy was as much a compulsion as Max had just attempted. If it was, I had no idea how to fight it.

How is Matthias deceiving you? Where are you?

Unseen finger tips touched my brow, caressed my cheek. I closed my eyes. We walked on sand and shingle, remembered the smell of sea and sea weed. I bent over and watched a fanciful hermit crab in an imaginary pool trying on a new shell.

See, she whispered in my head, *I can lie as well as you can. Don't try to hide from me like that.* She went away and I opened my eyes again, it had grown dark during that time and I was filled with an intense feeling of loss, as though she despaired of me. The thought that I might lose her was impossible to consider. I determined to put things right.

Morning came and with the light I seemed to gain a measure of self-possession. "Matthias," I began, "there are things I'm going to have to tell you but not yet, I've been wanting to but the time has never been right." My resolve died as quickly as it had grown. "We have to leave here; now that those two have arrived we have to expect a much stronger offensive. Even if we can hold them off for another day or so, there is no time to activate the scrolls as you wanted to. We must get away before it's too late—the scrolls are everything." *I was becoming as obsessed as Matthias,* I thought, *and could do nothing about it.*

"No. No, I know we have failed here. The moon wanes, the new phase will begin within a day. But how do we leave? Does anyone know of a way?"

"I agree the scrolls are important but what of my monks and the five hundred men who are guarding the walls?" asked Beorhtred. "Will these spawn of the devil overrun us completely?"

"Beorhtred, I do not like to barricade myself into a place like this. We have limited food, limited water and let us be honest with ourselves, very limited time. If there is somewhere else we can go, we must leave an hour or so before midnight, before the moon is high."

"In that case," said the Abbot ruminatively, "we have one more chance of ending this task successfully."

"Go on," Matthias said.

"We have links with a church where we could work…"

"Do not speak the name of this place."

Beorhtred nodded. "My congregation needs a place to go to. We have had some small success and the monks were heartened, they would welcome a chance to continue."

"Can misleading the enemy buy us all sufficient time?" I asked.

As midnight came and went, the farmers and the dozen or so monks were lined up along the stockade. Very quietly, we pulled the swing door up and tied it open. The cut that I had ordered made in the earthen defenses was like a passage into deepest night. The monks went first, laden with sacks of corn, dried meat, last year's fruit. After these went the farmers; it took an hour for them to go through and disperse across the dark plain and the still waters of the vale.

We waited until well into the small hours, showing a lantern now and then, walking the walls as though a force still occupied the hill. Then, when the mists from those same waters had risen high enough to hide us, we too went our way, Glastonbury still and empty behind us.

I had brought one of the fragments of the lantern; it had glowed the color of new cream in the palm of my hand, now it glowed within my purse.

Silver threads of water glinted everywhere around us. It was like a faerieland with pathways paved with silver coins. But it was dangerous: hidden beneath the fitful light of the last sliver of moon were black bogs, quicksand that sucked at unwary feet; foul miasmas that would breed the ague if our kerchiefs slipped from our noses. We went on steadily, gauging east as well as we could for an hour until we came to a firmer path.

"Well brother, I've got us out, where to now?" I asked.

"South for the moment, until we find somewhere to hide," said Matthias quietly.

"And then?"

"That depends on what you have to tell me."

"Ah. Perhaps this is the right time to tell you about Uncle Max at last."

Matthias looked blank. "The man with big hands?"

"A man, like us—an immortal who commands these ancients from our past. The ones you have been calling beast-men. Well, I'll tell you as soon as we find a suitable place to rest."

A short while later we were sitting around a small, almost smokeless fire in a narrow cleft between two rocks and hiding from the beast-men. This had a familiar feel to it.

"Uncle Max recruits these creatures—I think. I think—that is I thought—he sold them to local lords as fighting men. It just never occurred to me that he had a personal involvement in all this until I saw him in Aqua Sulis. The force that came to Glastonbury was probably called in from somewhere else and was acting independently until Max reached them with his own contingent. What his interest is in stopping this thing I don't know. Might you?"

Matthias sat back, leaning against one of the stone walls. He shook his head. "I don't know. Who is this Uncle Max? I mean what is he to you?"

I explained the relationship. "He must have been behind all this since before you left Hypolita Keep." I told him about Max and Morion escorting me into exile on their way to presumably—find him and his companion—Brother Ricard.

"And Morion?"

"Max's lieutenant. Morion developed a liking for me. I was strongly advised to go to Cordova and she's been checking up on my whereabouts every so often." I mentioned the rapport we had and I told him about the visions which seemed to be quite different.

As I explained. Matthias became agitated, sweat broke out on his forehead. "So she knows where you are? Where we are?"

I shook my head. "I've been lying to her."

"Hmm. She must have suspected something if she and… Max…" He paused for some moments. "I may share blame for the visions you've experienced. It's possible they were brought on by your nearness to the scrolls."

I nodded. "If that's so, it's a relief. I've never suffered such things before. I must tell you I'd begun to wonder if someone or something had cast a glamour on me."

Matthias wiped away the sweat with a sleeve, his eyes narrowed. "She and Max thought they recognized you at the Abbey but you misled them again."

"True."

Matthias smoothed an area of sandy soil and handed me a twig. "Draw me a map of our whereabouts."

"How big? How far do you want it to extend?"

"To the coast in the south and west. Do you know of a place east of Akeman-chester where there's a very old temple?"

I frowned. "A temple? No."

"From long before the Roman occupation. Something like those in France, at Carnac, close to where we met."

"Ah, a circle of standing stones. I believe I have seen them but they are to the south east."

I sat and thought awhile and while I did that, I went through my pockets. Two of last season's apples, was all I had brought with me. Matthias did the same and came up with another two apples and a cake of bread already hard and crumbling away. I began the map. The long peninsula to the west with its curi-ous claw-like ending, a large loop to take in the salt marshes at whose edge we camped and then a swoop out again where the fortress of Caerleon and another place called Venta had been. Then dots for Aqua Sulis, Lindinis—now Ilches-ter—and Glastonbury and a rather tentative prod for the old henge circle out near Sorviodunum.

Matthias gazed at it for a long time then looked up at me. "How often does this woman touch your mind?"

I was sort of surprised by the question, having expected his disbelief on the matter. "A couple of times over the last few days," I told him. "At the Abbey, during the attack and when we first came there; before that—not since we were in Normandy although she tried when we were on the road to Akemanchester."

"I think, perhaps, she knows you're with me, has known since we met or has had suspicions at least. We have to assume that anyway." He looked at my map again for some time and consulted his calendar, counting days, calculating travel times. He put his finger on the dot corresponding to the henge. "That is where we are going," he said.

"Whatever for?"

"It is a place of power, of very great power. In eleven days it will be even stronger. Other than that, I will not say since it is possible the information will be filched from your mind."

"Eleven days? Why eleven days?"

"The eleventh day from now commemorates the final visitation of Our Lord to his Apostles. We were at supper and His holy spirit came amongst us and touched each one of us. Our beings glowed, we were on fire though we were not consumed, flames leaped from our hands and from our heads."

Flames had leaped from our hands and heads just before we were sunk in the Gallic Narrows, it was a sight that seamen saw occasionally. I did not spoil his memory.

Matthias continued, unaware of my thoughts. "We went out and spoke to people passing by as though we knew each and every one of them. Everyone, no matter what country he came from, we spoke to him in his own language, telling him of our God and the Lord Jesus Christ. Pentecost."

Matthias was carried away with his account and only gradually returned to the here and now.

"It was then that we wrote the scrolls, while the Holy Spirit was with us."

There seemed nothing to say and we sat with our own thoughts.

"In eleven days is a special day of remembrance," he said at last. "A day of power. Very suited to what we have to do since the scrolls are written in just the same way that we spoke then—to everyone in their own tongue."

"And tomorrow marks the last time Our Lord was upon this Earth as a man. In His thirty fourth year; after returning from the grave, he ascended to His Father in Heaven."

I felt faintly embarrassed. Religions are full of these tales of death and return to life and to find someone like Matthias—intelligent, articulate, my friend— believing them was… well, *embarrassing*.

"Lord God!" Matthias uttered, looking at me with an expression which might have been amazement or incredulity. He took out his almanac and counted more days and then counted again. Afterwards, he just sat there looking at me while mixed emotions fled across his features.

"Well?" I said at last.

"The day you came by and like the Samaritan who gave aid to the Jew, you helped me when I had been left beside the road. That was Easter. I had forgotten."

"So?"

"The third day after Our Lord was executed. The day he was resurrected. Easter Day is the commemoration of that day."

I failed my friend. I could not see the significance in the coincidence but I said nothing. There are more than enough holy days in the Christian year for almost anything to happen on one of them.

"Never mind," he said, leaning forward and patting my arm. "It doesn't matter but you were sent to help me, of that there can be no doubt." He passed me the familiar night cup.

I disliked the thought of being manipulated by Matthias's aloof God even more than by the impersonal processes of fate, and I continued to wonder how much truth Morion's words held.

I dreamed but this time the visions were filled with thoughts of a supernatural being who was beckoning me to sit alongside of him. He spoke but not in words but thoughts. I was shown what would be my rewards for protecting Matthias and the scrolls and they made me cry that I should be considered so worthy.

In the moments between waking from the vision and gaining true sleep, I heard him murmuring.

Matthias finished the chant, put away the cup and herbs and sank to his knees. It was obvious the rite had taken it out of him but his God demanded all he could give to the cause and more. He just had to find the strength to finish the task.

XVI

e went west and a little south. When I queried this, pointing out that the henge he hoped to reach was to the east, Matthias said he wished to put our pursuers off the scent and so we travelled for two days, picking our path between the shining expanses of water and marveling at the sunsets, at the gold, orange, red, and purple reflections across the marshes. Seagulls and other birds wheeled above the waters, diving down and catching fish, their cries: plaintive notes among the wind's many songs.

We begged and where we had to, paid for food and drink. We came eventually to where the marshes became the Western Sea, where waves rolled in and winds blew from the edge of the world. Here too, the seagulls ruled the air in huge numbers, their calls no longer plaintive but peremptory, skimming the waves and taking their catch aloft with a jerk of wings. They covered the outcroppings and cliffs, sat on nests crammed into any crevice large enough to support their coming broods and carpeted the rocks beneath milky white with their droppings. We camped and watched the sun sink into the water.

"Yes," said Matthias in a thoughtful tone, as I settled myself into a particularly springy piece of grass, "tomorrow we shall go to that ancient temple we spoke of, near Ambrosia's fort."

That night Morion came to me, her first visit since we had escaped to the Abbey from Akemanchester. There was the now-familiar kiss of unseen lips, the caress of invisible fingers and the whispers in my mind which seemed both sadder and more caring than before. *Gerard my love. Where are you now? I want to come to you. Where are you going? Let me meet you there.*

And I, almost asleep, put my arms about her and drew her cheek to mine; I kissed her ear and whispered. *"Why do you need to know this, my dear? For Max's beast-men to come after me and kill me?"*

There was a sense of shock, even a little of fright in her thoughts. *"I would never see you come to harm."* There was horror in her words. *"Believe me, in these few meetings of ours, I have come to know you, more than you might believe. If it is within my power, I would save you from hurt."*

"Then why, Morion?"

"Maximus. He knows you're with the Christian."

"Maximus wants me dead?"

I could almost feel the violent shake of her head. *"Not you, my love; you are Max's only son—that's how he thinks of you, Gerard. You're the one he believes in. He knows he's going to die someday, accident or weapon—you're there to carry on and shepherd the Family into the future. You're his immortality, Gerard; he cares for you."*

Morion fell silent though her presence remained. Then: *"It's the other one, the Abbot of Hypolita, who is dangerous. I tried to tell you before... he holds the fate of the world in his hands and intends to sacrifice us all to that God of his. And by his actions he is killing Max and his kind and you and me and my kind."*

I lost her, shaken awake by Matthias. "Are you all right?" he asked. "You were crying out—a bad dream?"

"Uh, no," I said, torn between two worlds for I could still feel Morion's arms around my neck. I heard her final words to me and the thought that she may die left me shivering with an icy cold.

A final whisper blew through my mind, an afterthought perhaps, *"I know where you are, Gerard, I know you've been lying to me since I saw you in the flesh. But I forgive you for the sake of my love for you. Soon I will prove it to you."*

I looked around and gradually, the icy sensation faded, washed away by the flickering of the fire. I considered lying to Matthias, decided against it.

"It was Morion." I took a deep breath. "She must have seen this through my eyes, Matthias, perhaps she will guess where we are. When you woke me, she was still with me."

Matthias nodded, smiled even. "I'm sorry Gerard. Sorry I disturbed you. It doesn't matter about her knowing where we are; don't worry, I've planned for it."

"But the dreams and the visions are something else, something I have only suffered from recently. I wish I could explain why I am getting them."

Matthias coughed quietly into his hand and said, "I too have had the visions and, as I said once before, though I'm not certain, I'm sure it's because of our proximity to the scrolls. They give off a powerful aura, it affects anyone close enough. I see it as the power of God."

I pushed myself up to a sitting position and looked across the bar of silver the moon had spread across the waves. I could not bring myself to mention what Morion had said, this was not what Matthias intended, not what the scrolls were for. I knew that, I had touched the scrolls, even read a few words from one and had been given a sort of understanding. The purpose of the scrolls was benevolent, they had been written by good men—men like my friend, Matthias.

Some residue of Morion's certainty stirred. Could I have misjudged Matthias? Was he aware of the outcome that Morion feared—was he *really* planning to change the world and all of humanity in it? Matthias, I began to realize was one of these men who were so certain they were right that there was no room for doubt. I was filled with doubts, I think I had had them before.

"I've made a drink," said Matthias. "Ale and honey. It'll relax you, send you back to sleep and tomorrow we shall be at the standing stones. Remember that, it's important."

I slept but the following morning I didn't wake, not properly. Not asleep, not awake; not awake enough to think thoughts that would go where I willed them. I seemed to float or to fly and was certain that I was still asleep and dreamed.

Morion visited me in the middle of the day; I could almost see her frown. *What is it?*

I answered her not a word, sent her not a thought.

Are you ill, my Gerard? I know that you live, I feel you, see what you see, hear what you hear.

And I did hear. I could see and hear and to an extent feel—warmth and cold, smell—the musty odors of thatch, the smell of beer spilt on the floor over a generation, a tickle of smoke on the palate. Yet I could marshal no thought that did not come from somewhere else.

Sadly she kissed my lips, I as unreal to her as I was to myself and she left. Perhaps Morion had been wrong, perhaps I had died in my sleep as people do, for no discernible reason. Perhaps then, I was some poor ghost whose destiny was to skim across the world until it too decayed and grew old and died.

I shed ghostly tears and tore at my ghostly hair in despair at my fate. All the time though, I moved onward. Something drove me. Day or night, a pale disc of sun or moon told me of the passing of time and it was as though I trudged wearisomely onward across this expanse of desolate wasteland.

I waited and gradually realized why I waited, what I waited for. It was for Morion to come to me, and now I waited with some pleasure, some anticipation. The sun, a grey disc only just lighter in color than the cloudless sky arced above me and down and eventually was gone. Sometime later, an hour, two—it was difficult to think in terms of time—the moon, as dull as the sun had been, lofted among the scattering of flower petals which must be stars.

"Begone." The word was a shout, a curse. A tall shade stood before me. He struck his staff against a stone which gave back a mighty boom. "You are not of this place, neither from its past nor its future. Begone."

The place was a ring of stone gateways, solid against the grayness beyond and through each gateway was a half-seen land. In some views, the land was lush and green, meadows with a river in the distance; in others quite the opposite: sand, bare windswept rock and through still others were lands from nightmare: dark, star flung skies over restless oceans; glittering cities of stupendous architecture and night-time towers with a thousand windows ablaze with light as bright as the sun.

I came to realize that this was an ancient temple, that ancient place Matthias had asked me about; old enough to pre-date the Romans, the Greeks, the Egyptians. I *must* be dreaming unless it was still another vision? Was this actually real?

The figure, the Druid—for that is what he was—swung his staff at me, catching me across the shoulder. It hurt; the hurt alone surprised me as much as the overconfident priest's actions. I sprang to my feet, drawing my sword—a further surprise in this limbo dimension—the sword felt as always, sharp and solid.

I swung at the oak wood stave that was sweeping around my head and connected with a clang as though the wood was bronze. The shock ran up my arm, numbing the muscles. But the priest's astonishment was the greater; perhaps no one had stood up to his browbeating before. I changed hands, taking the sword in my left and slapped his knuckles with the flat of the blade. He dropped his weapon, his fingers as nerveless as my arm.

"Now begone yourself," I told him and kicked his staff away.

The Druid took a long knife with a twisted blade from some concealed pocket. It had the look of ritual about it.

"Gerard—fighting? Even now?" Morion had come while we were still engaged.

"This bully annoys me. It will not take long." Not that she could hear me, even though I could hear her gasp as he came at me again with the knife held in his two joined hands raised above his shoulder; a ceremonial movement.

The knife came down and I swatted it aside and it spun out across the grey sward below.

"You're too used to attacking corpses and sacrifices. Now leave me alone."

The Druid's figure wavered, wrathful but impotent. He faded.

"Gerard? Are you there?" Her lips on mine, a fiercer kiss than I had known, a sense of anxiety, even unease came with her words. *Where are you now, what is this place?* I perceived shock, greater unease. *What is happening to you?*

Try as I might, I could not make her hear my words. I had more in common with the Druid's shade than I did with the woman who I was sure now, cared for me. I felt her withdraw from me though the link was not broken and then she was near me again, her arms about me, even the feeling of her body next to mine. *Maximus knows of this place, he knows where you are. Wait for me, we will come for you.*

At least, I thought to myself when she had gone away, *I can move on now.* But in this, I was wrong. I stayed there, drifting aimlessly above the grey heath land.

But there *had* been a change, now I could think my own thoughts. Looking back, the ability had been there for some time, it had come gradually, I had just been unaware of the change.

The sickly moon had long since set when I became aware of still further change. Gradually my full sight was restored. The grey land I had become used to was replaced by a blurred kaleidoscope of colored shapes. Hearing returned; distorted but real-world sounds and feeling, cold and shivery; body and soul were finally re-united. My eyes opened on a somber grey cloudscape. I it was not easy to move my head but by straining my eyes I could just see Matthias tugging at the bridle of a reluctant donkey. To either side of me were the bars of a cart which hid much of what lay beyond.

I struggled to sit up but couldn't make it, I was incredibly weak—whatever it was that ailed me had drained all of my strength. However, my attempts to raise myself drew Matthias's attention. He stopped trying to persuade the donkey to pull the cart and came back to lean over the side.

"Awake at last? Thank God, I was beginning to wonder if you would ever actually recover."

He helped me to sit up and wedged some blankets in behind me. The stink I could smell was coming from me. "What's happened to me, Matthias? Have I been poisoned?" It was the only thing I could think of which might have brought me to this pass, I had never been ill in my long life—sickness was something that just did not happen to one from the Families.

"What happened to you?" He shrugged and shook his head and seemed different to how I remembered him, he side-stepped the question.

"In a day or so, we'll be coming down to the coast, things will be better then."

"Where are we?" He seemed unable even to cope with that and failed to answer the question.

The cart bounced over some exposed stones and tossed me about, I became aware again of my condition and winced at the smell. "Matthias, I stink," I said. "Have I aged overnight and lost control of my bowels?"

"Ill," he said, "you've been ill. I looked after you as best I could, cleaned you up every day but we have to keep moving, you know."

I took his words at face value for the moment. Why we had to keep moving was beyond me just then. "I'm hungry. Is there anything to eat? Thirsty, too."

Suddenly looking worried, he stopped and came and rummaged around in the cart, he came up with a chunk of dry bread and a stoppered jug of very watered beer. "It's been two days since I last came across a habitation, we're rather short of food and drink at the moment—what there is, of course, is yours. Just say when you want some more."

He set the donkey into motion again and the cart creaked and groaned its way along the uneven ground until somewhat after noon. We had reached the bottom of a shallow valley and the muddy streams all around us drained into a small pond which had collected behind a ridge of stone. A single, clearer stream emerged from the pond and cold though it was, it looked inviting.

"Matthias, I know you're in a hurry to get somewhere but I really am filthy. I have to have a wash…"

"A wash?" I thought he wore a vexed expression at first but I think his mind was on other things, he frowned, trying to understand what I had said. "Gerard, of course," he replied eventually. "I should have thought of it myself." Suddenly he was solicitous; he drew the cart up near the pond and carried me down the bank to the stream. "Is that all right? Can you manage there?"

I assured him I could and slowly pulled off my piss-wet and grimy garments. Matthias watched me for a moment and went back to the cart. "I'll start a fire and you can get dry."

I grimaced at the soap stone as it removed scabs and reopened sores on my shoulders and buttocks. Matthias pulled a small bundle of sticks from the cart and began to prepare a fire. He struck sparks into a box of paper fragments and had a small flame going as I washed. I was blue with cold by the time I had finished but I hardly noticed it, the pleasure of being clean surpassed the discomforts. I made a passable job of scrubbing my clothes as I had no wish to undo all of my good work. I wrung them out and carried them back as Matthias lifted me to my feet and supported me. I draped them across some bushes which partially sheltered the fire from the wind. The fire became hot enough to eat into the damp wood he had gathered from nearby and another bundle of twigs was drying off to make kindling for our next fire. Matthias was very organized, doing the sort of thing I had been doing during the previous weeks. And with that thought, my memory returned. It wasn't that I had actually lost my memory, just that the here and now had been so unpleasant up to this point that I had no capacity left to think about other things. Kernow, I remembered from somewhere was, the extreme south west, what I had known as Belerium during my army days. That was where we had come to.

We spent an hour there, drying out, drying our clothes and getting myself dressed and making sense of what I recalled. "Are we still being pursued?" I asked after a time.

He had been sitting hunched over his knees, his gaze on our little collection of flames. He raised his eyes to me. "We put them off the scent, Gerard. We have a breathing space; they think that we are days and days away from here."

We trundled on with me still as weak as an infant. Uphill and downhill and then, quite unexpectedly, I noticed the smell of smoke on the wind. We were laboring up a long but not very steep hill; a haze of smoke rose above it and was torn to shreds as soon as the wind took it.

Over the top and down the other side and there, tucked into the steeper side of the hillside, its nearer end being a shelter for animals, was a small farm house. Matthias pulled our donkey to the side and crossed in front of the byre. A collection of animals—sheep, two goats, an ox and a bedraggled dog watched listlessly as we came to a stop in front of the door.

Matthias bent and ducked under the low eaves, he knocked on the door and we waited. There had been grunts and screams within; now they ceased. There was a low voiced conversation then a silence which continued until Matthias knocked again. Footsteps, a bar being drawn on the inside of the door and the door slowly opening. The dark space framed a swarthy man with wild, unkempt hair, as wide as he was tall—though not so tall he would need to bend to pass beneath the edge of the roof.

He cocked his head up and to one side by way of asking our business. Matthias did not reply. "Well?" He said eventually.

"God be with you, my son," Matthias said. "I am a monk from the abbey at Saint Michael's Mount. Could you let us have some food for we are faint with hunger and dry with thirst?"

The man continued to stuff his undershirt into the tops of his hose and shook his head just as a woman came to stand behind him.

I guessed they had been taking their pleasure in bed; after all, there was little else to do in this place and with this weather. Had I been so engaged and interrupted, I would have shown no more friendship towards us than this man did.

Matthias had been an Abbot for a very long time though; it was more than possible that the sensitivities of the situation were lost on him.

"What ails your friend?" asked the woman from behind her husband, her voice pierced the ear as a spear might puncture a drum skin.

"Our brother is very ill…" Matthias began.

"Send them away," she said to her man. "We want no sickness here. Send them off."

Matthias held out his hand, a penny on his upturned palm and I watched cupidity war with the fear of sickness in the man's eyes. "Go and get them a loaf of bread," he said to the woman and she pulled her shapeless gown about her and shuffled back into the dark interior.

"Get them two turnips," he said and looking at our sad little donkey: "And a measure of barley."

"Brother Gideon *has* been very ill," Matthias amended. "He is getting better now. Perhaps we could sleep in your byre overnight?"

The food came, wrapped in two enormous dock leaves and the man reached out for the penny, careful to touch Matthias's flesh no more than could be helped. "Now get you gone. We've done all we need. I don't want you tainting my byre." The door slammed shut and now the sound of the rain falling was suddenly loud. Before the day wound to its dismal close, we spied a clump of stunted trees—little more than scrub bushes, really and Matthias exclaimed and shielded his eyes from the wind. "Now," he said, "if that is what I think it is, we should find good shelter tonight."

Mystified, I said nothing as he fought the donkey off the faint pathway and across the moorland to the trees. He forced his way through the bushes and a minute later came back again.

"Yes. Just as I thought." He leaned over and lifted me over the side of the cart and walked me carefully up the slight incline, through the bushes. Inside, there was a tumble of boulders and flat fragments of rock; at the center of these, some three or four yards apart were two upright slabs, almost the height of a man and a third slab making a roof: the remains of a large tomb. A tomb which had likely belonged to some ancient king or perhaps an arch priest.

We had a solid roof over our heads, we had a decent shelter and with a plentiful supply of dead wood from the copse, a fire was soon warming us nicely. Matthias went to get more wood while I sliced and boiled the turnips and when he returned, we ate. Matthias ate the hard and gritty bread, and—courtesy of the dour man and woman—even the donkey had grain to eat instead of the hard, wiry grass. I took the turnips as soon as they were tender enough to eat, thrusting them greedily into my mouth while they were too hot to chew, burning my palate in the process. I was almost comfortable, well enough to crawl if not to walk and able to perform the natural functions without soiling myself.

"What *did* happen to me?" I asked as the evening wore on and the cold stones had absorbed enough heat to reflect it back at us. "Did I eat something poisonous?" Illness had come as a dreadful shock to me; I could imagine no illness which was not also lethal.

"Yes, actually," Matthias said, looking out into the darkness beyond the tomb.

"What? Herbs? Mushrooms?"

"Look Gerard, I gave you a very strong sleeping draught."

"A *sleeping* draught?"

"I knew what I was doing. It was for the best, you know. It has helped us with God's work."

I sat there looking at him, not understanding what he was saying and not liking the sound of what I didn't understand. I continued to look at him until he met my eyes. "A sleeping draught? How long was I asleep? Hmm?"

"Six days."

"I thought I'd died," I told him. "I thought I was dead. How do you make a sleeping draught for someone from the Families, Matthias? Sleeping draughts, they simply don't work for us."

Matthias looked across at me, through a thin veil of smoke from the crackling flames. "I gave you poison, Gerard. I poisoned you to within a hair's breadth of killing you. I made your soul leave your body; I made your body so weak that it could no longer hold your soul." He looked at me with what seemed dislike in his eyes, maybe he hated me for making him admit the callous act he had perpetrated.

"I ask your forgiveness."

There was no tone of remorse in his voice. In fact, his words really didn't make sense to me until I had rerun them through my mind several times. When I did understand, I was very, very angry. If I had been capable of doing more than crawl, Matthias would have been dead; he would have died that night.

As it was: "Why?" was all I could ask.

"Your woman joined you there. Didn't she?"

"Yes. She did. And…" and then I saw it. "It was all for that then? To mislead Morion and Max?"

Matthias nodded. "Did it work? I think it did but you should know better than me."

"Oh yes, yes, it worked."

"Then it was worthwhile. All worthwhile. You have helped God's plan immeasurably."

"Matthias…"

He spoke quickly, in little bursts of guilty words. "It had to be done, Gerard. Had to be done, can't you see? The one you think is your woman is something far more than that. There is wrongness in her, a power I thought had died out in the World. It should have and will do when the scrolls are read. Do you honestly think our Lord intended for beast-men to walk the earth? They are an abomination put upon this earth by the Lord of Hell. Whatever you think of my actions, whatever you think of *me*, it was worth it. It bought us enough time to disappear entirely."

"'Whatever I think of you, Matthias? You have no idea, absolutely no idea."

He threw a few more twigs onto the fire. "You'll come round my friend, you'll see it in perspective."

My friend? In perspective? This was not the way friends behaved.

"Friends are not tools to use when convenient, Matthias. I thought you were my friend and I'd never poison my friend, no matter what the provocation."

The poison seemed to have flushed away the emotions Matthias usually inspired in me. I gradually became stronger but as I did my thoughts were trying to find reasons for my following this man, protecting him from all comers? What was it that had made me give up my feelings for my one true love to protect and fight for a man prepared to send me to within an inch of death's door?

"I'm sorry Gerard but it was all I could think of to do. They were drawing closer; in my own visions I could see them, almost feel their fetid breath on my neck. But it worked, Gerard, it worked. It's the *end* that matters, not the means."

The anger had drained me of strength. I lifted my arm just then and could barely clench my fingers into a fist. I let them open, let the arm fall to the ground and closed my eyes.

The next morning I was stronger, I walked a little, a mile or so and then rode in the cart for five miles more. I walked another mile and rested again and by degrees, coaxed my muscles into working order again. Towards the end of the afternoon, I was walking fairly steadily; supporting myself on the side of the cart. I could see the sea ahead and a long grey line which divided the ocean from the even darker sky, and at that point, my strength suddenly left me; I fell full length, my face buried in the mud underfoot. I felt myself lifted and laid carefully on the blanket in the cart.

The next time I wakened, I was on a couch with a warm blanket drawn up under my chin. My memories of all that had passed came back to me and I was dejected at the way I had been used. There was more here than Matthias had said, I don't know how he made me believe in him—more so than in Morion or my uncle who, after all, was virtually my flesh and blood. From this point on I was determined to watch him. Now though, I was more sorrowful than angry; Matthias's deceit had driven a wedge into our friendship.

"But you were chosen. By God. You were chosen to help me." He tried to tell me later that day.

"Friends do not make use of each other. God or no God."

At last, he had the grace to be ashamed.

Still, I was less angry than I might have been. I had learned something of Morion, I had learned that she cared for me and I had learned how much it meant to me.

We were in a harbor inn, my couch was in a side room and I was still so weak that Matthias had to support me out to the privy. I had tried to walk too soon, and brought about a relapse in my condition. I needed to rest.

He brought bowls of hot meat broth laced with herbs which helped to restore me and I did feel more kindly disposed towards him. By the third day I was able to sit up and swallow more solid food. As the day wore on, I felt better by leaps and bounds and I got up off the bed carefully and teetered to the window on shaking legs, a distance of five ordinary paces.

I drew aside the curtain and looked out across a rocky beach. Right before my eyes was the unmistakable silhouette of Mont Saint-Michel.

I was dumfounded. *All that way?* I thought. *All that way and already back in Normandy again?* I wondered what had become of the henge of stones.

I shook my head and hobbled back to bed, my mood swaying between frustration at abandoning our purpose and relief that it was over. The latter won out, whatever convoluted plans Matthias had concocted, he could play them himself while I would journey south as Morion wanted. I would meet her in Cordova.

XVII

ut it wasn't. It wasn't Mont Saint-Michel. This was Saint Michael's Mount on the Belerium Promontory, almost at the end of Britain. It certainly bore an uncanny likeness to the place in Normandy and, like that one too, it was reached by a land bridge.

As if my betrayal by Matthias had never been, I journeyed on. Some portion of my spirit rebelled but the larger part was happy to continue. Every night, my dreams were a welter of disturbed and rebellious thoughts. Every morning, I woke with a firm resolve to do my best for the cause.

Beyond the Mount and separated by a wide chasm was the land of Lyonesse: forever invisible from the mainland, forever hidden by a wall of mist.

As with Glastonbury, so with St. Michael's Mount—a place of power where extraordinary events took place.

We skirted the Mount and went—like all visitors—to look into the gorge which separated the almost-island from Lyonesse. As the mist and steam blew momentarily clear, it seemed bottomless until one's eyes became used to the perspectives. Near the center of the mile-long abyss I looked down into this huge gaping maw and it glowed; this was magma pure and simple, a huge red wound had been opened in the World's flesh down to the very blood and humors of its carcass. At either end, the sea poured into the gash, flashing into steam hundreds of yards above the melted rock.

Dizzy from the size and depth of this mutilation, we walked on, our donkey ignorant of the wonder that she beheld. Finally, we reached the monastery just beneath the church.

The place was deserted. The windows had no shutters, doors swung ajar. When we pushed our way inside, we found drifts of dry leaves carpeting the floor, the two or three rooms we explored led nowhere, the inner doors seemed to be nailed shut. Further along, within an archway were a pair of gates which at first appeared to be locked, we shook them and eventually, the left-most gate swung open.

"Hey. What's all this?"

Startled, I looked up. The man who accosted us was standing in a stable doorway beyond the gateway. He had a hay fork in one hand; he was leaning against the side of the doorway. From the corner of my eye, I saw Matthias looking at the crumbling crenulations above us.

"Your pardon," I said. "We thought the place was deserted. We are pursued by brigands and…"

"And found refuge. Well," he shrugged, "why not? I live alone, good company is always welcome. You *are* good company?"

"Exceptionally good," I grinned in as friendly a way as possible. Matthias came all the way through the gate, we looked around our sanctuary. Between the front of the stables and a larger building was an open space, most of it was paved with well-worn slabs of sandstone but there was enough unpaved area for a kitchen garden—unplanted at the moment but dug over, ready for cultivation when the season was more advanced. Up against the tower through which the gate led, several horse troughs had been filled with soil and planted with herbs but the most unusual feature was the dozen or more thorn bushes which grew from the cracks between the flagstones. These bushes bore small white flowers—from buds to full blooms to ripening seed heads, I was reminded of the supposedly magical bush we had left at Glastonbury. The smell of the tiny blossoms left me in no doubt.

"You can put your donkey in the stable over there; there are several residents there already but plenty of space for another."

Our willing host pushed the door open and we looked inside. A pile of soiled straw occupied one corner. Clean, new straw had been forked into the two stalls occupied by a pair of black stallions but the stalls with three somewhat more ordinary horses still needed mucking out.

"As you can see, I was just cleaning the place up."

"As a gesture of thanks, let us finish it for you. Where do you put the old straw?" Matthias volunteered our labor.

"Well now, it sounds a fair exchange to me. The door in the back leads through to another yard, there's a sled out there for the muck. I'll see to some vittles, you look as though you might be ready to breakfast."

"Breakfast? It's well past noon," I laughed.

"Still looks like you need to break your fast. I've seen more meat on a dead rabbit." He patted his own waistline then indicated mine.

"It's true," I said looking down and realized how much weight I had lost.

"My name's Matthias, this is Gerard," said my companion.

"Sulmed," he said and offered his hand to be clasped.

Matthias's concern for fair play went rather further than mine; nonetheless, we cleared the stable and settled our donkey in one of the vacant stalls.

"Those people who were chasing us," said Matthias thoughtfully between forking dung-filled straw.

"Yes?" I replied warily.

"Has the woman been in touch with you?"

"No. Not at all."

Matthias carried on working but he turned his back to me so I couldn't tell if he believed me or not.

When Sulmed had said he lived alone, he meant *relatively* alone, which meant there was no more than at least a cook and a housekeeper and maybe other servants. A good meal was served, a splendid meal laid on an ancient table in a dining room with flaking stone walls and carved statues whose features had long since crumbled away. We had been given a room each with soft couches and fine Turkish carpets. After breaking our fast—as Sulmed saw it—we rested for some hours. When we felt more awake, Sulmed showed us around his small domain.

"It was built by a distant ancestor of mine," he said, indicating the old and somewhat decrepit tower. "It wasn't the first of course, there's been a Sentinel tower here for as long as there are records, the foundations go back to the first one."

"Why build an abbey up here?" I asked. "Solitude?"

"Power," Sulmed answered. "The tower is built on a place of power."

I raised my eyebrows. "Ah. I've heard the same said of Glastonbury in Britain. Does it mean the same thing?"

"Oh yes. Places like Glastonbury and the Sentinel are connected, channels of power flow between them—and many other places."

"I have a feeling there's another connection too," Matthias suggested. Sulmed grinned and turned toward Matthias. "Really? Just what is it you believe?"

"An ancestor of yours visited Glastonbury I think. I think he also came here and built this tower—the first one, that is?"

"There is certainly a legend to that effect but as far as I know, it is not absolutely correct."

"No," I said. "Because you're one of us, I think. Shall I say an Amaranthine?"

Sulmed grinned again, engagingly. "I suspected you might be, you have the look but I haven't met another in a long time, now two come knocking at my door. Assuredly, *I* built the first one and later I *rebuilt* it."

"And the thorn bushes? The ones that bloom through all seasons?"

"True. I was there, too when the Jew came." He frowned. "Joseph?"

A few days later Matthias said, "Beorhtred and his monks will be here soon."

I had nearly forgotten about them, but yes of course, they had been following us at a distance; no doubt Matthias had been leaving them signs to show the way.

Beorhtred and his monks reached St. Michael's Mount, and we watched them ascend the ramp which spiraled around and around the hill.

I had already prepared to leave Sulmed's Sentinel as they reached the tower.

"Take care across the bridge over Hell's Divide," Sulmed warned me, "animals as well as men find it very unsettling."

I wanted Max and Morion to follow me into Lyonesse and I wanted to be away before Matthias started work on the scrolls. Suffice to say I didn't want a repeat of my barely conscious and scarcely-remembered visit to the henge of stones on the plain near Aqua Sulis. This time I went of my own volition.

If it was a successful deception, it would give Matthias and the monks time enough to finish their readings—another two or three days before they caught up with me and a similar time to return. Once these had been completed, of course, they and their militia would cease to matter. So, for now, despite my reservations which had eased somewhat, I would ride into Lyonesse and draw them after me.

XVIII

he bridge across Hell's Divide was a mile or more to the west. Laurel, the mount loaned to me by Sulmed, grew skittish as smells of decay and sulphur reached us; the birds had long since been left behind and there was no sign or sound of animal life. A deep bass rumble felt partly through the ground and heard partly though the ears made my horse more and more difficult to control and eventually I dismounted, covered her eyes with my coat and led her by the reins.

Before me, the horizon wavered as though seen across a summer beach. Another half mile and the ground became cracked and broken; rotten sandstone was peeling away in layers and opening into isolated plates with fuming cracks between. The pathway ran to the lip of the stupendous ravine from which a continuous gust of hot, foul air rose up to the clouds above. The air was difficult to breathe and I moistened a kerchief from the clay water jar in my pack and tied it over my mouth and nose. Unfortunately, I had nothing for my horse in this respect. Nevertheless I offered her calming and encouraging words.

At the bottom of the ravine ran a line of light, from this vantage it was a bright orange yet so distant that it was like a rivulet of molten iron—in reality, a maelstrom of primal magma welling up at the base of this great crack riven through the World's mantle.

This Hell's Divide itself was by no means the only wonder. Across the chasm, striding from edge to edge, was a bridge built by men.

A walkway, as wide as a man's shoulders, was suspended on upright ropes to two cables running between tall stone-built towers on either edge of the chasm. The cables ran over the top of each tower to be anchored into rock forty or fifty feet away from the edge. The nature of the ropes and cables was a mystery until I made a closer examination, instead of hemp or leather, the ropes were fashioned from several score—I judged—of thin bronze wires twisted into cords and the cords twisted into ropes. The higher cables were made in the same way with four metal ropes wound about each other and tied with metal clamps. It was not possible to guess how old the structure was; the bronze was green with thick verdigris and caked with soot and grime from the chasm's fiery breaths.

I led Laurel through the narrow portal which pierced the foot of the support-ing tower and set foot upon the shaky walkway.

My horse went wild, kicking and bucking until we were in danger of falling over the side. Hurriedly I backed up through the portal onto firm ground again and sought to calm her. I took off my coat and cloak and totally blindfolded her. She was till frightened by the swaying of the walkway but more or less manage-able, and the pair of us got across the chasm.

Beyond, in the land of Lyonesse and further from the chasm, the baked, rocky ground turned green with short grass and an occasional bush. Vegetation became thicker and we were constrained to a pathway which took us to a river—an overgrown stream really—leaping down the slope from higher ground.

I took Laurel to the edge to drink and hastily drew my sword when I saw the number of rat-like animals that wriggled out of holes in the ground as I approached. By the time I stood at the water's edge, we were surrounded by a semicircle of speculative carnivores and Laurel backed off, unwilling to drink.

I looked along the river, thinking of crossing. It seemed to broaden out and lose a little turbulence in the distance. In the other direction, the river appeared even more hostile. Well, there was no real need to cross; I could stay on the one side although the higher ground across the water was more inviting.

I kicked at the animals which were gradually coming closer; some of them were already in the water, swimming to close a circle about me. I turned to retreat from the river and one adventurous creature darted in to chew at my boot. I flicked it away with the tip of my sword but undeterred, it came back—perhaps boiled leather was a delicacy in these parts. I shook it off and kicked it away and when it returned, determined to chew its way through, I killed it. That really set things in motion, the rodents darted in towards me to get at the new corpse and Laurel, the reins tight in my fist, waded fetlock deep through fierce little teeth as every one of them tried to get a mouthful of their dead fellow.

"Vile creatures," I spoke out loud and wrinkled my nose. "Come on my friend, let's see if we can find safer drinking further on."

We did indeed find some pools of reasonably clear water and she drank thirstily, so much so I had to drag her away for her own good. There were also patches of lush grass here and there; I walked alongside as she cropped at the tender blades.

For myself, I found a few onions, one or two reedy vegetables to go with the bread and meat I'd brought with me but I wished Matthias was with me to charm a fish or two from the river.

Hungry, irritable, I looked for trees to make a shelter. There were a few soli-tary untidy-looking pines, of no use for my purpose—they seemed to be made exclusively of old knees and elbows. It appeared I would have to spend the night, when it came, out in the open.

Although I'd seen no recent signs of use, the path I followed was well-worn. It was quite possible that I would find a bridge across the river sooner or later. I remounted and moved on steadily, I needed to draw pursuit after me and past the work which must be proceeding at the *Sentinel*.

The narrow, straggly pathway I was following came quite suddenly to a bridge. To carry on along this side of the river meant riding through low brush and forcing a path where my progress would have been obvious. Whereas, if I crossed to the other side where there was a gatehouse...

I decided to do both.

I rode ahead for perhaps, half an hour, forcing Laurel through the ferns and low bushes. I came to a relatively bare patch of ground, made an inroad into the shrubs on the far side and then backed up. We turned about and returned to the bridge, treading along the same path we had made earlier.

We crossed the bridge slowly, my horse balked as the boards gave a little. I coaxed her across and off the far side.

As if by magic, a figure appeared and barred our way. "The fee is two fials— one for you and one for the animal." Greetings obviously were costly and not thrown away on one such as I. I nodded and dipped into my purse to bring out one or two of the coins I had earned over the weeks. "I think that one of these must be worth more than three fials—perhaps even more than the toll and a good meal at your house?"

The gatekeeper licked his lips and a look of regret passed across his face. "It is not permitted to take foreign money. The payment must be in fials."

"Foreign?" I looked at the coin I had proffered and, well indeed, it was foreign. Italian, I guessed, the inscription was in Latin. I chose another, this one in French and another—English.

"Will either of these suffice?" I held them out on my palm.

The gatekeeper shook his head, a magnificent pair of mustachios bobbed in unison. "The coin must be of good Saracen issue. I cannot take infidel money."

I was taken aback. It was rare to find scruples where money is concerned. "It seems that I cannot oblige you."

The other looked sadly at the coins.

"Look," I said, "I'll leave this coin here, on top of the hand rail. You can be generous and let me cross without charge and then do with the money as you see fit."

"You may not go on. You will have to turn back if you cannot pay me."

"Iron," I said. "Will iron suffice?" And I drew my sword and inspected the blade. "Very fine iron—fine enough to come between a man and his soul."

"If you care to look at the roof above you, you will see my son; he has a cross-bow. He is there to deter the users of force."

I nodded. The gatekeeper's son was fourteen or fifteen; he may have used the crossbow against a boar or a deer, but I doubt he had shot a man with it. "How many sons do you have?"

"Allah is generous. I have four sons."

"And where are the other three?"

The gatekeeper shrugged. "How would I know this? They are about their business elsewhere in Lyonesse."

"This is a pity," I suggested. "Your son," I indicated the one who sat on the roof with his legs on either side of the ridge tiles, "may kill me if I were to attack you, yet he cannot kill me fast enough to prevent your death. If he misses, your wives and daughters will be at my mercy, and your son will pass from this world without ever becoming a man."

"Your argument has reason and logic to it. I will call my son down. I will accept the money and you may go on your way."

"Could you provide me with something to eat as well?" Now that the moral dilemma had been dealt with, the gatekeeper took the coin with barely concealed eagerness. However, he had made his position clear, in case Allah was listening.

"I accept this for the toll, under duress. I cannot accept infidel money for food as well," he said, then he spoke to his son in a language of fast words and many syllables. The boy vanished from the roof and minutes later, came out to us with something wrapped in a cloth which he carried in both hands.

"Allah is merciful," said the gatekeeper. "Accept this food as a gift for which I do not ask payment." And the boy presented the cloth-wrapped parcel.

I took the gift. "This infidel thanks you for your generosity. May Allah light your way."

So went the odd transaction and when I had gone a little way, I stopped and opened the cloth. Inside was a loaf of bread, some cooked fish, oranges, and long white tuberous vegetables.

I allowed myself to preen a bit for my powers of persuasion were as good as ever. It had become a game, a contest in which I was an adept, pitching my skills as adventurer against the more stolid citizenry.

My meal was mouth-watering. I did not sprinkle Matthias's dried herbs across it, even though he had insisted I do so. Why should I? The food needed no seasoning. I fell to—as indeed Laurel did, too. On this side of the river, the grass seemed greener and there was considerably more of it.

A little later, we came to a broader and more trodden road which more or less paralleled the river at a distance of a mile or so. The surface was hard and dry and would hold little scent of our passing. I turned back to look in the direction of distant St. Michael's Mount then continued onward, riding until dusk and the need for a secure place to sleep became imperative.

A half-seen movement drew my eye off to the left: a grey blur, no more. A minute later, I saw the same thing again and then, because I happened to be looking in the right direction, I saw what it was—a grey wolf.

As though it knew I had seen it, the animal stood still on a patch of rocky ground. It gazed back at me and then moved off so fast that it seemed almost to vanish.

So, wolf country. Where there was one, there would be a pack within barking distance, sleeping tonight would require careful preparation after all. I decided to stop as soon as I found a suitable place and in any case, while there was still daylight. Mounted, I rode hard, intent on putting as much distance behind me as I could before dark.

I stopped at the edge of a copse of trees; there was a hint of something solid within and I dismounted to investigate. The something had been a hut, now it was four walls and no roof; in more northerly country it might have been taken as a sheep corral.

It would do. Some sword work to prune the undergrowth so that Laurel could share my refuge and we entered. There was dry timber all around—a fire, a store of wood for the night and a chorus of coughs and barks every time I came awake. The wolf pack was never far away, never asleep. We were away again at first light. Again, I forwent the sprinkle of herbs on my breakfast.

I had similar problems the next evening though I stopped a little earlier when I came across what seemed to be a perfect position. A tumble of rocks which, on examination, proved to be far from ideal—providing several opportunities for the animals to leap at me. However, behind the rock pile was a crack in the low cliff, a miniature box-canyon perhaps two yards wide—wide enough to coax Laurel into with a sack-full of oats. I hobbled her and went in search of fire wood—of which there was plenty with the dead limbs that had fallen from the scruffy pines. Placed in the entrance, this would form a secure barrier against any wild animals and provided I kept the fire burning well, I should rest easy.

Curious! I lit a small fire and then left my site to gather more wood, I did it several times. Each time, that damned wolf was out there, sometimes a hundred paces away, sometimes thirty, sitting, watching me.

Persistent! I suppose it might not have been the same one. There were others; half glimpsed, difficult to see in the failing light: quiet, watching.

Rather sooner than midnight, I was still awake, the fire was lower than I would have liked. I threw back the cloak and went to put more wood on the embers which, as I bent, diminished still further. My eyes were well adapted to the dark and I saw clearly; that wolf—or another—was pulling on the unburned end of a branch, tugging it clear out of the fire.

It saw me looking, saw me pull my sword out of the scabbard and sat down at the far edge of the firelight; a figure appeared behind it, a human figure.

For some time, I just stood and looked.

"Hello Gerard."

For some time, I just stood and looked some more. Not believing my ears let alone my eyes.

"Gerard, it *is* you, isn't it?"

"Morion?"

"Of course."

"Are those your friends out there?"

"The wolves? Yes."

"You'd better come through."

For some time, neither of us spoke. Sadly, she put her fingers to my face.

Eventually, I asked what she was doing here, in the flesh.

She answered me obliquely. "Where's your friend?"

"Matthias? Why would you want to know that?"

"Oh, Gerard, Gerard. You really don't realize, do you?"

"No."

"Thank the fates for that. I'd hate to know that you realized what was going on." She took a deep breath. "Matthias is one of the disciples of Jesus Christ."

"Yes, I know that."

She looked at me but probably couldn't see my expression in the flickering light. "And he has the holy relics which will destroy our world if he gets to use them. Now, I need to know where he is and stop him."

"Oh, come on Morion. This is superstition from a thousand years ago. Certainly there's power there but it's not going to do anything that spectacular. I know he can be a little strange but he cannot destroy the world."

"Not *his* world; his vision of what *should* be, but he will destroy *our* world—the one in which you and I and Uncle Max reside. Do you really want the whole world to run like a water clock? Hmm? Do you want to share and share alike with everybody else, to worship just one god…"

"I don't want to worship *any* god."

"No. But if Matthias gets his way, that's what will happen. This world will become a park, a garden party and none of my… of our kind will be left."

"Morion, that's twice you've told me this and I have great difficulty in understanding. What does Max have to say about your notions?"

"Max! Why do you think he's been chasing the mad Bishop of Hypolita for months?" She paused, "You seem confused, love of my soul. Has the warped one been feeding you tainted food, strange herbs or sleeping potions, perhaps?"

I stopped her. I had foregone the herbs the previous night and her words rang clearly through my brain. It was true; most days there would be seasoning or a cup he had prepared against this or that ailment.

"Has he—"

And again, I stopped her. There was the poison he'd deliberately fed to me, surely not the act of a friend—however misguided. And my willing acceptance of his motives…

Morion continued. "I think he will have been muttering strange words as you sleep, poisoning your head against us. Is that the reason for the deceptions you've been practicing against me?"

"I don't know, I only know that at times I can't think properly. I need to speak to Max, I think. I've known him since I was a boy and he doesn't get involved in wild chases like…"

"Exactly, Gerard. Come with me, listen to Max."

"Fine, fine. I'll come."

We left the following morning, joined by a dozen of Max's militia who seemed perfectly at ease with the wolves that Morion appeared to regard as blood brothers and sisters. They trotted alongside her like trained dogs. Even Laurel, my horse, was calm in their presence.

Going with Morion to listen to Max took time. Morion's wolves had followed my two day-old scent and Max was still no more than fifty miles or so from Hell's Divide; we had to backtrack some distance before we found him.

The wolves behaved in an oddly un-wolfish way, more like dogs with a high curiosity index, spreading out across the landscape and checking out anything which seemed suspicious. Several of them were not pure wolf—I assumed them to be cross-breeds until one of them came by me and looked up with an expression of pure hate. I recognized it; I had seen it in one of those visions I had had; I thought it had smiled or even grinned at me then, but looking back I knew I had been wrong. The animal had opened its mouth in revulsion and the same expression stretched its muzzle unnaturally now.

And suddenly, I knew what it was. The skull changed shape, it stood up on its hind legs, its front paws like clawed hands. "Mine," it said. "Woman is *mine*." And the final word was howled.

The form changed again, became wolf-like and unbelievably, leaped at me. The momentum knocked me off the horse's back; I fell and was dragged by my foot still in the stirrup as the frightened horse ran off.

I shook my leg free and dragged my sword from its scabbard at the same time. When the creature turned and came back at me I was still on the ground on my back, but I swung as well as I could. My blade, singing past the animal's ear and made it cower, suddenly aware that sharp steel could kill it.

It circled me, darting towards and away from me. I caught it on the shoulder as I struggled to my feet and blood streaked its silver fur. Again, it leaped as the sword hit the ground and for a moment, it stood against me, its breath hot on my face, teeth closing with an audible snap a finger's width away. I brought my sword up between us, hilt first, and cracked the pommel against its jaw; carrying the movement on, the blade edge cut a long gash up the rib cage and along the inside of its foreleg.

An instant later, Morion's whip snaked past me and snapped around the werewolf's neck, pulled the creature off me. "What's going on?" She hissed.

"*Mine*," said the jaws in a parody of speech. "*Takes mine.*"

I shook my head and heaved a huge breath of air into my lungs.

"What is yours?" She asked then turned to me, angry. "What have you done?"

"Me? It thinks I've stolen its woman. Its bitch."

Morion turned back to the wolf again. "You think you have a claim on me, Yusta?" She spat. "On *me*?" The animal moved off, its tail not quite between its legs.

I hoped she would never use such a tone on me, however foolishly I behaved. I didn't see the creature again until we reached Hell's Divide and Morion chose to say no more about the incident.

We met up with Max in the late afternoon. We three sat down, the wolves scattered and the beast-men took up lookout positions.

"So, Ger'd, what you do? Hmm?"

"All I've been doing is helping my friend get this God thing sorted out."

"This God thing?" Morion's tone was dismissive.

"Yes."

"Have you become a Christian?"

"Me? A Christian? An *anything*?"

"Tell us then, what is so important about *this* God thing?"

"It's…" What *was* so important? Occasionally, I had wondered the same thing and concluded that what *was* important was Matthias, and friendship. "The important thing is that Matthias asked me to help him."

"And Matthias is your friend?"

I nodded. "I thought so."

"You're sure?" Asked Morion. "Think about it carefully, you've killed and nearly been killed, you have travelled hundreds of leagues for someone you met purely by accident; or at least, I assume you did."

"That's so."

"Well just think about it then."

"Think careful," Max added.

I did that, I thought carefully. Morion rested her hand on my arm.

"It seems to me," I said at last, "that I just wanted Matthias to succeed in his purpose. I agree, he's fixated on this thing but I had nothing better to do, why should I not help him out?"

"Because those documents are dangerous, about the most dangerous things in the world."

"They're just plans, written by his God's disciples."

"Exactly. The trouble is…" A new thought came to her. "Have you read any of them?"

"No, oh. A fragment. A few lines, weeks ago. Why?"

"Because they affect the reader, they suborn the intellect."

"That's laughable. How can they do something like that?" Neither Morion nor Max was laughing. "It *sounds* laughable."

"Yet your friend believes they will bring his God's plans for the world to fruition, merely by reading them. That sounds laughable."

"Yes it does, but… that's why I never really considered them to be dangerous."

"But they are, my love. They really will bring about change, on a vast scale."

I shook my head. "Words, just marks on papyrus."

"But very powerful words."

"Memories," said Max. "Memory changes."

"Changes?" Now that it had been mentioned, it seemed something had altered—my perception of the scrolls perhaps. "Not memories. I suppose my attitude has changed, I seem to take the business more seriously now." I remembered the day I had looked at the scrolls, the hazy visions I had had. "Memories change?"

"The documents can change the world we live in. Ultimately, they will change everything, I promise you."

"I don't understand this," I said. "I really cannot believe that twelve rolls of paper can do what you seem to suggest," I frowned and then carried on. "Suppose you try to explain this to me again," I asked. "Tell me what it's all about. Why have you been hounding us all across the south of Britain? For what?"

Max's camp fire was now a mound of warm ash. Mentally bidden, one of the guards came with a jug of cold water dipped from a stream flowing down a narrow fissure nearby. It was bitter but we all drank thirstily.

"Your friend wants to try and fulfill the plans of his God. The plans that the Apostles wrote are plans to fix the future of the whole universe. That's you and me and everyone else, their future, fore-ordained."

Max laid his hand on my arm; his fingers wrapped around and held me firmly. *The twelve documents are truly the written records of the plans that the Christian God had for the Universe, Gerred.*

His words spoke directly inside my mind; strong, cultured, articulate and he had used my real name, my private name, my secret name, the name that had not been voiced in over a millennium.

They only need to be read and comprehended by a human being in a place of power to become real. Some of it has already been read; changes in history have already occurred; we who have lived through those events have memories of the incidents both as they were and as they are now. Both what is gone and what is to come will be changed.

There was no doubt about what he said. Communicating in this manner, Max's words brooked no disbelief; every sentence had the backing of absolute truth. He removed his hand. "Believe," he said.

Morion gripped my hand now. "Do you want to live in a world where everything is planned? Where, if this matter runs its course, everything will be fixed, anticipated, foretold down to the last detail?"

"Perhaps a God would know all this already."

"No God is *yet* so omnipotent. There have been many Gods, all foretelling what would come to pass, they have all gone now and their words have proved ineffectual but if these twelve documents are read by people who can comprehend them. Then there *will* be such a God. Max and your kind will be nothing but vague memories and I and my kind will become nothing more than fables and legends."

"But this God doesn't care; He has already turned His back on the world."

"That is the opinion of one man but even if it is so, this God's left pit-traps behind, maybe He doesn't care if those records change the fabric of reality, whether He's here or not."

I stared off across the sandstone pavement at the hazy line where rock met sky. I dropped my gaze, stared at my scuffed boots. "All this chasing about to stop a minor magic?"

"Minor!"

It had been my last argument but I had never heard Morion sound so angry, her eyes flashed and maybe her hair turned silver, I thought of the werewolf. Perhaps though, she was just exasperated.

"You want to be a puppet for the rest of your very long Amaranthine life, Gerard? Dangling on strings pulled by a machine?"

"Hades!" I stood up, as much to express my frustration as anything but perhaps now starting to truly believe. Whatever Matthias had done to me, it was still working. I was thinking words that were his, not mine.

"What is a world without unicorns, Gerard? A world where there are no phoenix, no faeries? No more me, no more you."

I sighed, realization at last dawning, I *had* become a puppet and all it had taken was for Matthias to tug at the strings. Morion was right, Max was right.

"Where is he, Gerard?" Morion had sensed my change of mind.

I nodded towards the north. "That way," I said. "We need to return. Perhaps we can reason with him."

"Matthias must be stopped whether he'll listen to reason or not."

"I'm convinced," I told her. "Matthias already has more than a head start on us; he's back at the *Sentinel* with a half-dozen monks reading the scrolls."

I had joined her by this time and was checking the saddle on my mount; she looked over her horse's back at me. "The Sentinel?"

"There's a tower on St. Michael's Mount, they call it the Sentinel."

I bent to tighten the buckle. When I straightened up, Morion was already in the saddle; Max too had climbed onto his enormous horse.

"Led me astray. Fox-sly." Maximus was looking at me as I mounted Laurel, a slight grin on his face. "Two times."

"Twice? Ah, that first time was Matthias. He told me afterwards that he'd poisoned me, commanded my soul to go where he wanted it to."

"And this is your friend?" asked Morion, disgust loud in her tone.

"He was my friend, yes." I tried to justify his actions. "He thought the end justified the means."

"Friends don't do that. *My* friends don't do that."

"No, I know. I guess I'm as bad though, I lied to him, I knew you were searching for us but I didn't know why so I didn't tell him who you were. If it comes to that, I lied to you, by pretending to be far away from where I was. Uninvolved."

"The reasons were different though and as you say, you didn't know what was happening. I suppose *we* must take the blame too, for not telling you. Many of the men Uncle Max recruited died at the Tor because of us." Morion spoke sadly.

"A litany of mistakes," I replied.

We rode steadily, the sound of the guard marching behind us a steady beat of pounding feet and I pondered on Max's words. I had definitely been acting on the age-old feeling shared by all humans: that of judging a person by how much I liked him when there were more important considerations.

The decision was made to stop and rest. Both of us had missed most of a planned rest period and we were tired. This time, we camped in the mouth of a small high-sided valley which by now was in shade. Two of the guards made a fire and set water to boil. Another brought out provisions, I was pleased about that because mine were gone.

It had become habit. I had resisted it over the two previous nights, I brought out the packet of herbs Matthias had given me. Truly, I intended to pitch them away into the darkness.

"What's that?" Asked Morion, wrinkling her nose against the slight odor. "What, by all that's good and fresh, is that?" She snatched the stuff away and tested a pinch on her tongue. "This is what your *friend* has been giving you?"

"Hmm. Yes."

"It's a wonder you still have a mind to think with. Anyone else, an ordinary one, would be a gibbering idiot…"

Later, one of the guards came across with a cup in each hand. I could see the steam coming off them in the firelight. Morion took one and I took the other, a herbal tea—I thought it was mulled wine until I smelled the aroma. I raised the cup to my lips, and as I did so I saw Morion's hand come up underneath and quite deliberately tip the scalding liquid over my shirt.

"Corruption, woman." I jumped up, holding the drenched cloth away from my skin until it cooled. "What did you do that for?" I was shocked and more than a little angry.

"Because I've just realized, that's for running us around in circles at Akemanchester."

"Me? Akeman…" I thought back. "Ah. Yes, of course," I said. "Those must have been your guards who caught us for a while."

She nodded. "They don't understand the finer points of holding prisoners."

"Rest," said Max. "Leave after midnight."

After midnight, we moved on, the moon was bright and it was almost as easy to ride in the silvery light as in daylight, it was also easy to doze off while we rode and my mind insisted on going back over the last weeks of travel.

"Were you and Max responsible for those incidents off Finistaire?" I asked Morion after one such catnap.

"Finistaire?" I saw her raise her head to look at the stars as she thought. "Finistaire?"

"When we took ship across the Gallic Narrows."

Morion's jaw dropped and her hand covered her mouth. "*You*? You were there…" She thought a moment more. "Of course you were," she continued to look at me with big, shocked eyes, then she spoke again. "We never knew. You were telling me that you were on the way to Cordova, as I recall."

"Well, yes, I suppose I did. So it really *was* you and Max responsible for those storms?"

"Max. He comes from a time long before us, Gerard. He can still talk with the elementals, you know. They had tremendous powers when the world was younger but I don't think they're interested anymore."

I noticed the phrase, reminiscent of what Matthias had said about his God—*not interested anymore.*

"Max *can* wake them up though. Now and then," she added.

"And the fire beings at Glastonbury?"

She nodded. "Those, too."

It is perhaps a shameful thing to relate but neither she nor I gave a thought to the several score of other souls who had lost their lives that first time. *Ephemerals—though they would not be aware of it, at least they would live again. It was of no consequence.* Such was the Amaranthine philosophy. Only *we* mattered in the long run, the true men; those who would control the world someday.

Just before dawn, we came up the final scarp before descending to the rift separating us from St. Michael's Mount and the mainland. We stopped and I set a small fire going to make the herb tea Morion favored. Max walked on to the bridge and was examining it while below him, in the depths of the canyon, the lava clamored, its light reflected off the clouds of steam rising into the lowering sky.

I was more or less asleep but I saw him return. Something—not Max's movements—something disturbed me, though I could not have said what it was, Morion leaned companionably against me and breathed quietly. The guards were silent shapes a few yards away. Finally Max sat down, his back ramrod straight, legs crossed and tucked beneath him. Presently, he snored quietly.

Nothing else moved, there were no animals, no birds or bats here.

The lava roared more loudly than before, crackling and banging within the chasm's confinement. Still its roaring grew and moving Morion carefully away I climbed to my feet and walked the hundred or so paces to where the bridge led out over the depths.

"What's the matter?" Morion had woken and followed me.

"I don't know, I thought the lava sounded louder than before but now that I'm here, it's the same. I can hear something though, can't you?"

We returned to sit by Max again, a rumbling mountain of a man.

"Something," she said. "I can hear something." She tilted her head and swept the fall of hair away from her ear. "Like a tempest, coming closer."

I nodded. "Or a cataract."

"A tidal wave?"

"Not here, we're too high."

The noise persisted, its source still obscure. It persisted and grew; in fact we began to feel it in the ground. "It's an earthquake." Yet the kettle which still stood on one of the hearth stones showed nothing. The water within was as still as a mirror.

"Change," rumbled Max. "Scrolls; changing."

As we tried to make sense of his words the noise rose and rose: it was like a stampede, a thousand elephants stampeding across the baked earth, all the hoofed animals of the world charging across the deserted clearing we occupied. It had sounded like this when I first read that fragment of the scrolls back in Gaul; like but unlike, as like as the settling dew is to a tempest. Morion's hand took hold of mine and gripped it fiercely and… blackness. Blackness with fiery points of light like falling stars streaking the black sky in all directions, pulses of fire rising from the unseen horizon. My brain was being flayed with sensations I could never afterward describe, my mind was being peeled of its onion skin layers, I was being exposed naked to every hazard that Matthias's God could fling at me. I was dimly aware of both Morion and Max being subjected to their own spectrum of pain and re-forging; behind them too, in the far, far distance were other souls, other minds which were being forcefully reshaped.

Gradually the herd of altered memories moved beyond us, trampling through the future, re-making the world as Matthias and his brethren had foretold it would be, wanted it to be. Our senses returned to us—to Morion and to me, that is.

Max was lying on his side, drawn up into a parody of a fetal shape; his eyes were tightly shut, his fists clenched, his breathing a series of tortured gasps. Whatever demons had flayed his brain, they had left far more damage behind than we had suffered. Clearly, Max's re-forming had been on a huge scale compared to ourselves; his birth had been an era before that of Jesus Christ's.

Although hours must have passed, it was still dark and the guards lay sleeping. They had not lived through events which had changed and thus, changed them; only people like us, who had lived for centuries or millennia would be so affected. Max, whose age was an order of magnitude greater than ours, was most affected. Morion seemed to have escaped lightly.

However, this was not how it ended.

Suddenly I saw that my brain contained two sets of memories, those of the real events and those from what the scrolls had laid down. I reeled as the awfulness of what I remembered welled up into my consciousness, I fell over as my senses were overwhelmed and I must have just lain there and gibbered for afterwards, Morion told me that she could get no sense from me for hours.

"Am I dying?" I shook my head; it felt tight, too small.

"Dying, Gerard? Of course not."

"I already died, Morion, I died."

"And yet you didn't," she stroked my hair. "You're here, with me."

"But I did…" And I told her the way of it, dying on the golden sand at the edge of that terrible sea in Judea.

A little later, I was able to stand and went across to Uncle Max who was still in a coma. Morion marshaled the guards and I went off to find some trees or saplings to make a stretcher for Max. The guards carried him across the gorge and we brought the animals, across, blindfolded. We set out for the *Sentinel* tower.

There were more mindquakes as we marched, though most were minor ones, changes too small to find. Morion and I walked together, the guards four abreast in front of us.

"Why didn't you come to me these last few weeks?" I asked her.

I could feel her grin when she turned towards me. "I did."

"I don't remember."

"Think of early mornings like this, when the air was cold, didn't you ever feel a warm presence?"

I thought back. "Perhaps."

"I said nothing to you. I needed to catch up with you and to achieve that I couldn't let you know. You were difficult to touch, you seemed ill."

I clasped her to my side as we walked. "I was almost dead."

Dawn came with a weak yellow sun shining through the wavering air rising from the chasm behind us.

Max was no better; he was locked in some inner conflict between what had been and what was. Morion and I talked over his condition and finally, we came to a decision. She went to the four most reliable guards, took hold of their wrists and spoke earnestly to them for some time, both by word of mouth and signs and by mental pictures and urgings. When she was satisfied that they knew what to do, she let them go. The guards took up Max's unconscious form and left us; Morion had ordered them to take him to the mainland, recalling for them some place they had stopped on the way here. Somehow, they would have to tend him where we could not.

We were certain that only a small part of the scrolls—perhaps even only a single scroll—had been read completely. We had to get to Matthias and prevent the process from continuing. Now I knew that Matthias's way would mean the end of life as I knew it and all that mankind had achieved would be destroyed. Everything we had ever built would fall and crumble, everything ever written would disappear and nothing would be left; not the Families, not even memories.

We started up the hill followed by the remaining guards. It was quiet, dawn only just breaking. Near the top of the stepped pathway, a sudden loud and raucous screech nearly stopped our hearts. Looking round, we saw a huge raven sitting on a bough with one bright black eye fixed upon us; it opened its beak and gave vent to another shriek which broke off into what sounded like a fit of terrible coughing. We drew breath again and came up to the tower of black stone: the *Sentinel.*

We came to the gate where the portcullis was drawn down; we dismounted. Morion's horse followed her up to the grille, nuzzling against her shoulder; mine, sensing familiar ground, bent its neck and tried to find something worth eating among the wiry grasses and heather growing between the slabs of soft rock.

"There are no windows."

"No," I replied. "They're in the western wall, the other side."

"What do we do then? Shout and attract some attention?"

"Is that what we want?"

"No," she grinned.

"Well, I'm going to climb this wall. It's old and the mortar's fallen out and nobody's chasing us."

I thought she might have told me to take care but she didn't; I suppose she already knew me better than that. I threw my cloak across the saddle and pulled the baldric round so the sword hung down my back, then I began to climb.

There were plenty of hand and foot holds and presently I pulled myself over the ancient battlements around the roof. Steps led down inside and I found the alcove where the winch was riveted into the stonework.

The spindle squeaked as soon as I began to wind it. The pavement was worn by generations of boots; pools of water lay in a depression. Cupping my hands, I poured some on to the bearings and the squeak disappeared leaving only a low grating noise.

"All right, that's enough."

I jumped but it was Morion who had spoken; as soon as she could, she had squeezed through the gap as it opened.

"I want it high enough to get out in a hurry."

She nodded and I continued until the portcullis was high enough to duck under. We went round the outside of the yard, threading our way through the thicket of thorn bushes which had seeded across the southeast corner; wind-blown leaves and straw deadened the sound of our footsteps. We crept across the porch protecting the main door. It wasn't locked, we entered silently and closed it behind us. The vestibule was dark and deserted but there was light under the great doors into the hall; again, we crept across the gritty paving. What was best to do? Rush in or open up a crevice to see what was going on?

XIX

oth, as it transpired. Morion eased one of the doors open a finger's width and we put our eyes to the gap. Sulmed and the Abbot Beorhtred were sitting on one of the wooden benches, the Abbot on the seat itself, Sulmed on the high back with his boots on the seat. Matthias was winding one of the scrolls onto a makeshift roller while a monk was rubbing his eyes and bending again to—presumably—read the text.

Sulmed must have heard something or perhaps felt a draft of air. He looked around, jumped from his perch on the back of the seat and came towards us at a run, taking up a sword from a side table as he came.

I slowly opened the door a bit further and waited as he dashed across the room. He came towards the door, his sword leading the way and as it came between the edge of the door and the jamb, I pulled the heavy door closed, trapping the blade. I felt Sulmed's head hit the other side and then I opened it again, catching the sword as it fell from his grasp. Morion's whip coiled around the reeling man's chest and pinioned his arms to his side.

"Gerard! You made it, thank God." Matthias straightened up and his ready smile faltered a little as he saw Morion behind me and then realized what had happened to Sulmed. "Gerard?"

I looked at the heap of scrolls resting on a table. "How many of these things have been read?"

"The monks find it very tiring, it affects their eyes so just this one so far, and about a third of another. We'll get better, we'll make some more rollers tomorrow."

"I'm sorry, Matthias." I shook my head. "I think it's time to put a stop to this thing for good."

"My friend, why? What's got into you?" His smile faded some more.

"My *friend*, these scrolls are rewriting history."

"Well, here and there perhaps. Minor things—things that the authors had to guess at, perhaps."

"Things they wanted to be true, Matthias. Things that never were."

"All to the greater glory of our God, my friend." Matthias's smile went completely now; in fact, his gaze turned unusually grim. "And that is what counts."

"Truth? Doesn't that matter anymore? Reality?"

"Truth is what God says it is. Truth is God's will."

"Oh no." I shook my head and I nodded, glancing at the papyrus stretched between two rollers. "Propaganda," I said and stared at the hieroglyphics. *All this shall come to pass before Byzantium falls...* I read and would have read on if Morion had not put her hands in front of my face.

"Stop it," she said fiercely. "Don't look at it—it changes you, just by reading it. I can see in your mind how you've changed already, not as bad as Maximus but bad enough that it will take us weeks to unravel. If you still believe your friend Matthias has the best interests of you and the rest of humanity, ask him why he doesn't read the scrolls himself."

"Well Matthias? Why don't you?"

"I don't need to, Gerard. I wrote one of them, I know."

"I'll tell you, Gerard," she said, "it's because he knows the damage the reading alone will do to him, he fears to do so."

I nodded and her hands went away. I wrenched my gaze away from the scroll and back towards Matthias. My sight had become hazy, I saw visions before me, misty views of palaces and temples, lines of richly clad men and women walking across park land, chanting, shaking systrae and beating small drums. Through the transparent visions I saw Matthias draw the horrid blade he had taken from one of the guards so long before.

I shook my head, trying to clear my eyes and see what was real. A flash of reflected light told me Matthias was attacking and I side-stepped as I drew my own sword. He would have harmed me but his hand jerked and his weapon fell to the floor with a strident clang of steel on stone. Morion had used her whip to strike his wrist but there would be no more immediate help there—I could hear her and Sulmed scuffling behind me. My blade came free and vaguely, I could see Matthias picking his up from the floor and then he was at me again. I parried, felt his sword slide along my blade and disengage; I riposted, was parried, too.

It was all automatic, by feel. I simply could not see what was happening properly. Between us and beyond were great insubstantial pillars and I could not help pulling my attacks to one side or another to avoid striking these mirages.

A cold line made itself felt across my ribs on the right hand side. Matthias—clumsy Matthias—had got past my guard and drawn blood.

"Friendship, Matthias? Is this what has become of our friendship?" And I lunged, feeling something at the extreme end of the move. Had I hurt him?"

"My God becomes before all of that, Gerard."

Either I had cut him or he was suffering pangs of conscience because his voice sounded tortured.

I saw a bright line of light and blocked it. It took every last ounce of strength I had to stop it and then to return the riposte. I felt his blade turn uncertainly and followed through with a reprise, felt a momentary resistance, I brought my back foot forward, and lunged again and fell, my strength gone completely.

If I had been able to see Matthias plunging his sword down at my chest, I could not have moved. I waited… waited… waited. Nothing happened for a long time then a figure entered my blurred vision, something flickered in the light, bright; somehow I knew it was sharp, a blade. It came down in what seemed like slowed time; I reached up and took hold of it with my left hand, reaching for the handle with my right. If the edge had cut my hand, I was not aware of it; I simply wrenched the sword from whoever held it and slashed at the wavering shadow above me.

There was a terrible scream that turned somehow into a howl. Another scream, this time from a different throat and a long drawn out growl. My eyes were seeing dreadful visions, things that never could have been: silver, sharp claws and white teeth tearing, blood, gouts of blood. Then all this went away.

"Gerard?" I started. I thought perhaps, I had gone to sleep and all the incongruous, unbelievable images were dreams. "Gerard, what's the matter?"

It was Morion, not as I had dreamed her.

"He's dead, Gerard" She fumbled with my clothes. "You've a slight wound on your side, hardly more than a scratch."

And then I knew. "He used one of your swords, Morion. The poisoned ones."

She gasped.

"I think he's killed me, too."

But I didn't die, after all. I was still reliving the savage attack. I didn't want to live, not with memories like this. Despite his betrayal, I still could not help but remember him as my friend, even though that friendship was artificial, the drugs he had given me still twisted my perceptions. I tried to halt my breathing but my chest moved up and down, contradicting my will. I concentrated on my heart, willing it to slow and stop or speed up and burst; neither urge had the slightest effect. I went on reluctantly, living.

"Morion," I shouted, or thought I did for I could not tell if I had made any sound at all. No one came.

The vitality of my Family had overcome the venom and forced me through the pain. I was to continue living.

I climbed laboriously to my knees and holding on to furniture, I went about the room, I was alone. Briefly I wondered about Sulmed, I had no idea how long I had lain in the poisoned coma—where were the others, had I been left for dead?

I had been moved at some point and by accident I discovered the room where Matthias and I had fought, Here he was, dead, his throat a mass of raw, red meat with the blood running across the floor. I knew what I had seen was true and that I still lived despite the poison I had taken from the blade he had wielded.

With so much damage to his throat, he had died the true death, the Last Apostle, gone. Next to him, I saw Sulmed. His head had been severed and lay beside him. Blood had run in astounding quantities.

Morion? I searched and eventually found her; alive, but slumped in a high-backed wooden chair turned away from me. She was very still, unconscious or asleep, exhausted by whatever had gone on after I... then I remembered again.

I shook her gently and suddenly, she was falling, overbalancing. I caught her and lowered her to the floor—rather, in my weakened state; I collapsed beneath her and cushioned her fall. I managed to put my hand across her mouth as she opened it to call or to scream in case there were enemies still. Her eyes found mine; I felt her lips smile beneath my hand. I moved my fingers and kissed her mouth.

She had leaped to protect me, changing as she screamed, silver fur shining, teeth gleaming, a long, lithe, lupine form already closing on the friend who was about to kill me.

"Thank the Fates you still live," she said.

"Thank the Fates for you, too. I have to thank you for my life, Morion. I saw you, my love, I saw you change."

"We have to get rid of the scrolls," she said at length. "We have to burn them so they can never be used again."

"They cannot be burned. I've seen it tried."

"We have to take them somewhere then, bury them."

I agreed. "What about Beorhtred and his monks?"

"Beorhtred's dead. Perhaps the monks took his body away with them when they fled back to Glastonbury, perhaps, I don't much care."

The opened scroll, the one they had been reading from when we had arrived, was still stretched on the windlass machine.

I slashed across it with my knife to release the tension and lifted the nearest roll off the frame and laboriously slotted it into the case with the others. I tugged the other half from the box which held it and wrapped the loose paper around the bundle. A few characters came into focus…

… final hours of the old…

That is all I remember reading and a great hall of judgment reared itself up before my vision. Blacks and grays predominated, tall pillars and walls covered in black and grey hangings receding into the distance; in front of me stood a judge in scarlet robes and a scarlet skull cap with a black rod, as black as the blackness between the stars at night. He was angry, seething with a rage that washed over me like scalding water.

What he said to me I don't know. His voice was like rocks falling from a high cliff, each word crashing down round my ears, grinding all before them. The vision repeated itself a thousand times, beginning anew each time, I tried to shut my eyes, to shut out the powerful glyphs from the images in my brain. I forced my fingernails into the flesh of my palms; I bit my tongue in the hope that the pain would distract me long enough to break the spell.

Somewhere in there I must have succeeded for the tirade paused, the scarlet figure resolved itself into the red habit of the dead Abbot who sat in a corner unnoticed until now. The black and grey wall hangings were six monks who had crept into the room as the seizure had taken me, they had not run away after all.

Pace by pace they came forward despite the determined looking lady brandishing two swords behind me. Confident, perhaps, that their God would protect them or even take them straight to Heaven, they ignored her and fell on me. I was still not very strong and not able to put up much resistance.

They looked around as three of our guards squeezed abreast through the doorway. The monks lost their holy zeal and ran, leaving Max's militia trying to puzzle out what was happening.

"Gather up the rolls, they've got to be destroyed," I told them and sat down, just as soon as I could walk without falling over.

"Acid?" She wondered aloud.

"Perhaps, who knows? Is there any here?"

"I don't know. So what now?"

"So think."

We thought and came up with the same idea we had thought of earlier—if the scrolls wouldn't burn, they could certainly be buried.

Our horses had been left to wander; they still had the saddles on and had obviously not been fed except for what they had found among the perpetually flowering thorn trees growing between stones. Sulmed's animals were in an even worse state, probably not having been looked after for days. We turned them loose, pulling hay free from the bales and pouring oats into a basket where they could get at it. There was water in troughs and our good deeds done, we left with the scroll bag tied across the back of my saddle. I was slowly regaining my strength but even so, Morion rode ahead leading my horse while I did little more than slump in the saddle.

It took us an hour to reach the chasm, trying to look casual and ordinary to the people who lived and worked on the Mount. None of them followed us, none of them showed the slightest curiosity about us and our small contingent of semi-human militia.

Below, the walls of the chasm fell away in rugged columns and niches. Small shrubs clung to pockets of soil caught in the upper reaches of the cliffs but below those few yards, the stone was bare, devoid of life. We stood on sandstone which had been weathered by the winter winds and cracked by the heat from below. We tied the horses to the remnants of a fence and went out onto the bridge.

From there, it was possible to see beneath the sandstone slabs to where the rock was dark slate reaching down as far as we could see. The far side was granite, black and glittery with bulges and hollows and misshapen knobs as though it had at some time been as malleable as potter's clay. Separate colors were lost as the gaze travelled down, the rock becoming more and more illuminated by the brilliant orange of the magma filling the very depths of this great break in the earth's fabric. It wasn't really possible to distinguish where the redness of the chasm walls ceased to be reflection and became hot enough to glow with light itself.

Morion unbuckled the case and hoisted it onto her shoulder.

"What are you doing?"

"I'm going to…"

But it was not me who had asked.

"It's time I killed you now." The voice came from behind me, ragged, forced, ugly. I turned. It was Matthias, his clothes stained with his blood, his ruined throat closed, his feet and legs covered in dried mud.

Like me, he had recovered from his wounds and followed us. He had the same vitality as I had, that even the terrible wounds Morion had inflicted would heal eventually. I wondered if Sulmed had restored himself too, reattached his severed head… I shuddered away from the thought.

Wearily I tugged my sword from its scabbard; it seemed to weigh ten times its usual weight. I guessed at what Morion intended to do with the pernicious writings. "Quick Morion! Get rid of the scrolls now!"

I heard her step onto the bridge behind me and I took a step towards Matthias, coming to an unsteady fighting position. My former friend nodded and pulled that damned envenomed sword out and swung it. Dully, I parried, riposted, parried… The metal clanged and each clash jarred my arm and shoulder.

I could see Matthias's eyes glancing over my shoulder, his gaze divided between me and Morion's action. Eventually, it was too much for him, he summoned some last reserve of strength and simply battered my guard away, he hacked but I managed to interpose my blade somehow and his weapon slid along mine but his lunge went past me. It was a move I had not anticipated.

He slashed at Morion who, with far quicker reflexes, simply ducked. Matthias's blade clanged into the ropes which supported the bridge, generating a shower of sparks from the bronze wires.

The heavy weapon bounced; the shock of the impact jarred Matthias's arm and sent his whole body spinning further out across the bridge where he teetered, but recovered his balance. I followed him onto the swaying bridge as he dashed back towards Morion, lifting his sword high and grabbing at the rough corroded lines hanging from the suspension ropes.

Morion had pulled the scrolls halfway out of the tight fitting case; now it lay between her feet as she pulled the whip off her belt and struck out at Matthias. The whip coiled around his hand like a sentient snake then around the metal line he was grasping and bound the two together, he could move no further and I staggered towards him over the heaving foot boards. Matthias looked back at me, transferred his sword from his bound hand to the free one and slashed at the whip. The coiled leather was immovable, it would not unwind. He tried to saw at it with his dangerous blade but its leather was as tough as the bronze wire it was bound to.

What had possessed Morion to empty the case I could not have guessed; "Kick the case over," I shouted, "don't try to get them out, kick it."

Matthias lost all restraint. With a great howl which drowned out the continuing grumbling of the swirling lava below us, he hacked through his left wrist, a spray of arterial blood soaked his face but he leaped, careless of the great drop, towards Morion. Too late, far too late.

The case was already falling, turning, twisting, diminishing, a black dot against the eye-hurting glow of magma. We all watched its descent, even after it had fallen too far to see; its splash hidden in the all-pervasive glare from the center of the earth. Matthias sagged against a line and slid down to the foot board, I knew from my own experience that poison from the blade was coursing through his veins even as his life blood was pumping from the end of his severed arm. Could he survive even this? Morion too, was hanging onto a rope, too drained to do more than gaze down past her feet. Then…

"Look," she said and pointed feebly.

Perhaps that case of power-filled glyphs had still been falling until this instant for now, there did seem to be a splash. What must have been a huge mushroom shaped fountain of lava rose from the distant surface and settled slowly back into the magma. A cloud of hazy air rose up, expanding, thinning to near invisibility and as it passed us, my head was filled again with images of stern Gods and lovely angels but they passed as the cloud rose above us.

Again, the eruption happened below but more powerfully and this time, it kept rising until it seemed to reach slowly upward for us with a vast exhalation of roasting hot breath. Whatever unearthly power was contained in those twelve scrolls was bursting open the earth's bowels, releasing the forces which made the world turn.

"Morion," I shouted, suddenly fearful. "Come past us, get to the edge."

"You go," she gestured, "I'll follow."

"I have to try and get Matthias off here."

No matter, it was already too late. This was a real eruption, the rocky edges to either side were shaking, the bridge jumping up and down beneath us like a living thing. Huge flakes of rock were peeling away from either wall and crashing down into the upwelling lava. One of the suspending ropes broke on the far side and our bridge was suddenly twisted out of shape.

I clambered over Matthias and got hold of Morion by the collar of her jacket and—finding the same last reserve of strength that had come to Matthias earlier—I hauled her along the bucking bridge and tugged her bodily onto the ground.

Matthias was still huddled there, his arms clasped around a supporting rope. Blood ran from his severed wrist and his face reflected the pain he was suffering. I got down on all fours and began to edge out along the foot boards.

The remaining tie fell on the opposite side as the cliff gave way. I hung on for dear life as the structure fell; hooked my feet behind two of the supporting lines. There was a huge crash and jolt as I was dashed, upside down, against the cliff. A wave of boiling heat swept up from the molten rock, red hot fingers reached towards me. I couldn't breathe; the gases were foul and hot enough to sear the inside of my lungs, my body would not let me breathe and yet I could do nothing as the lava got nearer and nearer. Below, his clothes smoldering, Matthias looked up at me. His eyes were dark pits in his ravaged face, the wounds that Morion had inflicted were dripping blood. Matthias clung relentlessly to the red hot strands of metal with his right hand, he reached up to me with the stump of his left arm and I thought he mouthed "sorry" as he failed to reach me. I moaned with pain as I crawled vertically down towards him, I stretched out and still could not reach him.

My sight was almost gone, the heat was affecting my eyes—then I could no longer see him. I tried to blink to clear my vision but it changed nothing, he had gone—he had joined his treasured scrolls.

Then the lava began to fall away again, to recede.

There were scrapes and jars and I was tilted this way and that. Morion had managed to convey commands to her guards; they pulled what was left of the bridge up bodily and me with it. At length, I lay sucking in gasps of cooler but still foul air. My hair had blazed away, the skin on my face was a mess of burst blisters; my hands were red and raw and my clothes were little more than soot and charcoal and my eyes still worked dimly after their near roasting.

Across what had been a chasm, there was now only a field of molten rock, glowing into the far distance, barely distinguishable from a sky of roiling orange and black clouds laced with lightning. The far side, the interior of Lyonesse, had sunk thousands of yards below its former level and had relieved the flow of lava which, otherwise, would have risen to the very lip of the chasm. Even as I watched, the molten desert was sinking slowly and the Western Ocean was laying claim to the land beneath growing clouds of steam.

I think I gave up then, losing consciousness. Lyonesse was returning to the sea and all who lived there were dead or dying.

I was sometimes conscious of being carried, sometimes of being dragged where the path had fallen away. Once, there was the cool sensation of water being poured over my head and shoulders and my hands. Later, there was an inn which had been Nefeli's and I remembered it as having been close to the end of the land bridge out to the Mount. Now it looked out over a bay swirling with murky red waters. I regained awareness and health to find Uncle Max sitting on a bench at the side of my bed.

"Ah," he said. "Wakes."

"You're well?" I asked Max.

"Wellish," he told me.

"Morion?" I asked.

Max nodded. "Wellish also."

Someone, Nefeli, came to light candles in black iron sconces with bulbous glass shades. She brought a tray of cool drinks and small cakes; she dropped the blinds over the windows.

The bench creaked as Max rose ponderously. "Won the battle, Ger'd, the war still to win."

"Still the *end days*, then? Armageddon's only postponed?"

"Still." And Max left me alone.

Later, with the darkness, Morion came to lie next to me, where she belonged.

THE END

The Story Continues

The Pope's Magician
Book II: The Amaranthines
Coming 2014

ALSO FROM ADELE ABBOT

Of Machines & Magics

COMING SOON FROM ADELE ABBOT

The Pope's Magician

WWW.ADELEABBOT.INFO

ADELE ABBOT graduated from Manchester University, where she majored in law. Her interest in Fantasy was first fired when she came across the Lyonesse series by Jack Vance. After several false starts and plenty of encouragement from friends and family, she began writing her first book, *Of Machines & Magics*. While shopping for a publisher, Adele began work on another fantasy, *Postponing Armageddon*, which she entered in the "Anywhere But Here, Anywhen But Now" contest for aspiring debut novelists, sponsored by Sir Terry Pratchett and Transworld Publishers. Out of more than five hundred entries, *Postponing Armageddon* reached the prize shortlist of just six novels.

In addition to pursuing a writing career, Ms. Abbot is a full-time law partner by day. She currently resides in Yorkshire in the United Kingdom with her son. Find out more at her website, www.adeleabbot.info.

About
Barking Rain Press

Did you know that six media conglomerates publish eighty percent of the books in the United States? As the publishing industry continues to contract, opportunities for emerging and mid-career authors are drying up. Who will write the literature of the twenty-first century if just a handful of profit-focused corporations are left to decide who—and what—is worthy of publication?

Barking Rain Press is dedicated to the creation and promotion of thoughtful and imaginative contemporary literature, which we believe is essential to a vital and diverse culture. As a nonprofit organization, Barking Rain Press is an independent publisher that seeks to cultivate relationships with new and mid-career writers over time, to be thorough in the editorial process, and to make the publishing process an experience that will add to an author's development—and ultimately enhance our literary heritage.

In selecting new titles for publication, Barking Rain Press considers authors at all points in their careers. Our goal is to support the development of emerging and mid-career authors—not just single books—as we know from experience that a writer's audience is cultivated over the course of several books.

Support for these efforts comes primarily from the sale of our publications; we also hope to attract grant funding and private donations. Whether you are a reader or a writer, we invite you to take a stand for independent publishing and become more involved with Barking Rain Press. With your support, we can make sure that talented writers thrive, and that their books reach the hands of spirited, curious readers. Find out more at our website.

WWW.BARKINGRAINPRESS.ORG

Barking Rain Press

ALSO FROM BARKING RAIN PRESS

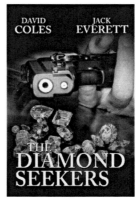

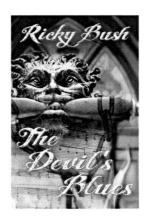

Lightning Source UK Ltd.
Milton Keynes UK
UKOW05f0120120813

215192UK00001B/10/P